2012

PARALIGHT PUBLISHING

Speed
OF LIGHT

LEE BAKER

LEEBAKERONLINE.COM

ISBN 978-0-9833742-1-3
Library of Congress Control Number: 2011913747

Printed in the United States of America

First Edition, August 2011

Book design by Sandman Studios (www.sandmanstudios.com)

Cover art by Kienan Lafferty and Christian Perry, © 2011 Paralight Publishing

Air Supply song "Lost in Love" lyrics used with permission of Graham Russell

www.leebakeronline.com
www.speednovel.com

For Drennan

P r o l o g u e

The police car pulled to the curb in front of the police station, and the crowd converged. Camera lenses bumped and scratched against the windows, and faces of reporters pushed forward to get a view of the backseat. I felt a surprising calm considering the situation I was facing. Officers from the police station forced the crowds of reporters, cameras, and media personnel to the side, clearing a pathway into the building. My attorney gave me a reassuring look and stepped out of the police car. I followed, and questions flared from all directions.

"Did you fire the gun?" demanded a blurred face to my right.

"Is your son okay?" questioned a woman being held back by an officer.

"Did you murder your wife?"

"No comment," my attorney responded.

"Did you murder Cole Trace?"

"Are the allegations true?"

"What were you thinking?"

"No comment. He has no comment," my attorney responded repeatedly as we pushed past the crowd of reporters and into the station.

The police lieutenant, who resembled a brick wall more than a man, directed us to a conference room and said, "Please take a seat, and don't worry—the cameras are off." My attorney and I took a seat as he turned to the other officers and said, "I need to talk to them alone." They exited. He shut the door, sat across from us, took a deep breath and said, "You had better tell me everything because there's a hornet's nest outside this room bigger than anything I've ever seen; and if I'm not on your side, your life is over."

He was right. I had just committed crimes that could keep me locked up for the rest of my life. He needed to understand that I did it to save lives—his included. I was not the murderer he thought I was, and the world I lived in was different than his. I had changed during the speed of light test flight, and my mind was no longer confined in the same way his was.

I looked at the police lieutenant and said, "When you close your eyes, the world around you disappears and is replaced with a calm blur of avoidance. I did that with my life. I closed my eyes and refused to see what was happening around me. As a result, I lost and gained everything. I know that is an odd statement, but it's true."

"You closed your eyes?" queried the police lieutenant. "That's all you can say? You resisted arrest. You attacked police officers, Pierce."

"There is more to this than you can imagine," I answered.

"Try me," he said.

I cupped my hands over my eyes, and the world around me went black. Slowly light appeared, and I could see blurred images. A serene face came into focus. I took comfort from the smile and knew what I needed to do. I removed my hands from my eyes, reached across the table, and grabbed the police lieutenant's forearm.

"Don't close your eyes," I said, "I'll show you."

"You'll show me?" he asked.

"Just do as I ask. Keep your eyes open," I said confidently as I looked into his eyes. I concentrated on the day of my anniversary, and clear images formed in my mind. He stiffened, and I could feel the connection I was making flow from my hand to his arm and into his mind.

"What are you doing?" he demanded, tensing as I saw the, now familiar, shimmer of energy lift off my skin and ripple through the air around me. The lieutenant's eyes widened. The solid table top below our arms rippled, and sinews of light rose from the surface. It dematerialized into threads of soft light that streamed down to the floor. Green, manicured blades of grass grew from the white laminate tiles. The color spectrum ranged in a single blade of grass was perfectly discernible and hypnotizing in its beauty. The police lieutenant's head cocked back in disbelief.

"Look around you," I answered as the walls of the small room disintegrated into wisps of light. They reconstructed themselves into a sidewalk stretching beside a road. Blue skies arched over our heads. The sharpness and brightness of the colors around us should have been blinding but instead were comfortable, natural. When the transformation was complete, we were standing outside a quaint whitewashed café with an outdoor seating area.

"What is this?" he asked, his face astonished.

"This way," I said. We walked toward the café and I saw myself sitting at a table across from my wife, who was speaking to me. I had my face buried in my hands, covering my closed eyes. The morning sun cast a glow on her smooth skin, and the blue desert sky enhanced the azure of her eyes. A breeze stirred the long, dark hair that rested on her tanned shoulders, framing her prominent cheekbones and arched brows. The ambiance of the small café with hand-painted artwork and whitewashed walls accentuated her beauty.

"That's you?"

"Yes, and Catherine, my wife," I said, as my heart wrenched inside me, "This was our wedding anniversary."

I was a different person back then. I had lived in a different world. Catherine had been the center of my life, but I had not wanted to hear what she was saying. The most difficult part about watching the moment was that, as I had sat across from her at that table, I had no idea it was the beginning of the last day of her life.

I should have listened.

Chapter 1

I could hear her voice in the darkness, "It's coming together. The case is solid. The banks have confirmed the transactions and Cole has made headway with the witnesses. We're getting together this afternoon to connect the dots."

The words pounded at my head like Chinese water torture. Any other subject would have been bearable. I pulled the palms of my hands from my eyes and lifted my head to see Catherine sitting across from me, framed by the whitewashed walls on the outdoor balcony of our favorite café, waiting for a response.

"I'm listening," I said through a forced smile.

"Cole figures we almost have enough on Paralight to take it to Vanessa," she continued proudly. My mind swirled with the thought, and I did not want to consider it. That would mean they were all involved—the whole family. It would not stop from any side. The worst part of it was that they were all attorneys; and when you get attorneys together, a simple subject becomes unbearable. I loved my job, and I did not want the beautiful three to shake it up.

Cole was Catherine's brother, Vanessa her twin sister. The three were living works of art—all unfair to the world. I had met them my senior year of high school when the Trace family moved to Phoenix. Their presence was a shock to the system. Catherine and Vanessa Trace were twins, but not identical. They actually looked quite different, but both had unfair symmetry and light olive skin. Catherine had sleek, dark-brown, almost black hair and striking blue eyes, and Vanessa had thick, light-brown hair and golden-brown, penetrating, cat-like eyes. Cole Trace looked as if he had stepped out of the pages of *GQ Magazine* and complemented his little sisters. The opinions and attitudes toward the new Trace family were polarized. You either loved or hated them; and whether you loved one or the other, was primarily based on your gender. Girls hated the twins because the boys' eyes wandered and, in many cases, flat-out stared whenever they were around. Guys hated Cole because girls floundered like lovesick, star-struck groupies when he entered a room. With this going on, the three generally kept to themselves.

I didn't have much to do with school and was more involved in flying than anything else, so I didn't get into the drama of the Trace family. However, I was not blind and would have been very happy if the twins had noticed me. I was of average height and had an average build. I liked to think I was handsome, but there was no indication that my thinking was correct, as I never stood out enough to get the attention of any of the girls, least of all the Trace twins. My eyes were not brown or blue but some sort of hazel that mixed the two, and my hair was not dark or light; it was right in the middle—a cross between blonde and brown. Everything about me in high school screamed average, and I was not involved in anything noteworthy in the school social arena. I felt as though I blended into the lockers; and whenever one of the twins was nearby, I froze or turned the other way. Socially, I was a misfit who spent most of his time focused on airplanes.

Airplanes were my life. I was an only child, raised by my father who was a pilot of sorts and who worked as a mechanic at a small airstrip on the outskirts of Phoenix. I spent most of my time either helping fix planes or flying them with my father. I can't remember life without airplanes and was basically raised on that small airstrip. My mother had left us when I was one, and I knew very little about her as my father avoided the subject.

My father did not have enough money for daycare so I was passed around the small staff at his work. In my younger years, I was mostly raised by Bonnie Hatch a kind woman who was the secretary at the airstrip—which meant that she didn't do much. Occasionally the phone would ring, or people would come through the front door, but no task required more than a few minutes. I became her focus, and she became my substitute mother. When I was old enough to pay attention for sustained periods of time, I followed my father around as he maintained the planes. I became his assistant and would get him the tools he needed or find the parts required for a certain repair. I was flying planes with my father far before I was old enough to get a pilot's license and became fluent in the controls of everything from old bi-plane dust croppers to luxury private jets. School was a distraction from my passion for flying, and I would spend much of my time drawing new designs for airplanes or daydreaming about my next flight.

One fortunate day, Cole's father, who was an attorney, was flying out on a business trip with a client and had brought Cole with him. A storm kept the plane grounded for four hours, and Cole wandered into the hangar where I was working. I showed him the plane I was working on, and we talked. I didn't know what to think about him when the conversation began, but as the hours rolled by I realized he and I had a lot in common. There was a human being behind the handsome face. By the time he left, we had agreed to hang out on the next weekend. I went to a movie with Cole and the Trace goddesses and somehow was able to be myself. They accepted me for who I was. Catherine and Vanessa commented that it was refreshing to be with me because I was not a pawn in the social arena of high school. From that point forward, the four of us were our own clique. I actually had friends at school. My life changed. Suddenly, other kids wanted to get to know me. Even, then, I knew it really had nothing to do with me and everything to do with Catherine, Vanessa, and Cole. Thirteen years later, I was sitting across the table from my wife, Catherine Black, no longer a Trace, dreading the fact that three members of our clique would soon be focused on bringing down my career.

"You don't have much time, Pierce. Put in your resignation and cancel the flight."

"Did you know it's our anniversary today?" I asked, intentionally trying to derail the discussion.

"I seem to recall we got married," she replied with pursed lips. She knew what I was doing.

"We did, yes. Nice day, wasn't it?" I was all smiles.

"Perhaps this will be my last chance to celebrate it with you." She was smiling, but there was a steely glint in her eyes. The glint implied that I was committing suicide by not quitting my job, and the smile let me know she was about to dive again into the subject of Paralight.

My mind rushed to *PLEASE don't bring up the monkey. I can't bear it.* "Then let's make it a good one," I said. I stood up and kissed her quickly, not letting her take the discussion any further down her road. "I've got to get back, but I'll see you at seven." I turned and fled quickly before she could say another word.

I was a safe distance away when I looked back and smiled. She didn't smile back. Her eyes narrowed, letting me know that the conversation had been postponed, not concluded. This conversation or hints toward it were constant. She thought I was going to die and wanted me to quit. She also thought my company was corrupt and would soon be exposed. The attorney who would do that job was her brother Cole.

As I drove my old Pontiac to the guard gate at Paralight, I pushed the conversation with Catherine out of my mind. A familiar excitement rose inside me. It always did. I waved to Alex in the guard booth and he opened the gate. Located on the outskirts of Phoenix, Paralight was a mirrored-glass office building with large hangars extending behind it toward the desert. The grounds were well groomed, a drastic contrast to the desert. The grass was green and the trees lush, providing ample shade for the rows of cars parked in front of the building. I turned away from the manicured, above-ground visitors' parking lot and drove down the decline to the underground parking where I found my favorite spot. It was the corner nearest the elevators. The reason it was my favorite was because I would park at an angle and get more space than any other spot, and I had a very short walk to the elevators.

People have been madly curious about what happens at Area 51 or in the government's technological research facilities; but if you asked the average person in Phoenix about Paralight Technologies, you would get a blank stare. Prospective employees of Paralight were required to sign detailed confidentiality and non-disclosure documents that absolutely prohibited saying anything about what they did at work beyond the information on Paralight's website. It provided information on the company's research in creating technologically advanced headlights for cars and boasted modestly about its numerous manufacturing contracts with both national and international automotive industries. The rare person who had heard of Paralight would comment, "Don't you make headlights?" The truth was much more interesting.

I took an elevator from the parking garage to the main level, then walked into the large foyer and waved at a few familiar faces as I made my way to the ornate executive elevators. Inside the elevator, I scanned my employee's card. A panel under the elevator buttons slid up, revealing a separate panel with a glass screen. I scanned my index finger on the screen, and the elevator descended. When the doors opened, I walked down a short hallway that led to "Scarlet."

Scarlet was the name assigned to the underground development hangar at Paralight. It was approximately the size of a football field and had three tiers of walkways running around its entire perimeter. Each walkway was about two stories high. On the far end of the hangar, large doors opened to a tunnel leading to the desert hangars behind the Paralight offices. On the floor of Scarlet were many different projects ranging from hovercrafts of various sizes to a sleek jet fitted with the technology to travel at the speed of light.

Since the inception of the company, the founders had a passion for understanding the properties of light. Over time they developed technologies that allowed them to convert matter into light, embed the information about the properties of the matter into the photons, and then rebuild the matter from the information. Two months previously on the deserts outside Phoenix, Paralight had performed a test on the speed of light jet with a monkey in the cockpit. The plane burst into an explosion of light on one side of the horizon and appeared on the other side in a seemingly simultaneous burst of light followed by a thunderous blast that rivaled the strongest electrical storms. Before the test flight, the jet was known as LP-6, or Light Plane version 6. After the flight, it was renamed Stormlight.

The mass of the jet and the monkey were converted into photons with the information about their structure embedded, they briefly traveled at the speed of light, and then were rebuilt in the new position. The test was a great success. The monkey, Cartwright, became an instant star at Paralight, and the scientists feverishly worked to compile all of the data and reports. The secrecy of the project rivaled that of the Manhattan Project, and many of us wondered why Paralight did not make a public announcement of this great success. However, the positive results of the test flight with Cartwright pushed forward the date for the human test. I was the human—selected to be listed among the greats in the history of this world. That is what I wanted. I wanted to be the first man to travel the speed of light. I would not let my wife and her brother take that away from me.

I had started working with Paralight several years previously, thanks to Cole's recommendation. He had then been part of their in-house legal team, hired shortly after his graduation from law school. Paralight had started Scarlet ten years before I joined the company. In conjunction with the technologies surrounding light, it was building its own planes, hovercrafts, and flight-related technologies. It needed test pilots, and I was hired because I was an experienced pilot and had technical and mechanical experience.

After a quick stop in the locker room to put on my pressure suit, I made my way to the simulation room, a large circular space with criss-crossing bars that intersected to create the metal mesh of the walls. Within the mesh, were thousands of lights that, when turned on, created holographic environments in which to test experimental planes and increase the skills of pilots. A ramp led to the center of the room where a mechanical arm held a cockpit with two seats. I was scheduled to do a routine skills test flight through diverse terrain. I sat in the cockpit, secured my buckles, pulled on my helmet and turned to see Kendall, my flight partner, securely belted in behind me. Kendall had been a helicopter pilot in the Gulf and Iraq wars and built himself quite a reputation for flying under difficult conditions. The ramp pulled back from the cockpit and retracted through the metallic mesh of criss-crossing bars. I looked to the window of the observation booth where I saw the technicians watching. They signaled that everything was ready.

"There'll be a flaw today. I know it," Kendall quipped through the microphone in the helmet.

I smiled and pulled the visor down over my eyes. As I looked forward, the world around me changed into a desert runway. I thought, *I'm the luckiest man in the world to be paid to do this. Millions of people dread going to work, but I get paid to play the most expensive and visually stimulating video game ever created.* After Kendall and I flew for twenty minutes at mach speeds through canyons and mountain ranges, the lights dimmed and the environments faded away.

"Again!" I said.

"My turn," Kendall smiled as I looked back to the observation booth.

"Give it a day. I don't want you to be embarrassed following my perfect run."

"Perfect if you don't know the meaning of the word," Kendall grinned as I unbuckled myself.

"Careful, Kendall. I'd agree with Pierce," chimed in another voice. I looked back and saw Jack Jones standing behind the technicians. Jack was the executive over Scarlet and was responsible for our secret division at Paralight.

"Make it real and give him some gunfire," retorted Kendall.

"I'm okay without guns," I responded, "I have a strong allergic reaction to death."

Kendall and Jack both laughed. Soon Kendall and I had switched places, and he was preparing to fly the course. Jack said he had a meeting with a red pen and a contract on his desk. As he was leaving the observation booth, he said, "Happy anniversary, Pierce!" I was initially startled that he would remember—then shrugged. Everything was on the computers, and I was sure an automatic reminder had popped onto his screen. Still, it was a thoughtful gesture.

Following Kendall's ride in the simulator, we spent the afternoon testing one of the new hovercraft models, designated X1.

It was a four-seater and was having problems with cornering. Our testing gave the tech crew more headaches than solutions. We thought it was amusing to see them turn white as their minds spun around the amount of work it would take to reevaluate and implement our suggestions. We tried to cheer them up by saying it was "job security."

I took a shower in the locker room then went to my small office which was adjacent to the locker room and sat at my computer to write my daily log to Jack. It was mandatory to tell everything you thought during work. "Inspiration comes from thought," Jack would always say, "Tell me everything." He wanted our deepest thoughts, but I made clear distinctions between work and my personal life—I never wrote about anything outside of work in the logs. My personal life was mine.

As I pulled up to my small house, I saw Cole's car parked in front. It was starting to rain, a rare but welcome phenomenon in the desert. I thought the rain was appropriate because, although he is technically my best friend, I dreaded the sight of his car. I knew he and Catherine would be in her office plotting against Paralight. This was the last thing I wanted to deal with on my anniversary. I wanted Catherine to myself for the evening, and I believed that I had outmaneuvered her at lunch, securing a night free of any Paralight legal discussions.

Cole had put me into this awkward and frustrating position with Catherine. He'd been laid off three months earlier after six years with Paralight. Because his relationship with the head of the legal department had soured, his boss wouldn't give him a good recommendation, which had sunk his chances of getting hired on at top law firms or as legal counsel for other major companies. Basically Paralight had ruined his career, but instead of finding a way to play nice, Cole insisted that Paralight was misusing the funds from a U.S. military contract that he had helped draft. He claimed that executives of Paralight were falsifying records, documents, and test results to cover their fraud. I didn't think his evidence was persuasive. As I saw it, he had begun a personal campaign to redeem his injured pride by exposing Paralight and had convinced Catherine to join him.

Catherine relished the opportunity because it gave her an escape. The year after Catherine graduated from law school, she was working with the fourth largest firm in Phoenix as a corporate attorney and we found she was pregnant—a surprise to both of us. Her first plan was to continue working; but halfway through the pregnancy, we learned that the baby would be severely mentally handicapped. The next few months were very difficult for us emotionally and financially. We had just purchased a home based on our combined salaries, but Catherine felt she needed to take care of our son rather than advance her career. My problem was that she earned double what I did. If she quit her job, we could not afford the home we were in and the lifestyle we were creating. She won, as usual. We sold the home and moved into an apartment.

After Danny was born, he became her life. She took care of him full-time. When I got hired on at Paralight we were finally able to breathe a little financially and were able to afford our simple house. Life looked great to me and I was passionate about what I was doing. Going to work at Paralight was exciting and exhilarating. Although Catherine never outright said it, I knew she felt jealous that I could accomplish my dreams and work in an environment that was stimulating to me in every way. She loved Danny, and he was the focus of her life, but she was also extremely bored. Each day was the same, and progress was either nonexistent or slow. Some nights when we talked, tears would come to her eyes as she explained how much she loved Danny but desperately needed something to think about. She craved the times we would go on dates for the mere fact of being able to have a conversation with another adult. She read voraciously and would discuss her books in detail with me. She loved in-depth conversations about the characters and the moral decisions they made. At nights we would often read chapters together, and I enjoyed the depth it brought into our relationship and the stimulation it meant to her mind. She had a love for classic literature and history and would learn all she could about a person or situation, examining every aspect from all angles. That is why she loved the law and the idea of being a trial attorney. She was an investigator, curious by nature. Figuring things out was her passion. I loved this aspect of her and thoroughly enjoyed these conversations—until recently. Then it seemed as if the moral decisions of everyone in history were pointed toward Paralight.

When Cole asked Catherine to examine the records and documents in his case against Paralight and help him develop a criminal case, it gave her a new lease on life. She dove into the materials and felt she finally had something to do that would make a difference in the world, help her brother, and employ the full range of her mental resources. I begged her to take up tennis or to write a book—anything but this—but nothing I said could change her mind. The two had been gathering information against Paralight for several months with the goal to taking a watertight case to Vanessa, who was working her way up at the district attorney's office and making a name for herself as a prosecutor.

Catherine was convinced I worked for criminals. She and Cole had boxes of evidence and information and the details became the subject of most conversations. Cole also convinced her that the speed of light plane with the monkey was a failure and that Cartwright had died. She believed I would die if I tested the plane and constantly pressured me to leave Paralight before the test flight. At that point, I made my decision. It was hard to argue with most of the evidence she was gathering, and I had very little understanding of the financial, legal and research aspects, so I just stayed away from it all. I closed my eyes and refused to listen.

But the monkey was another story. I repeatedly told her that I had seen the test flight with my own eyes, that I was still in contact with Cartwright, and he was perfectly fine. I told her that I might not be as smart as she was but my eyes worked just fine, maybe even better than hers. My line of reasoning did nothing, because when Catherine was convinced of something, you had a better chance of convincing her that gravity did not exist than changing her mind. I found that not approaching the subject or quickly steering away from it was the only way to keep my sanity and happiness.

I walked into the house to see Janet, our babysitter, sitting in front of the television with Danny at her side staring out the window. He was six and had not said a word in his life. Janet, our sixteen-year-old neighbor down the street, had become more of a nanny than babysitter since Catherine's dive into exposing Paralight. She was overall a good girl and perfect for our situation because she had a lot of time. She was attractive and spunky, but she had a slight learning disability and dyslexia that slowed her down at school. When she was drowning in school, her parents pulled her out and were homeschooling her. Because times were tough for her family, her mother got a job and was not home to do the schooling. The timing was perfect for us, since it coincided with Catherine's crusade against Paralight. Catherine and Janet's mother worked out a deal that Janet would continue homeschooling through internet courses and could do them at our house. The truth was that Janet watched more T.V. than anyone I knew, but tending Danny was not a difficult task as he rarely did anything but stare out the window or at the wall.

"Danny! I'm home!" I said as I came through the door. Sometimes I would get a slight movement from him but most of the time there was no reaction. I walked to him and crouched down to look into his far-away eyes. "Danny, I was flying today and I'll take you soon if you'd like." His stare remained constant. "You do any reading today?" I continued directing the question to Janet. No response. "Janet?"

Her mind took a few moments to click from the "O.C." rerun she was watching, "Sorry, what?" she replied.

"Did you and Danny read?" Janet and Catherine had made a deal that the two of them would read simple books together. Janet's mother had found that if Janet wore reading glasses she could focus more on the words and it freed her from some of the effects of her dyslexia.

"Mr. Brown can moo, can you?" she said with a smile, quoting a Dr. Seuss book sitting next to Danny. "Danny is having trouble mooing but I think he liked it."

"I can moo, Danny, can you?" I said. Danny's eyes were still in another world. I kissed him on the cheek. "Catherine and the bloodsucker in the office?" Janet smiled and her eyes went googly as she nodded. She had a crush on Cole and thought he looked like Edward Cullen from the movie *Twilight* which she had watched more than was humanly possible. Whenever Cole entered a room, Janet would go silent and blush.

"I heard that," answered Catherine's voice from the small study behind the living room.

"I thought tonight was our night, not the vampire's," I said as I walked into the study to see the dry erase board covered with information for their case. Boxes and files covered the desk and floor. Cole thought it was funny that Janet was so smitten and liked the comparison to Edward.

"Oh, no, Cole's coming along to dinner and I thought I'd sit by him," quipped Catherine.

Cole looked at me and smiled, "One of these days you'll thank me for what we're doing."

"You're right, I will. Thank you," I said. Cole smiled to himself and I asked Catherine, "You said something about dressing up, right?"

"Yes, I'm dressed and that's five pages, also five more for not listening at lunch." Catherine, in a beautiful black dress, smiled widely considering the ten pages she had just accumulated. At nights, when Catherine and I read aloud to each other, "five pages" was part of our agreement. Whenever I wouldn't listen to what she was saying—or more precisely when she thought I wasn't listening to her—I would have to rub her back while she read five pages from whatever book we were reading. At the time we were reading Shakespeare's *Hamlet* and she insisted that this story line would help me to make quick decisions because delay and avoidance can be catastrophic. How right she was.

"Lunch, yes, I'll give you that, but not about dressing up. I brought it up so obviously I was listening," I argued.

She shrugged, indicating that she wasn't going to argue the point.

"Five pages then," she stated with a dreamy smile.

I turned to Cole. "I'd ask you how you're doing, but that may get us into an area that Catherine doesn't want to discuss tonight."

"No, no, darling, Cole and I would both like to discuss it," Catherine teased.

Cole stood up, "I know when to keep my mouth shut. You guys have fun. I'm on my way out." He made his way out of the study.

He stopped in front of Danny and stooped down to eye-level, "Danny, you take care of Janet. She may get scared here tonight." He kissed Danny on the forehead and smiled at Janet. Janet's eyes nearly rolled up in ecstasy and her face turned scarlet, but she smiled at Cole. With that, Cole was out the front door, and I was upstairs changing.

The rain was pouring, when Catherine and I left for dinner. She had made our evening's plans but had refused to give me any hint of what we were doing. She knew I would dig it out of her if we talked so she refused to say anything other than directions.

"It's our anniversary. Say something, anything," I said.

She shook her head and bit her lip, not letting a word out.

"Please, anything! Tell me how good I look, how charming I am," I continued.

"Left," she said with a smile.

"Left?"

"Left," she said again.

"What does that mean? You left something home?"

"Left! Turn left here!" she said in a panic.

"Oh, *turn* left," I said smiling as I yanked the wheel. The car slid on the wet road, barely making the turn. Catherine gave me an out-of-breath "you're crazy" look but kept silent.

"Three words—that's great. Eight years of marriage and I get three words. My girlfriend here can do better than that," I pulled the handle on the car door.

"The driver door is ajar," said the female voice from the car. We were driving Catherine's car, an older model Lexus loaded with features.

I then pulled the door shut, "That's five words I believe. Five and I've had to make no commitment, nothing. She'll do it again, too." I opened and shut the door again.

"The driver door is ajar."

"I have the right to remain silent," Catherine stated.

"You do, but there are consequences," I replied.

"Consequences? You're not getting anything out of me. I'm saying nothing."

"Severe consequences," I said with emphasis.

"I'm not scared."

"I don't scare you?" I questioned.

"I didn't say that," she smiled warmly, "but I'm not scared." I took her hand, and she squeezed mine. I looked over at her. Her mesmerizing face was calm and loving. In that moment, all the hard work of my life was worth the expression on her face. I had everything. The next moment I lost everything.

The passenger window behind her shattered and glistening pieces of glass slowly flew past her face and her body was thrust through the window. The crash was deafening, metal tearing into metal, and everything that made sense in my life vanished. My life went black.

I woke in my car with my cheek on the steering wheel. A woman was outside the driver's side window and told me she was a paramedic. My hands went to my face and wiped blood from my eyes. Red lights were flashing and through the rain I saw an ambulance. Several paramedics were loading a stretcher into the ambulance. Catherine was on the stretcher. I struggled to get out and my seatbelt held me tight.

"Sir, stay in the car, we'll help you out," said the paramedic.

"Catherine! Catherine!" I screamed through the rain and I saw her head turn slightly. She looked in my direction. I yanked the seat belt off, pulled myself out of the car and, against the demands of the paramedic, ran to the ambulance.

I jumped into the ambulance as the paramedics were closing the doors. They began to work on her. She was losing blood, and they were working hard to stop it. Machines were going and they were yelling to each other but all I could see or hear was Catherine. I concentrated on her eyes. "You're doing great, Catherine. We're almost there."

She looked at me with a smile but a tear ran down her cheek.

"It's okay, you're going to be okay," I said to her even as I doubted my words.

Her face was white. The glow inside her was fading and being replaced with desperation and fear, "I'm scared, Pierce."

"Don't be scared. You'll be okay." Tears welled in my eyes. Her statuesque face attempted a smile and then her eyes changed.

She was looking at me but she wasn't. My heart strained and the nerves of my body fought against the reality my mind was trying to register. I touched her face but there was no reaction, "Catherine, can you hear me? Catherine?"

I looked at the paramedics and the sound of the world around me returned for a moment. There was a solid line and a constant tone on the heart monitor, "Catherine! Please, Catherine! Can you hear me?"

The paramedics pushed me to the side, barking orders and reports, working feverishly. Silence took over again and numbness engulfed me. The rest of the night was a horrific emptiness. The hospital recorded her as dead on arrival, and I had papers to sign in the cold, sanitary offices. Police officers had me fill out additional papers because the other driver had fled the scene on foot. It was a hit and run. I arrived home in a cab. It was still raining. The house was cold, the rain was cold, my hands were cold, and I could not feel my heart. Nothing was there. Everything was gone. The walk to the doorway seemed an eternity. As I reached the door, Janet opened it. Tears were running down her cheeks. She hugged me and I could see her lips, trying to say, "I'm sorry," but the words would not come out. Her tears turned to wrenching sobs.

"Thank you for watching Danny," I said. I fumbled a twenty-dollar bill out of my wallet and handed it to her.

"If there's anything…" she couldn't finish.

"I know, thank you."

Janet nodded and left.

I walked to where Danny was sitting and slumped down in front of him. He had her beauty in his face. He stared blankly, and for a flash I thought of her face as she faded away.

"Danny," I said quietly. Nothing changed. There was no reaction. His eyes were as distant as Catherine's had become in the ambulance. Catherine was gone, and Danny was never really with me. I loved my son, but I had never felt so alone in the universe.

I braced my back against the wall and my legs gave way under me. I slid down the wall and was stopped by the floor. A full realization of the accident and Catherine's loss fell upon me, and tears rolled down my cheeks. The pain flowed out of my body through my eyes until exhaustion took over and I again returned to blackness.

Chapter 2

Rock formations whipped by outside the cockpit, and the visor on my helmet displayed my position in relation to the other planes—two fully armed F-22 Raptors. To the United States government, the jet I was flying, Stormlight, did not exist. It was the jet that Cartwright, the monkey, had been strapped in for the speed-of-light test. I was flying low over the deserts to avoid any detection, but I had been detected. Stormlight was a futuristic airplane no one outside of Paralight had ever seen, and it was flying in United States airspace. Because of the secrecy of the tests we were performing, I was not allowed to respond to their demands for identification, and they had been cleared to engage. I was being attacked by the United States Air Force. Stormlight had no missiles or weaponry, and I was all alone.

The controls of the jet were smooth and tight, the reactions instant and precise. It was everything we had designed it to be. A projection on the visor showed the Raptors diving in pursuit. I descended into a canyon and zipped past the red-rock faces. Clouds of sand burst off the cliffs as I skimmed near them. The Raptors were following in close formation. They were fast. If I were to survive, I had to increase speed enough to out-fly them. I pulled away from them and they did not follow, instead they pulled up out of the canyon and targeted me from above. The first missile zeroed in on me. I hugged tight to the canyon floor, and the missile caught the edge of a cliff, exploding into a cloud of rock and fire.

My visor informed me that the other Raptor also had a lock on me. The canyon extended into a straight-away, and this missile would trap me. I pulled up out of the canyon and banked to the right. The second Raptor released its missile, and I could see it approaching. My thumb flicked up a switch cover over a white button, and my visor informed me the system was ready. I saw the missile approaching and pressed the button, engaging light speed. Everything burst to white and instantly I was flying high above the ocean, the Raptors hundreds of miles away. I smiled, rolled my jet, and descended until I was only meters above the waves. The pressure of the speed of the plane and the vacuum left behind caused a wake on the surface of the water and threw a swirling plume of mist into the air that appeared to be chasing me. Then the world around me faded away, and the criss-crossing bars of the simulation room were again all around me.

The cockpit pulled itself back into the center position in the room and came to a full stop. My turn on the simulator had ended, but I did not move. I dreaded the fact that I could no longer drown myself in the fictional world the holograms created. The simulator was my escape and coming back to the real world was always difficult.

I had sunk myself into my work after the accident and Catherine's death. Not thinking about it was the way I held myself together. Nights when I went home were the hardest. The funeral and the preparations for it were, to that point, the most difficult times in my life. I did not cope with the loss of Catherine well at all. It all seems a blur to me now. Cole and Vanessa did most of the preparations. Catherine's parents were in town, but whenever I saw them I was at a loss for words. They seemed to be satisfied with giving a hug and remaining silent. I avoided the subject of Catherine and did not attempt to face her loss. My father stayed at my house for the few days before the funeral and his presence was helpful, but I was still alone. There was an emptiness that no one could fill. I spoke at the funeral and had prepared a talk about the wonderful things Catherine had done in her life, the love I felt for her, and my admiration for her focus on our son Danny. When I got up to talk, tears came to my eyes and I could not see the words I had prepared. I am not the best speaker and I cannot quite remember what I said but something came out, mostly emotion. Seeing her casket lowered into the ground seemed to me the most unfair act any person could do. Guilt bit my insides. I had been driving the car when she died. I couldn't stop the questions. *If I had been driving slower, would the hit-and-run have missed us? Was I driving recklessly? If I had done something different, would she still be alive?* I wanted to go back and change that night and have her at my side again, but the casket going into the ground made her death final. She was gone, and I could not get her back. The guilt bit deeper because I knew she was a better person than me, yet I was the one who had survived.

For the first couple days after the funeral, I became a recluse. I could not seem to put my sentences in an understandable form and avoided speaking. The loneliness was unbearable. I found some solace upon returning to work as my mind became occupied with something other than my loneliness, self-pity, and guilt. Janet had been a lifesaver. She had stayed at my house full-time and had taken care of Danny while I was not register-ing the world around me; but with the test for Stormlight ap-proaching, I decided to put him into a care facility. Janet, not needed, went back to her home. The decision was hard and it added more loneliness and guilt to the hollow life I was living, but I felt it would be best to have him in a facility on the off chance something unexpected happened during the test flight.

Of all places in the world, I felt comfortable only in the sim-ulation room. The holographic projections were so lifelike it was impossible to distinguish them from reality. It was ironic. I felt comfort being in an unreal environment. I could step out of the real world, which was filled with emptiness, and relax in a fic-tional world created by lights; but the flights always came to an end and I had to face reality again.

"Light speed was a cop-out," said Kendall through the mi-crophone on my helmet.

"Put missiles on Stormlight and I'll fight," I replied.

"Now there's an idea," said Kendall thoughtfully. We re-viewed our flights in the visual room, which was down the bal-cony from the simulator. I always enjoyed the walk to visual because I could look out to the right and see the wide expanse of the Scarlet hangar and it gave me a feeling of accomplish-ment knowing I was an essential part of the program. The small conference room marked 'Visual' had many large panel screens, and we could review and critique the simulations step-by-step. Kendall had been shot down by the Raptors and still insisted my run was flawed because I had to resort to light speed. I told him that losing the entire plane was more flawed than pushing a white button and returning alive and with a hundred million dollar plane.

After the review in visual, I split away from Kendall and went through a barrage of tests. The light speed test for a human flying Stormlight was scheduled for the next morning, and they needed to be sure I was healthy in every respect. I had to leave the site for a CAT scan then I returned to the Paralight exam room. This room was a combination of a research lab of a wacky scientist, a computer technology company and a doctor's office. Computers and monitors were everywhere along with three hospital beds, tables with instruments, a treadmill, and cages with monkeys in them. One of the monkeys was Cartwright, the speed of light monkey.

A tall, thin scientist named Carter, who had the personality of a petri dish, was running the tests. With him were two assistants, neither of whom I knew. Carter had been at Paralight long before I was hired, and I had to interact with him for only a few minutes every quarter. He was not a pleasant man; and by the end of my sessions with him, I was ready to speak with someone who understood the existence of human beings around him. He was all about research and his lab. People were instruments and he dealt with them as if they were just another tool. I could understand why his assistants did not last long. The treadmill slowed, and Carter came over to take the electrodes off me.

"Hey, Cartwright," I said to the monkey with a smile. Carter looked at the monkey with disdain, let out a disappointed burst of air, and continued his work.

"He's still healthy, right?" I asked Carter.

"Hold still," Carter commanded.

"Cartwright, he's fine isn't he?" I questioned again.

Carter peered at me with annoyance, then looked at the monkey and quipped, "That monkey right there is perfectly healthy."

"How am I?" I asked.

"You'll do."

"I'll do?" I answered with a slight laugh.

"Yes, you'll do," he answered stoically as he turned to his computer screens. "Put all this away," he ordered his assistants who quickly followed orders. Without looking in my direction he continued, "Your report will be to Jack within the hour."

I had an impulse to speak with the new assistants, but they worked in silence, not looking up. I walked out of the room. I met with Jack in his office where two attorneys from the legal department had me sign away my life but also make the arrangements that would take care of Danny if anything were to happen to me on the test. The two of us then walked to the boardroom on the top level of the building. Members of the board had gathered, waiting to discuss the speed of light test flight with me.

The boardroom was modern, sleek, and beautiful. Black ergonomic chairs surrounded a brushed chrome and mahogany table. Seated around it were well-dressed men and women. Two chairs at the end of the conference table were empty. Jack took one and motioned for me to do the same. I knew all of them but rarely saw or spoke to any of them. Jack was the only one I had consistent communication with, and I always felt he was fighting for me and appreciated my talents.

"Einstein said it wasn't possible," began Mr. Turnbow, the president of Paralight, "How does that make you feel?"

"I figure if a monkey can do it, why can't I?" My reply broke the awkwardness as several of the executives laughed.

"You're comfortable being the first?" the woman in charge of international marketing questioned.

"I trust those around me. Jack here has never led me wrong." Jack's expression showed his approval with my comment.

The questions continued for a few minutes until Mr. Turnbow finished the brief meeting with, "Tomorrow's a big day for all of us. Thank you, Pierce." He then turned to Jack, "Let's make history, Jack."

"We will. I am very confident this will be a large turning point for Scarlet. We'll see you all tomorrow."

"Thank you for your time, gentlemen," said Mr. Turnbow.

Jack and I nodded, stood up and left the room. As the door to the boardroom closed behind us, Jack turned to me and said, "Well done. Come early tomorrow. Everything must be perfect."

I nodded in agreement.

Part of the long marble hallway with large windows opening to a view of the skyline of Phoenix was sectioned off with small orange cones and a short, mentally handicapped janitor was mopping. Jack looked at the janitor with disdain, "Aren't you supposed to do this at night?" he demanded. The janitor looked at Jack helplessly as Jack continued, "Get this out of here. They're having a board meeting and will be out shortly." He then kicked some of the cones out of the way. The janitor backed away and hid his face.

Jack finally seemed to realize he was mentally handicapped and in frustration said, "Great, the one that can't think." Jack then moved in close to the janitor's face and said quietly but with force, "Put these in your cart and go! I don't want anyone to see this mess, or you."

The mentally handicapped janitor quivered and then scrambled to pick up the cones. Jack walked down the hallway and around a corner. I watched in shock and pain. Jack had always been cordial and supportive of me. I had never seen him behave so cruelly. Was it the pressure of the flight? Whatever it was, I felt indignant. The poor janitor was innocently trying to do his job.

I picked up several cones and took them to the janitor. He shrank away from me, so, moving slowly, I put them on his cart and said gently, "You know, you do a fantastic job. I don't think I've ever seen such clean floors."

The janitor smiled cautiously.

"My name is Pierce. What's yours?"

"Jonathan," he replied in soft tones.

"It's a pleasure to meet you."

"You, too, and thank you. I'm sure you clean floors good, too," he said in a complimentary way.

I felt strangely close to Jonathan, and my heart ached as I wished Danny could speak with me as Jonathan did, "Thank you, Jonathan." I helped Jonathan pick up the remaining cones and walked with him to the janitorial area. He was quite pleasant and I enjoyed speaking with him.

By the time I pulled into my driveway, the sun was going down. I walked into the empty house and was reminded, again, of my loneliness. The air inside seemed thicker than the outside air, and it caused my heart to burn. I wished Danny were there so I could at least look at him. I grabbed a piece of bread from the pantry and ate it as I went upstairs to my bed. After the imperfections in the ceiling thoroughly bored me, I turned to stare at the family photo on my nightstand. Catherine and I were smiling, and Danny had a pleasant, comfortable look on his face. Memories flooded my mind, and I felt stifled again. I had memories of her, but I did not have her. Next to the picture was the play we were reading together, *Hamlet*.

I needed some sort of reprieve from my mind. I sat up, bunched my pillows behind my back, picked up the book, and started to read. I liked the plot. I also liked the way Shakespeare wrote. Hard to understand, yes, but very creative and well thought out. I acted out in my mind the aspects of the story, and creating the images in my mind helped me remove myself from the depression I felt living in my own life.

When I woke up early in the morning, the book was resting on my stomach. I got up, took a shower, went down to the kitchen, made a simple breakfast and continued reading. Before long I saw a familiar car pull up in front of my house. It was Cole.

Not this morning, I thought. *Please, leave me alone today.* I put the book down, stood up, picked up my car keys and had opened the front door before Cole could knock.

"Hey, look who's here!" I said with false heartiness.

"You've gotta listen to me," he said.

"I know, I know. The monkey's an imposter," I mocked.

"Just this once—listen, please. Three lab assistants saw it die and they'll each testify."

"I agree. I don't think his story made sense either," I said as I walked past him and toward my car.

"It's not a game, Pierce. You can't do this."

"It's the perfect crime. Who'd question the monkey?" I said with sarcasm.

"It's fraud, Pierce. It's more than fraud. It's a house of cards. The whole thing is coming down. There is much more at play than you can imagine, and they'll do anything to cover it up."

"I have quite an imagination," I replied with a smile.

"Catherine knew it. That's why—"

My finger quickly went up, "Not there." I was firm and resolute. He told me at the funeral he thought Paralight had sent the hit-and-run driver. After that, I had had enough. I blew up at him and told him he had brought misery to my last months with my wife and I didn't want anything to do with him. The next day we made amends, but I made it clear I did not want anything to do with his case against Paralight. "Don't go there. I'm sorry you were fired; and from what I know, you should still have your job. I still have mine. If I leave or get fired, what else do I have?" With that I got into my car and started the engine.

"You have Danny."

He was right. I still had Danny. I saw sincerity in his eyes. He was genuinely interested in me and my welfare. "Dinner's on me, I'll call you later," I said as I pulled out of the driveway. Cole stood silently and watched me drive away.

It was a relief to get to Paralight. I pulled myself out of the miserable world of my personal life and started work. The locker room was empty as I put on my black flight suit. I always liked dressing because I felt and looked like a superhero. The suit was tight fitting, black, constructed to constrict as speed and g-forces increased and was wired to monitor every part of my body. The scientists would use the information to evaluate and improve the machines I tested. As I exited the locker room, Jack was waiting in the hallway. He smiled brightly, and we walked down the hallway to one of the hangars together. Inside the hangar were several hovercrafts filled with scientists and Paralight personnel. As I walked in, there were smiles and a few comments, "The first man!" yelled one of the assistants to Carter. I smiled because I had always wondered if they did have personalities.

"Way to go, Pierce!" shouted Kendall. I smiled at him and the others with their beaming faces.

"Thanks," I replied as I stepped into one of the hovercrafts. There was applause from everyone. "Okay, thanks—enough of that. You realize this is not a huge deal. It's a fast trip." Everyone laughed, and with that the hovercrafts zipped out of the hangar and across the desert. It was not long before we approached a small test runway with a small control tower. This is where I had watched Cartwright make history and was where I would take the fastest step humankind had ever experienced.

The formalities were nonexistent. The crews and scientists rushed into the control tower to man their respective positions, and I got into the cockpit of Stormlight. After the cockpit was closed and sealed, and I had secured the helmet on my head, I sat and waited.

It wasn't too long before Randall, the head of operations, came through on my systems, his face on a screen in front of me, "This will be easier than you thought. We'll control everything from our end. Just sit back and enjoy."

The systems engaged on the panels in front of me and the plane taxied down the runway. "You're the boss," I answered.

"All systems are go. Begin take-off." The plane accelerated, and I was quickly airborne. The plane headed south for some time before circling around and heading north. "Pierce, enjoy the trip," Randall said.

"Forgive me for not bringing back T-shirts."

Randall smiled, "Increase speed."

The speed of the plane increased drastically, and I heard the crack of the sonic boom. My suit tightened around my body, constricting my blood flow. The speed continued to increase, "Engage."

A bright light flashed in front of the plane and engulfed everything. All motion was slowed by millions. My hands turned into sinews of light which spread up my arms. I could see the dematerialization of coils in my flight suit and in the blood veins in my arms. Chemical compositions reformed and shed unnecessary particles. Photons sped off in organized patterns, and my existence flowed with them. I could simultaneously feel the ground below, the atmosphere above, and the emptiness of space in the solar system. I felt the awe and astonishment of the scientists in the control tower and the electrical charges flowing through the instruments that were displaying the readouts of the test. Everything around me became unified in a clear moment of enlightenment and understanding. The inherent cloudiness of my human mind and faculties disappeared and I, for a brief moment, felt the understanding of pure intelligence and existence course through me. There was a unity in my being and the endless universe and I knew I was not alone.

In a large, crackling explosion, my world of understanding, unity and enlightenment collapsed back into mortality and the confines of my body. The overreaching understanding and union I had with my surroundings became splintered and chaotic. Pain coursed through every nerve, and I saw the stitching of the chemical compositions of my body reuniting and forming. The sinews of light attached to matter and pulled it into precise shapes, reassembling the plane and my body back to the forms they had had a millionth of a fraction of a second before.

A final shock of power swept through my system, and the light was gone. My muscles contracted, and I hunched over. The feeling of claustrophobia overtook me, and I gasped for air. The cockpit squeezed me into my seat, and I thrust my hand up to push it away from me. As I watched my hand, another appeared next to it—but it was different. It was covered with hair and flailing. I heard screams. Inside me, something was struggling to break free. I screamed and struggled to break free from the belts strapping me to the seat. Hairy hands and then feet flailed and kicked out of my body. I snapped the belt off my chest, jumped from the seat and into the instrument panel. I was not alone in the cockpit. Cartwright was there with me, screaming at the top of his lungs and my head seared with pain. Suddenly the plane was gone, and I was alone. Light collapsed all around me, and then it was dark.

Chapter 3

Blackness increased and decreased. I vaguely remember blurry light and unfamiliar faces. When I was able to focus through the blurry world around me I would find that my surroundings kept changing. I would wake up in different places with a biting headache. One time I would be in a living room, another time outdoors, later still in a nightclub. The people I saw were strangers, and I had no idea what they were doing or why I was there. None of it made sense. The longer I tried to stay awake, the more the pain would increase. Eventually I would close my eyes, and the pain would subside.

Finally I opened my eyes to no pain. The actual coming into consciousness was a long-drawn-out process, and the blur that filled the room cleared over the space of hours. When I could make out my surroundings, I was in a small white room with a bed and a simple nightstand. I sat up on the bed, and blood rushed to my head. I felt the numbing of a blackout absorbing my body and quickly returned my head to the pillow. A short time later, a doctor came into the room and sat next to me.

His words were cloudy but I could understand them, "I'm Dr. Reed," he said. "You have been in a coma for two and a half months." During our first conversation, the headache returned and the cloudiness of his voice took over and I again fell into oblivion.

As time went by, I was able to focus and gained comfort in the white surroundings of the small room. Dr. Reed told me to try not to think when I was awake. I became quite good at not thinking. As long as I kept my mind clear, the headaches would not come. He also told me that Danny was okay. The most important thing I could do was sleep. The dreams and headaches would subside as my mind healed from the trauma of the test flight. He also explained I had first been taken to St. Joseph's Hospital, but as my mind was showing strange, unsteady patterns they had transferred me to the Kensington Mental Hospital where he, Dr. Reed, could personally oversee my recovery and make detailed diagnoses and reports for the company which would provide a better understanding of the influences of the speed of light test flight. He assured me I was not to consider myself a mental patient, but a patient who had suffered a trauma to his mind. The interviews with him were for scientific progress and understanding.

I slept a lot and the nurses were nice other than a large oaf of a male nurse named Marshall. Marshall brought in the morning meals and without fail would make a comment intended to put me down. I had a dream one night that I was on a playground and the children were laughing at another child, calling him "Mars." The next morning when Marshall brought in the food, I slipped and called him Mars. He went ballistic.

"You're a freak!" he yelled, "Just like everyone else in this place and you better watch out!"

"I'm sorry," I said apologetically.

"You're right you are," he sneered, "I'm in charge of the food around here and I can make your life horrible." I remained silent and he left the room. From that day forward, I refrained from talking when Marshall came and instead looked at the wall. Therapy or "scientific" sessions with Dr. Reed were pleasant and we progressed to where we would walk around the gardens of the facility for our discussions. I was eager to return to work and my life, but Dr. Reed explained that the board of Paralight had specifically ordered no contact from anyone other than Dr. Reed until he felt the recovery and scientific evaluations were finished. Paralight had legal authority over my health, and Dr. Reed was constrained to follow their wishes, but he did assure me that the test flight had been a great success: I was the first human being to travel the speed of light. The world did not know this, and the board was waiting until the proper moment to release the information, but my physical health and mental stability were important aspects of the study of the speed of light.

It was, in total, one day shy of four months from the date of the test flight when I found myself sitting across from Dr. Reed for my final session. It was a rather comfortable session. Dr. Reed asked questions about what I would do and where I would go. I gave generic answers. He told me he had contacted the institution taking care of Danny and had scheduled for Danny to be released to my care again. I told him I appreciated his help and looked forward to being with Danny. As always he concluded with the question, "Anything you'd like to say?"

"I have to admit I'm looking forward to anything but white," I answered.

"Go home. Look at more than white walls. Come back, visit with me tomorrow and tell me about it. I have scheduled you in at four o'clock."

"Thanks, Dr. Reed."

With that Dr. Reed stood up, shook my hand and led me out the door. Marshall stood in the hallway with a bored, clumsy expression on his face. "You're letting him out?"

Without acknowledging the comment, Dr. Reed said, "Drive him home."

Marshall nodded and walked with me out of the building, across the courtyard, and to a gray van. I intentionally avoided his gaze and sat in the far back. Marshall got in and drove through the courtyard. The large metallic gates opened for the van, and he pulled onto the street. It was refreshing to see cars on the streets and the world in full motion. I had been cooped in the white room and gardens of the institution for so long I had forgotten the energy of the outside world.

"See anything I don't?" asked Marshall with a smirk.

I was tired of Marshall and I had ignored him long enough, "You," I replied.

"What's that supposed to mean?"

"Yes, I do."

Marshall's brow furrowed and his head tilted with confusion, "You do what?"

"See something you don't."

"Huh?"

"I see something you don't," I repeated.

"What's that?"

"An unfortunate man."

Marshall squinted and I could see fury building in his face. I stared back at him and slowly his expression relaxed, "You're the one from the nut house." He smiled to himself and stuck his elbow out the window.

I looked out the window again and took in the scenery. It wasn't long before we pulled up to my house. I opened the door and stepped out.

"I've driven enough of you home to know that they'll lock you up again tomorrow," said Marshall with a jerk of his chin.

"You think so?" I asked.

"You're all freaks. It's in your brain and it'll ooze its way out. Everyone at the mental hospital is mental."

I pulled the sliding door shut and walked to the window, "Where are you going?"

"Back to work," he replied.

"According to your definition, what does it make you if you are at the mental hospital?"

Marshall considered the question for a long moment then sneered, "You'll be back, Mr. Mental." He put the van in gear and pulled away.

I took a deep breath and walked up the pathway to my house. The lawn was mowed and green—someone had been taking care of it. There was a note on the front door. I pulled it off and it read:

> *Pierce,*
> *Welcome home. We have taken care of every-*
> *thing. Have a good night's rest and I will see you*
> *in the morning.*
> *Rick Alstead from Paralight*

It felt good to walk through the front door, smell the familiar wood, and know I was home again. As I walked into the kitchen I saw Catherine standing at the stove, but then she was gone. I blinked my eyes and looked again but I was alone. Loneliness caved in on me like a suffocating cloud. I was in my house but I was not with Catherine. She was gone. I took deep breaths but claustrophobia forced the walls of the house to smash into me, and I struggled to breathe. I ran from the house and the crisp out-side air rejuvenated my lungs. As I sat on the steps and waited for my body to recover, I ached to be near my son. There was comfort in the thought of Danny. For me he represented stability. The house was nothing more than materials without life in them, and I had been without my son long enough. Determined to ease the loneliness, I ran back into the house, found the keys to my car and drove to Danny's care facility.

As I entered, the staff was warm and welcoming. They let me go to Danny's room and spend some time with him. It was comforting to see him and touch his face. He stared at the wall and I talked to him for about thirty minutes. He didn't respond, but it made me feel good. He was a part of me and Catherine. Being with him again filled some of the emptiness inside. The administrator of the facility confirmed they would bring him to my house the following day at two o'clock and I thanked her for all she had done.

When I returned home the sun had set, and the silver of the moon was my light to the front door. I turned on the lights and went into the kitchen for a glass of water. Coming home was not as traumatizing the second time. I saw *Hamlet* on the table and picked it up. I opened the pages. Skimming several passages brought more calmness to my mind. From what I understood,

Hamlet had troubles with loneliness, too, and I felt he would empathize with me.

I thought about the last time I had read the book and how I had rushed out of the house past Cole. It had been four months since I had seen Cole—or anyone not connected to the hospital, for that matter. I took the book with me and went upstairs to my room, determined to get in touch with Cole the next day and catch up. I smiled with satisfaction at the thought that I would be vindicated. Despite Cole's doomsday predictions, the flight had been a success, and I was okay. It felt good to smile. It also felt good to sit on my bed. I opened the book and read. It was not long before Hamlet and his concerns, along with mine, faded from my mind and I was asleep.

I woke slowly in the morning to my comfortable and warm bed and took the time to relax and think before I moved. I missed my wife—I longed to see her by my side but knew it would not happen. I pondered my future, and the fact I would be returning to work shortly. My life would be different when Paralight announced the success of the speed of light flight. I would be forever recognized as the first pilot to fly the speed of light. It would be in the history books. I would have fame and popularity. However, the thought was hollow. The great moments of life have value when you share them. I no longer had Catherine. She was the person who had given value to my accomplishments. Danny didn't understand those accomplishments, but being with him had calmed me. I was a father and there was a deep connection with Danny even though it was one-sided. I needed him in my life.

As I was contemplating my situation, I turned and looked at the familiar family photograph on my nightstand. We were all dressed casually and sitting together on a rock near a river in a park. Red and orange autumn leaves blanketed the ground. The photographer had met us at the park, and I had carried Danny to the photo shoot location. That morning Catherine and I had been at our usual odds over Paralight and had had an actual quarrel. But while we were walking to the river, we decided we wanted to remember a wonderful moment every time we looked at the photos, so we created a "moment." We decided to replace the argument with a created story. Our story was that we had gone to I-HOP for breakfast and had watched the sun rise in each other's arms. She added that I had given her a card and a rose—and that she hadn't hinted about either one of them to me. My contribution was that she had bought tickets to a film I wanted to see and had slid them into my hand just as the sun rose. Whenever we looked at the photograph, we would talk about how great the sunrise was and how thoughtful our partner's loving gesture had been.

We were both smiling in the photograph. As I stared at it, I could see the life and vitality in Catherine's eyes. Even Danny had seemed pleased and relaxed. I remembered the happiness of creating that moment. Catherine had been wonderful that day. I missed the great times, and I also missed the fights and the tension. It was all part of the package of "Catherine." I missed her. I missed our life together. The image captured her personality and life so fully I became entranced. I couldn't take my eyes off it. Her smile shifted a little. Well, I knew that was impossible, but I kept looking. Her smile widened. A strand of her hair fell into her face and she brushed it back into place. I blinked my eyes several times and refocused on the picture. The images of Danny and me blurred. Catherine stood up. The sweater and jeans, she was wearing rippled and transformed into a beautiful black dress. She stood and walked toward me still smiling.

Shocked, I stood up from the bed and backed myself into the wall of my bedroom which faded away like wisps of a cloud. My eyes were still locked on Catherine, but I could tell that my bed was fading from sight, to be replaced with a lavish sofa. I stepped to the right to avoid a chair that was materializing right where I was standing. In the center of the new sitting area, was an ornate coffee table upon which sat a bucket of ice, a frosty bottle of Amour de Deutz champagne, and a set of champagne flutes.

"Higher," I heard behind me. The voice was familiar, but I didn't believe it. I turned to see Vanessa tilting her head and squinting as she looked at a large banner on the wall. Catherine was standing against the wall, holding one side of the banner. It read: *Happy Anniversary, Pierce and Catherine.* Holding the other side of the banner was Cole.

"No, Catherine, higher!" insisted Vanessa.

"Then look at her, not me," Cole said exasperated, "You hold it."

"I've got the tacks," replied Vanessa with a smile as she stood back surveying the banner.

"Catherine?" I asked. I could hear the astonishment in my voice as I walked toward her. She did not hear me, nor did Cole or Vanessa. Catherine was full of life. The image in the ambulance when her life left her returned to my mind. It was nothing like what I was seeing. Warmth and excitement washed over me as I stared in awe. I walked over to Catherine as she was holding up her side of the banner and cupped her cheek with my hand, but my fingers passed through her face as if nothing were there. Were they there? Was I? What was happening?

Catherine turned to Vanessa, "Hurry, my arms are dying." Vanessa hurried to Catherine's aid and tacked the banner in place. Catherine stood back to look at it, "Perfect!" she beamed with a wide smile.

"Not perfect, tack my side," said Cole.

"What else?" Vanessa said to Catherine without a look at Cole.

Catherine smiled, "We've got the champagne..."

"...the table's set and matches are on your side..." continued Vanessa.

"The tacks!" interjected Cole.

"I can't think of anything and we've got to go."

"Funny. This is funny. I'll let it go," warned Cole.

"Oh, the sitter. Did you call her?" questioned Vanessa.

"Janet's there already, no sitter needed," Catherine said as she opened the door.

"I'll drop it! I will!" yelled Cole.

Vanessa followed Catherine out the door and shut it. Belatedly, I leaped forward, passing through the door. The two sisters were in the hallway, laughing contagiously as Cole shouted inside the room.

"I'm your ride, Catherine!" he yelled. "You're going nowhere without me!"

Catherine opened the door and looked at Cole with surprise, "Oh, Vanessa, that side doesn't have tacks on it."

"It doesn't?" Vanessa smiled as she walked toward Cole's side of the banner. I walked back into the room following her.

"You know we're in a rush and you stand there wasting time." Vanessa tacked the banner.

"Very funny. You two are hilarious."

Catherine and Vanessa burst into laughter again. I watched in amazement. This is what Catherine was planning for me the night of our anniversary—the night she had died. She had organized this room for us and somehow I was now seeing what they had done.

"Everything set?" Vanessa said to Catherine.

"I think we're done."

"I'm done," said Cole, "I've had enough of both of you." Cole exited followed by Catherine and Vanessa, both with large smiles.

As I stood in the room looking around, the banner faded away to wisps of light which reorganized themselves into the walls of my bedroom again. The ornate hotel room slowly disappeared and soon I was standing next to my bed with a biting headache. My vision faded to blue and a numbing feeling crept across my forehead and down my face. I collapsed onto my bed to recover from the painful light-headedness and found that I could not hold onto my consciousness. The world around me went dark.

I woke sometime later and opened my eyes to see the photograph on my nightstand. It was the same. Catherine, Danny, and I were all in the picture. I sat up in my bed and contemplated what I had just experienced. I had been in that hotel room with Catherine, Vanessa, and Cole. It was the night of my anniversary. I saw them all. My hand had gone through Catherine's cheek. It was so clear, but how was it possible? Could I have collapsed into sleep and had a very vivid dream? I shook my head slowly.

I had not been in that room on the night of my anniversary. Neither Cole nor Vanessa had told me anything about it. I rubbed my eyes and face. It was the strangest and clearest dream I had ever had—but *had* it been a dream?

I got out of bed and grabbed my cell phone, determined to find out if Cole and Vanessa had helped Catherine with the preparations for our anniversary and if so, what the room looked like. I called Cole and heard an automated message saying his inbox was full. I got Vanessa's voicemail and left her a message. I had no idea where Cole would be, but Vanessa was easy to find during business hours.

It was not long before I was walking down the stuffy hallways of the district attorney's offices. The walls were close together and gave me claustrophobia. The worn carpet reminded me of an old folks' home and even had the stagnant smell of decay to go with it. I was relieved when I arrived at the door, its frosted window sporting latex lettering reading "Vanessa Trace - Assistant District Attorney." The door was cracked open, and I could hear Vanessa speaking on the phone. Her voice was firm, and she was obviously not happy with the person on the line. "You represent a criminal; and as far as I can see it, fraud is fraud." She listened for a moment: "I'm not naive enough to believe that. Of course, he's done it before."

I lightly knocked on the door, and she looked up at me. Her creased brow softened and she smiled, waving me in.

"The contract was a farce, he kept the payment and the title company allowed him to sign the documents. How many others have fallen into his trap? The whole ship is sinking. Call me when we see the same picture." With that she hung up the phone, smiled, and rushed to me, "Pierce!"

"Remind me not to cross you," I said as she gave me a warm hug.

"It's great to see you. You look great. Sit down, please." She picked up a stack of disorganized files off one of the folding metal chairs in front of her desk and cleared a space for me. "How are you feeling?"

"You mean after being sequestered in the nuthouse?"

"I would have phrased it better, but yes."

"I'm great. I'm fine. You?"

"Busy, as usual, but I'm good," she said, looking at me with her striking Trace family eyes.

"I have a question. Not a question, really, but . . ." I faltered, and began again, "The night of our anniversary . . ." I paused again, groping for words. I could see sadness wash over her face. "You and Cole were with Catherine at the Windsor Hotel. You hung a banner above the bed that read 'Happy Anniversary, Pierce and Catherine,' the table was beautifully set and a bottle of Amour de Deutz was being chilled. Cole and Catherine were holding the banner and you had the tacks. You tacked Catherine's side, left Cole holding his, and the two of you left the room. You both thought it was pretty funny."

Vanessa looked at me with surprise and a mischievous smile, "Catherine told you?"

"No, I couldn't get a word out of her."

"Cole?"

"No. I dreamed it, I guess. But I was awake and it was so clear that I thought I'd run it by you and Cole."

"You dreamed it, but you were awake?"

"Yeah."

"How did you do that?"

"I don't know. I was looking at that photo of me, Catherine and Danny—the one by the river—and Catherine started walking toward me and brushing her hair to the side. And next thing I knew I was in the hotel room with you three."

Vanessa squinted and sat back in her chair trying to absorb what I was saying. "That's a little freaky to me."

"Me, too."

"Cole and I never brought up the hotel, considering the accident."

"But it happened, just like that?"

"Just like that—down to the tacks on the banner."

"You're right. It's freaky," I leaned back in my chair and tried to make sense of what I had seen.

"What are you doing now that you're out of the nuthouse?" I smiled at her, "Tomorrow I'm going back to work. This afternoon Danny's coming home, but I still have time to catch lunch with Cole."

Vanessa's face paled. "You didn't know? Cole's been missing since about the time of your flight. No one knows where he is."

"Missing?"

"Not a trace. He vanished."

"You don't know anything?" I asked.

"Nothing. I've done everything I can. It's been in the media and searches have been made everywhere."

"I'm sorry."

"It's okay. I'm okay. You can't change fate."

The phrase caught me off guard. It hit her, too, and she recognized the uncomfortable feeling coming from me. Her eyes dropped to papers on her desk and tension wrapped around us like a blanket. The phrase was exactly what she had said to me years ago and the scene flew vividly into my mind. We were sitting in my car late at night. We were holding hands, and it was the most awkward experience of my life. Vanessa, Catherine, Cole, and I had been inseparable after high school. Cole always said he knew I would become part of the family because he knew what was going through the minds of his sisters. Catherine was more outgoing than Vanessa and generally took charge in conversations. Vanessa held back and would say surprisingly charming things that enchanted me but kept her true feelings close to her heart. Vanessa had left for a couple of months on a study abroad course. During that time, Catherine and I had moved forward in our relationship, and it was clear to both of us we would get married. Catherine had not mentioned anything to Vanessa because she felt we should tell her together and in person.

As fate would have it, Cole and Catherine both were unavailable on the night Vanessa returned from the study abroad. I picked her up at the airport on my own. During the drive home, she asked me to stop the car; and I pulled into a small parking lot on the side of the road.

"I've had a lot of time to think while I have been gone, Pierce," she said, her voice warm with sincerity. "It's strange when you go away hoping to find something wonderful and realize everything wonderful in your life was already with you. I have realized I have everything I want, and it is right here. It is right here, right now, Pierce." She took my hands and looked me in the eyes, "I mean it, Pierce. Everything I want in life is in this car right now. I'm in love with you Pierce—I have been for years. You are the only person I have ever had these feelings for and the only person I will ever love."

My heart sank. I looked back at her eyes, seeing nothing but hope and sincerity and knew that my next words would change her life forever. I tried to think of something graceful and loving but my mind was a blank. Finally I stammered, "Thank you, Vanessa. That is the kindest thing I have ever heard from anyone."

"It's true, Pierce," she continued, "I know it now, and I need you to know how I feel."

The image of Catherine appeared in my mind, and I wanted to cry for Vanessa. "I have something to tell you, too." My voice sounded hoarse in my own ears. "Actually, Catherine and I have something to tell you, and we felt we needed to tell you together and in person."

"You and Catherine?" she asked, and I could see in her eyes she already understood.

"Yes," I answered. There was a long pause and I could see tears well up in her eyes.

"You love Catherine?" she added.

"I do. We're getting married."

She took a deep breath, bit her lip and turned away, so I could not see a tear roll down her cheek, "I'm sorry," she said, "Please forget what I said."

"Vanessa, what you said was one of the most wonderful things I have ever heard. I'm flattered you would think that way of me and had things been different…" I did not know how to finish the sentence.

"This is very embarrassing. I shouldn't have said anything." I touched her cheek and gently turned her face back to me, "Vanessa, you will always have a special place in my heart. I love you and your family. I always have. I'm in love with Catherine." I felt like a criminal. I had stolen from her a moment she had been dreaming about. She had declared her love to me and had wanted it reciprocated and I had taken the dream from her. "Catherine and I want you in our lives. I'm sorry I had to tell you this way." There was another long pause. I repeated feebly, "I'm sorry."

She looked at me and said, "It's okay. I'm okay. You can't change fate."

I didn't know what to say, and we sat together in silence for about a minute. I then started the engine and drove her home. The drive was long, and both of us remained silent. As we stopped in front of her house, she turned to me and said, "I'm happy for you both. I'm a strong girl. Please know you won't see me like this again."

Catherine and I got married and Vanessa dove into her career. She never got married and rarely dated. Catherine and Cole constantly said I was the reason.

The messy papers on her desk could not cover the tension, and finally she looked up and broke it by saying, "It's been a horrible few months. It's our mom and Cole's kids who have taken it the hardest. Mom's really lost it. I fly to San Diego to be with them whenever I can. Jackie's held herself together, but they had no insurance because of his layoff from Paralight. She's working two jobs, and her mother is looking after the kids. Speculation was he couldn't handle it—being fired, the lawsuit, Catherine's death, and your coma—but I don't believe that. Not Cole."

"No, not Cole," I said as I stood to leave. Vanessa came around her desk, and we shared an awkward hug. My mind was spinning. How different my world had become!

Chapter 4

Rick, a smiling, small man from Human Resources at Paralight was at my home when I returned. He asked me where I had gone so early and before I could answer he explained he was given the task of getting me anything I needed and had been taking care of my life while I had been away. He had been in charge of paying the bills on my house, attending to its maintenance and organizing my mail. After explaining that he had purchased a new lawn mower when my old one had broken, he showed that he had stocked the fridge and bought new clothes for Danny.

"Thanks," I said, "Thanks for everything."

"You're welcome," he answered in relief as if I were judging his performance.

"Relax, take a seat," I said.

"I'm fine standing," he said with his large smile stretched across his face. He then went around the house dusting and arranging areas I did not think needed any attention. I thought his attention to detail was overkill but appreciated that I was not alone in the house and let him work freely.

When the care facility brought Danny home Rick insisted on helping Danny to the house and carefully asked me every detail of his care. He then prepared dinner for us and made sure our sheets were changed. Janet came over and Rick sat her in the study and conducted an interview with her that was much more detailed than Catherine and I had ever undertaken. Upon his satisfaction that she could properly attend to the needs of Danny and our house, he noted her cell phone number and left for the night with his over-exaggerated smile stretching across his face.

Janet came early the next morning and was happy to be out of her house. She fit right in; and in no time was comfortably sitting in front of our television with a glazed expression. Danny was also staring with glazed eyes but his attention was on the wall. I had brought *Hamlet* down from my bedroom and was reading to Danny. Every so often I would review what had happened in the book and watch for some movement from him. I never saw so much as a twitch, but I didn't give up. As I read, I came across a phrase spoken by Polonius about Hamlet, "Though this be madness, yet there is method in't." Catherine and I had discussed this phrase when we had been reading the play. There are a lot of positions you can take on Hamlet's sanity. Catherine argued that he really was crazy, but it was in layers. Some layers kept in touch with the world around him and others tossed him into the recesses of his mind. She believed that his mind had risen to a new level when he had seen his father's spirit and, as a result, was no longer living completely in the same reality as everyone else in Elsinore.

I stood up and went to the fridge for a drink, then returned, rubbed my eyes, and again picked up the book. I opened to the page where I had left off. How had Hamlet felt? He probably struggled against the conviction that he was crazy. His father had been murdered. The visitation from his dead father's spirit made it clear that his uncle had murdered his father and married his mother to become the king. Being surrounded by such a conspiracy would be enough to drive anyone mad. How would I have felt in that situation?

I had been staring at the page without really seeing it, as I processed this thought, but suddenly I was paying attention. A letter on the page had just twitched. The movement surprised me. It was the "H" in Hamlet's name. I blinked and stared hard. I saw another twitch. I knew it was impossible, but it never occurred to me to close the book or close my eyes. As I looked more intently, the "H" moved again. I continued to focus on the letter, and slowly the "H" lifted off the page and floated in the air in front of me, followed, more rapidly, by the "a," then the other letters of Hamlet's name. The complete name floated in the air above the book. The "H" transformed into a lower-case "h" and the lower-case "a" next to it transformed into an upper-case "A." The "h" moved to the back of the name, and the name "Amleth" now hovered in the air in front of me.

Other letters rose from the page of the book and ordered themselves around "Amleth" forming the phrase, "He is Amleth and he was never mad." I reached out to touch the letters, and they moved around my fingers as if they were feathers floating in the air only to return to their previous positions. I looked through them to Janet and Danny. Janet was still gazing, rapt, at the television. Danny was still looking at the wall.

"Janet," I said, "Is Hamlet's real name Amleth?"

"Huh?" she replied, her eyes not leaving the television.

"Amleth, is that Hamlet's real name?"

"I have no idea. Who's Hamlet?"

As I stared at the phrase in amazement, more letters rose from the book and formed another phrase, "Madness is relative." I moved my head from side to side and ran my hand under the letters. Yes, I was seeing them hanging in the air. They were definitely there.

"Janet?" I said.

"Yeah."

"Do you see anything here in the air?" I asked. Janet pulled her eyes from the television and looked at me. I circled my hands in the air in front of me around the suspended name and phrase. I ran my fingers through the words and they smoothly moved around my fingers and returned to their positions.

"No, nothing," answered Janet as she returned to the television.

More letters floated to join the others forming the word, "Corrington."

"What's Corrington?" I asked.

Janet shrugged without taking her eyes from the screen.

More words formed, "Brick wall, metal gate."

"Brick wall, metal gate?" I said, this time more to myself.

Another phrase formed, "Get the pen. Do not delay."

"It's telling me something," I said to Janet.

"What?"

"The book is telling me something."

"Yeah, that's what they do," she replied.

"Get the pen. What does that mean?"

"It may be a stretch, but it probably means get a pen."

"You don't see this?" I asked.

Janet looked over at me again, and I again ran my fingers

through the phrases in the air above me. Janet looked at me as if I were nuts then paused unsure of what to say.

"See what?"

"There are words, hanging here in the air," I stated.

"Where?"

"Right here."

Janet got up, walked over and looked closely at the air in front of me.

"In the air?"

I nodded. "Yes."

"Right there?"

I nodded again.

"You want me to say there are words hanging in the air?"

I nodded again. Janet tensed a little, then dropped her shoulders and confessed, "Okay, yes, I've smoked pot, but never meth, shrooms or crack. I stay far away from hairspray, glue, paint and gasoline. They play with your head. I have friends who see words in the air, but I don't."

I stared at Janet, stunned. "Thanks, Janet."

Janet nodded, "I'm glad I got that off my chest." She then returned to the television.

As she slouched back on the sofa, my eyes returned to the words hanging in the air in front of me. I closed the book, and the words fell and faded away. I went into the study and logged on to the internet. I googled "Amleth" and what immediately popped up was: "Amleth, Prince of Denmark: Written circa 1185, but based on an older oral tradition. It describes the same players and events as does the Shakepearean play." I smiled to myself, "Hamlet is Amleth."

I searched for "Corrington" and the results were extremely varied and had nothing to do with Hamlet or Amleth. I also searched for many variations of "brick wall, metal gate" and "get the pen, do not delay" only to get nothing of consequence from any combination of searches.

After exhausting an hour or so, I left Janet and Danny to get to my appointment with Dr. Reed and drove into the parking structure across the street from the Kensington Mental Hospital. A large red-brick, wall extended around the hospital, making it impossible to see what was going on inside the gates. I crossed the street and glanced at the street sign: "CORRINGTON STREET." I paused, staring at the sign. Corrington was the name of the street I was standing on? Perhaps I was going crazy. Surely I'd seen this street sign before without noticing it, and my subconscious, knowing I would be coming to this appointment, had just given me a reminder—like the dentist's receptionist calling to remind me about an appointment? Okay, so it was a little weird that it had been spelled out by letters hanging in the air in front of me, and it didn't explain how my subconscious knew that the historic Hamlet had really been Amleth, but the explanation there was probably just as simple. My heart was beating a little faster than usual, but I deliberately focused on telling myself everything was normal. I didn't need to show up for an appointment with a psychiatrist in the early stages of a panic attack complete with hallucinations.

I turned away and walked down the street toward the main gate at the west entrance. *"Metal gate."* I stopped walking. I was following the brick wall to my right that led to the ornamental, metal gate. The words had come in the right sequence: *"Corrington, brick wall, metal gate."*

How could it be coincidence? I thought. I was walking down Corrington next to a brick wall and headed for a metal gate. I could almost hear the next words: *"Get the pen. Do not delay."*

I saw a pen—an ordinary ink pen—on the ground in front of the metal gate and the world around me slowed to a crawl. My heart pounded in my chest, and my limbs went numb. There was something important about that pen, and I knew I had to act. I quickened my pace, rushed to the pen, and bent down to grab it.

CRACK! A bullet hit the gate right above my head. Without thought, my body lunged through the gate and into the courtyard. A second shot hit the gate again. I rolled behind the brick wall. A third shot hit the brick wall. I scrambled to the wall and held my back to it. My heart was pounding, adrenalin racing through my body. I took a few quick breaths; and as the panic and numbness decreased, I seized control of my senses. I had never in my life been shot at and the feelings were overwhelming. *Who would be trying to kill me?* My mind scrambled to make sense of the situation. I took a few more deep breaths then ran quickly along the wall into the cover of some large bushes.

In the bushes, I saw a thin woman wearing the white clothes of patients of the hospital. She was obviously hiding but didn't seem to be afraid of me. I thought it odd that a patient would be in this section of the grounds as on the south side of the building was a fenced in garden area where patients were allowed to roam. The west entrance was open to the outside world and was therefore forbidden to patients.

"Someone is shooting at me," I said.

"They don't need guns," she asserted with certainty. "Guns are the least of your worries."

"You know who it is?"

"They have seen you and now they are after you too."

"Why are they after me?"

"They want what you have," she said as her eyes scanned the brick walls in fear. "They're on the move. Soon they'll be inside the walls," she continued.

"What do I have?" I asked.

"We need to get into the building fast." The woman grabbed my hand and pulled me with her, running parallel to the wall. Her hand was icy cold. I was sweating, but her grip was so frigid it almost hurt. We rounded a corner in the wall and soon I was sure the building blocked the gunman's line of fire. We ran through a clearing and I saw Marshall with two staff orderlies on the other side of the open lawn area. I followed the woman into the bushes on the other side and she pulled me close. Her other hand pressed against my back was just as cold as the one still gripping my hand. The chill traveled across my back and through my body. I looked at her face. It was distorted with fear. "They're coming!" she whispered, her voice quivering with terror.

"Where?" I questioned.

"By those gates," she replied. I looked toward the hospital's north side gates and saw dark, cloaked figures approaching. "Do you see them?"

"Yes, what do they want?" The world around me had changed from afternoon to night. It couldn't have been four o'clock, but the blazing Phoenix sun was gone. It was dreamlike. I was in the same grounds that I had been in a moment before, but now it was night. I could see stars in the sky and the moon was casting a silver glow onto the world around me.

"They want me," she replied. "They want to kill me." The fear in her eyes was terrifying. More figures came into the courtyard, and I scrambled from my hiding place, breaking from the woman's grasp. As I thrust through the bushes, rays of light again pierced the foliage; and I stopped with my back against the wall. I looked toward the north gates, and it was no longer night but day again. The woman was several feet from me, and she still looked in fear toward the north gates. I followed her gaze, but the cloaked figures were gone. There was nothing but green grass and the brick wall. I wondered if I had dreamed the stars in the sky, the silvery moon, and the shadowy figures. They had looked so daunting and real. The terror in the woman was real.

"We need to make our move," she said in hushed tones, "The faster we run the better chance we have. Are you ready?"

"Sarah! Sarah, come out!" yelled a familiar voice from the clearing. I leaned to the side and saw Marshall, followed by hospital orderlies and Dr. Reed. "Sarah, we know you're in there! Come out!"

She looked back at me, "Marshall and Dr. Reed think I'm crazy. They'll try to keep me here. If I'm in a room, they'll be able to get to me. I need to get out. Let's go."

I shook my head, "No."

"We have no time," she insisted.

"No."

The woman looked toward Marshall, then again toward the north gates. She bolted from the cover of the bushes toward the side of the hospital building.

Marshall, Dr. Reed, and the orderlies saw her. Marshall yelled, "Sarah, don't run! Stop!" She kept running, but Marshall and the two orderlies bounded after her, caught her, and yanked her to the ground. She struggled, screaming, "Get your hands off me!" It took all three, holding her tightly, to keep her pinned down as Dr. Reed pulled out a syringe and came to her.

"Let me go! Let go! They're here! They're here now!" she screamed.

"Sarah," said Dr. Reed soothingly.

"No! Don't do this!"

"Sarah, you know I need to do this."

"They were shooting at us—both of us," Sarah motioned to me in the bushes. Dr. Reed, Marshall, and the orderlies all looked toward the bushes. I stood up and stepped out. "Just ask him."

All attention turned to me. "Pierce, was someone shooting at the two of you?" questioned Dr. Reed.

Marshall looked at me with a smirk, telling me he knew I would be back. If I said someone was shooting at me, I would be immediately readmitted into the mental hospital with Sarah and kept there, pending an endless string of sessions with Dr. Reed. Judging from the fact that a few moments before I was in this same courtyard looking at stars rather than blue skies, they had every reason to believe I was crazy. What was true anyway? Someone *had* shot at me outside the gate. I was sure of that. Or was I? I was also sure that a few moments earlier, it had been night in the courtyard, and cloaked figures were approaching. Cloaks? What was that about? This was the twenty-first century, not the Middle Ages. No one shot at me when I was with her, so I could truthfully answer no to Dr. Reed's question. Perhaps I was crazy. I needed more time to figure out what was going on.

I felt my options drain away. I looked at Dr. Reed and said, "No, no one was shooting at the two of us." It was the truth according to what I knew. However, guilt coursed through my body. Sarah looked at me in disbelief.

"Liar! He's lying!" screamed Sarah, as she redoubled her efforts to break free.

"Hold her," said Dr. Reed calmly as he injected her with the sedative.

"No! Don't do this! No, please!" screamed Sarah again. She stared at me, and her voice dropped. "How could you do this!" she demanded. "They were shooting at you. They were shooting at you…You liar…You saw them…They were shooting…" Sarah slumped into unconsciousness as Marshall and the orderlies carried her away.

Dr. Reed came to me, standing outside the bushes. I explained that I saw her when I came into the courtyard. She had asked me to help her. Dr. Reed didn't seem to be unduly curious about the information as we walked to his office. As I sat down, he asked, "Why do you think Sarah included you in her story?"

The answer to his question was, *Because I saw what she saw*, but I was not going to say it. Instead I shrugged, "She's your patient."

"She's plagued with night terrors and has been since she was a child. She also sees them in the day. She describes them as pure evil and horrific. Today was the first time she mentioned shooting. You have any ideas why?"

"I understand you have many patients, but I came here for me," I said, changing the subject. I saw her night terrors. I saw those shadows; but if I told that to the doctor, then Marshall would be right and I would be locked up again.

Dr. Reed smiled and nodded. "Right. You. How was your first night home?"

"Good," I said, deciding to be very brief.

"Tell me about it."

"It was good."

"It was good?"

I nodded and smiled.

"Anything more?" questioned Dr. Reed.

I shook my head, "No."

"Has anything abnormal happened to you?"

"Abnormal?"

"Seeing things that should not be there—timelines not making sense—events seemingly happening out of context of the real world."

Interesting way to put it because everything he mentioned had happened. "I slept well last night. It was good to be in my bed. No night terrors," I said with a smile. It was true. I had slept well, and the only night terrors I had seen were during the day.

Dr. Reed straightened up and smiled back at me. "I've spoken with your office at Paralight, and they are looking forward to your return. You're a hero now, and I suppose you'll be a celebrity when everything goes public."

"It will be nice to get back to my life," I responded with a smile.

Dr. Reed stood up and walked around the table to shake my hand, "Then let's not waste time. Call Melissa and get in my schedule for next week." He then motioned to the door.

"Thank you, Dr. Reed," I said. He put a friendly hand on my shoulder and walked out of the office with me. As we walked down the hallway to the hospital's entry foyer, I could see the metal front gates, where a gunman had missed me three times, through the large glass doors. I had no idea if I was crazy and had dreamed up that experience; but if someone had been shooting at me, then he would be able to see me clearly through the doors of the foyer. I stopped and stepped out from under Dr. Reed's hand to one side of the foyer behind a pillar.

Dr. Reed looked at me strangely, then said, "You've made wonderful progress. You're an interesting study, and I look forward to what happens with Paralight."

"Thank you."

He smiled and gestured toward the door. I did not move.

"Is something wrong?" Dr. Reed asked.

"No, nothing's wrong."

"I'll see you next week."

"Great, next week," I said, smiling. I stayed behind the pillar.

"You're not leaving?

"I am," I assured him.

"You may leave," he encouraged with a smile.

"I know. Thank you," I said, unmoving. The awkwardness was profound but it was becoming clearer to me that I was not willing to bet my life on the chance that I had imagined the shooter. "You're free to go, too," I said encouragingly.

Dr. Reed looked puzzled but responded seriously, "I am, yes."

"You are," I repeated, hoping he would end this ridiculous situation.

"With your permission, I suppose I will." He was frowning uncomfortably. He hesitated, then turned and walked back toward his office. At his door, he looked back at me and waved. I smiled and waved back. He slowly entered his office.

I turned back and walked a few feet to an intersecting hall-way. I continued down the hallway, passed a lounge and headed toward one of the hospital's back exits. As I was about to round a corner, I heard Marshall's voice and several sets of footsteps. I ducked into a closet and pulled the door shut. After I heard them pass by, I quietly opened the door and continued down the hall. I was in a wing housing the patients' rooms. I glanced in the windows as I passed, most rooms empty, but then saw Sarah lying motionless in a bed. Late afternoon light streamed in through the barred exterior window. In the distance, I could see green trees and the red brick wall which surrounded the hospital. Sarah seemed deeply unconscious, but her face was still lined with fear. The lines on her forehead were deep, betraying a lifetime of worry and stress. I wondered what it would be like to struggle against her fears and concerns; and as I stared at her, a chill, much like the chill of her touch, engulfed me. The air rippled above her body and the sunlight streaming in through the win-dow faded. The room went dark. The trees on the other side of the glass were now black and glistened with silvery moonlight.

She stirred in her bed and awoke, curled against the wall and looked around in fear. A scratch outside the window caused her to jump, pull the blankets tightly around herself, and push herself back into the corner. I heard more scratching from the window, and a black shadowy hand grabbed the bars. The fingers were dark, muscular, and tipped with claws. Another hand appeared, and a ghastly, cloaked creature leaped through the bars and the window into the room. It crept across the room as if it were stalking Sarah. I could see more details than I had outside. The creature's skin was a dark black, but dully shining, like metal. The eyes were deep caverns with a haunting hollowness. Several other cloaked creatures crawled through the window and out from under the bed and scaled the walls around Sarah. The first of the creatures pulled back the cloak from its dark face. It exuded evil. It emitted a spine-chilling roar, revealing razor-sharp teeth, and crouched to lunge at Sarah. Tears streamed down Sarah's face, and she screamed.

Heat rushed through my body, chasing away the chill. I yanked on the doorknob—locked—then banged on the door, "Sarah!" I shouted. "Sarah!" I smashed my shoulder into the door and reeled back. The sunlight had returned, the creatures had vanished, and Sarah again lay unconscious.

I heard running footsteps coming down the hall. "Who's there?" yelled Marshall's unmistakable voice. I sprinted the last few yards down the hallway and out the back door, jumped over the railing of the steps, and hid under the overhang of the porch. As I pressed myself against the concrete, trying to calm my breathing, Marshall and several orderlies burst through the doors and scanned the yard. After a few moments, Marshall said grimly, "Whoever it was must still be inside."

They went back into the hospital, and I remained motionless for several minutes trying to figure out what had just happened. Those creatures must have been Sarah's night terrors. Only nightmares could come through locked windows and ooze up walls from under her bed. How could she have survived, living under those circumstances since childhood?

I discreetly went through the hospital's back gates, darted across the street, and ducked into an alley. Perhaps everything that had happened from the shooting to Sarah's night terrors was created in my mind and I was in no real danger, but I was not going to take any chances. If the shooter was still out there, how could I disguise myself? Was it safe to retrieve my car? If I went home, would I be leading killers to Danny and Janet? At the end of the alley I saw a superhero sweatshirt in a store window. I slid inside and bought the sweatshirt along with a matching baseball cap. I pulled the hooded sweatshirt over my shirt, put on the baseball cap and pulled the hood over the cap.

"You look cool, man," said the store clerk admiringly.

Feeling better, I made my way to the parking structure and, stooping, ran along the rows of cars until I reached my Pontiac. I saw no one, heard nothing. As I drove out, I was braced for a bullet to shatter a window or to pierce the door, but nothing happened.

Chapter 5

The normalcy of the drive home should have calmed me, but my hands were still shaking as I stopped at my house. Naturally, I was in shock. Questions of reality and sanity filled my mind. Someone had just tried to kill me. A sniper had shot at me, and my mind was catching up with the fright of the situation. I had also just witnessed some sort of demons or creatures as they stalked a crazy lady at the mental hospital—but why? If they had succeeded in tearing Sarah apart, then she'd be dead and permanently free of them, right? But they did not tear her apart. When I left the window outside her room she was again asleep—not torn apart, not dead. They were the craziest part, but they were just too realistic.

I realized that I was no longer willing to explain away what was happening as my insanity. No matter what was happening, I was accepting it as real: nightmare creatures, a killer hunting me, and all. My acceptance added another layer to my shock and drained the feeling from my limbs. I took a few deep breaths, and my racing heart calmed a little. If someone were after me for any reason, then I needed to protect Danny while I figured out

what was happening—and Janet. I looked around the neighborhood suspiciously, eyeing each spot where I thought someone
could be hiding, then stepped out of the car and rushed through
the front door.

Inside, the same time warp was playing. Janet was watching
the television, and Danny was staring out the window. "Janet,
time to go home," I said. I rushed up the stairs, threw clothes
for Danny into a backpack, and grabbed cash from a drawer in
my room. I ran back down the stairs, "Up, up, now," I said as I
quickly picked up Danny, grabbed Janet's hand, and pulled her
toward the front door.

"Mr. Black?" questioned Janet. She then looked at my outfit,
"Hey, nice hat."

"Danny and I are leaving for a while."

"What's going on?"

"Can't explain. We'll talk later," I said as I pulled her through
the front door, locked the door, and then carried Danny toward
my car.

"Wait, why the rush?" she asked puzzled.

I threw the backpack into the car, put Danny in the passenger
seat and buckled him in, "Thanks for your help, Janet."

"Mr. Black, this is strange."

"Thanks, Janet," I said as I got into the car, put it in gear, and
pulled away.

"Mr. Black? What's with the outfit?!" she yelled as I drove
down the street. I glanced back at the corner. She was walking
slowly toward her house. I felt bad leaving so abruptly and not
telling her anything, but I also felt that the less she knew; the
better off she would be. She would be okay.

As I left my neighborhood, I realized that I didn't have any idea about where to take Danny. I was driving aimlessly, trying to think, when it occurred to me that the sniper could be following me. Adrenalin slammed my heart again, and I went on ultra-alert. I drove through many neighborhoods constantly looking to see if anyone was behind me or if I could recognize cars from one place to the next. The rush hour traffic, even in quiet neighborhoods, was both a help and a hindrance. I stopped several times and waited to see if a car I had seen before would drive by. Eventually I was sure that no one was following me although, in a way, that was even more puzzling than a tracker would have been. As I drove by an elementary school, I thought of Bonnie, the secretary at the airstrip who had basically raised me, loved me, and followed my progress all the way through high school. Bonnie had even come to my graduation from high school and later my wedding, but I couldn't think of a way that anyone would now, years later, connect me with her. She lived in Laveen, just outside Phoenix. I didn't call. I just drove to her house.

I grabbed the backpack, lifted Danny in my arms, walked to the front door, and rang the bell. I felt odd standing there; but when the door opened, Bonnie's face lit up. "My little Pierce?" she said with a glowing smile that stretched her wrinkled skin.

"Yes, hi, Bonnie," I said with a smile, "This is my son, Danny."

"Oh, my dear, come in and make yourself at home."

I stepped through the door. It felt like coming home. I had always loved her. She had taken a special interest in me, but I always wondered if that was just how she treated everyone. I never knew a child who did not love her. Her warmth and acceptance flowed to everyone around her. She asked about my flying and talked to me with the same love and interest she had when I was a child. She was interested in Danny but seemed neither shocked nor repelled by his condition and his nonresponsiveness. I told her about Catherine's death, said some peculiar things had been happening recently, and said I needed a new place for Danny for a few days.

"He must stay here," she said instantly.

Relief flowed through me. I had not even asked her directly. "Thank you so much, Bonnie," I said. "I've been at a loss as to what to do."

"Say no more," she said, "You're my family, Pierce. He's my family."

I never viewed it that way, but I could see she did. My heart warmed. I knew she was sincere. We spoke more of Danny and his needs and she actually thanked me for trusting her with my son. She set Danny comfortably on her sofa with a blanket and pulled out a book to read to him. I told her I would be back in a couple days and quickly left. As I walked to my car, the sun was setting and a brilliant orange-yellow band stretched across the horizon. I looked back at the window where Bonnie was standing, smiling and waving. I drove away thinking that this world wasn't so bad as long as people like her existed.

The drive was beautiful with the sun setting across the desert. Dusk had always been my favorite time of day in Phoenix. Catherine and I used to sneak off at dusk and spend hours on the hood of my car looking at the stars. The brilliant colors of the sunset had faded by the time I reached my destination. Now that I had assured Danny's safety, my top priority was finding out if I was crazy. I was quite sure the creatures haunting Sarah were from her mind and not real, but the vision I had had of Cole, Catherine, and Vanessa setting up the anniversary banner in the hotel room really had happened. The strange things I was seeing and experiencing had some form of truth and reason to them. I needed to find out what I could count on. Somehow Hamlet or Amleth or the book itself had warned me of the shooting outside the gates of the hospital on Corrington, and I was quite sure the bullets had struck the gate and wall of the hospital.

It was night when I parked my car a street away from Corrington and crept down a side street until I could see the brick wall surrounding the mental hospital. There were very few people on the streets. A couple walked hand in hand on the opposite side of the street from the brick wall and a block away a man in a business suit walked briskly toward a parking lot. I crossed the street and walked to the front gates of the mental hospital. I held my breath as I ran my hands along the bars of the metal gate and then saw a bright indentation where the paint had been knocked off. It was definitely the mark made by a bullet striking metal. I ran my finger across it. Relief and fear filled my mind at the same time. The good news was that I wasn't crazy. The bad news was that someone had genuinely attempted to kill me. I could not fathom who would want me dead. I continued searching and saw another indentation on the gate from the second bullet. In the brick wall near the gate, I saw a hole where a bullet had embedded itself into the brick.

Clear evidence of an attempted murder, I thought. I knelt down, pulled the keys from my pocket and dug into the brick. As the bullet fell into my hand, I examined it to see if it could give me any clues about who had shot it. My mind ran through detective movies and ballistics crews in shows on television.

I focused all my attention on the bullet. The air around it rippled and the bullet quivered, then rose from my hand and hovered in the air. I dropped my hand and looked at the bullet in awe. It was impossible, I knew that, but there it was, hanging in the air just like the letters from *Hamlet.* As I continued to watch the bullet, it returned to the wall and the dust fragments I had cleared away from the hole in the wall rose from the ground and returned to the wall, making the hole appear just as it was when I first saw it. As I stared in wonderment at the scar in the brick, I saw my shadow appearing on the wall. A light was glowing behind me. Alarmed, I turned. The sky was a brilliant orange-yellow—the sunset I had just seen as I was driving into town. It was vivid and clear. I looked around me. Cars and people were racing past at incredible speeds. They were merely blurs in front of me. Shocked, I realized something even stranger. They were all going backwards. The sunset colors faded, the sky turned blue, and the sun rose in the sky. I turned back to the wall and saw my shadow creep down the brick wall as the sun continued to rise. The world around me slowed. I saw myself diving in reverse from behind the wall and coming to a standstill in a crouching position. I saw a cloud of dust speckled with small crumbs of brick rise from the ground, cluster around the bullet-hole in the wall and slowly go back into the brick wall. The bullet emerged from the wall leaving no hole and moved backwards through the air. I stepped back to allow the bullet to go past me. It was moving in a straight line, slowly enough that I could trace its direction. It was backing toward a half-open window on the third floor of a hotel across the street. Now the people and cars on the street were at a standstill. Everything was practically motionless except the bullet slowly heading toward the window.

I ran across the street and into the hotel. I rushed up the stairs to the third floor and dashed into the open door of a room. It was empty so I rushed through the wall and into the next room. I'd found the shooter. A man with dark brown hair was aiming a sniper rifle out the window, its muzzle end-heavy with a large silencer. As I watched, the bullet reentered the rifle. Two more bullets reentered the rifle. Time stopped and I looked at the man. I had never seen him. Why did he want to kill me? It couldn't be personal, so someone had hired him—but who? and why? Motion started again, and a bullet shot out of the rifle with a muffled pop. I looked out the window to see myself dive behind the wall. The rifle popped twice more. Dust kicked up from the brick wall.

The sniper muttered something and stood up, a frustrated look on his face. Rapidly he disassembled his rifle, packed it into a briefcase, and was out the door in just a few seconds. I followed him down the hall, down a stairway, and out the hotel's back door into an alley. He calmly walked down the alley, opened the trunk of a blue Ford Taurus, put the briefcase in the trunk, and climbed behind the wheel. I moved through the closed passenger door and sat down next to him. The man drove out of the city and into the suburbs. I kept mental track of his turns, thinking I had a good chance to find the neighborhood again. He turned onto Chandler Way, parked, took his briefcase out of the trunk, and entered a house: Number 133.

I was filled with fury. This man had attempted to murder me, though I was a complete stranger to him, then had driven home like any workman going home after his job. I closed my eyes and took several deep breaths to calm myself.

My mind cleared in what seemed to me a flash of bright light; and when I opened my eyes, it was dark again. I was on my knees in front of the brick wall with the bullet in my hand. I reached into my pocket and pulled out the life-saving pen I had picked up off the street and wrote "133 Chandler Way" on the back of my hand. Still boiling inside, I rushed across the street, down an alley, found my car and started driving—retracing the journey I had just taken with the sniper. The turns and neighbor-hoods were clear in my mind. I felt an odd anticipation to see whether the house on 133 Chandler Way was real—but I already knew the answer. As I rounded the last corner, my headlights shone on the street sign: "Chandler Way." Chills coursed through my body. I was actually driving to the house of a hired killer. I pulled to the side of the road, turned off my headlights, quietly closed the door, and walked down the street. I recognized the house immediately and felt the hairs on my arms rise. The blue Ford Taurus was parked in the driveway and lights were on in the house. I pulled out the pen and wrote down the car's license plate number on the back of my hand. Then I crossed the lawn and cautiously looked in the living room window. A man was sitting on a sofa in front of a television casually watching. He had dark brown hair, but I could not see his face. I crouched and moved closer to the window so I could see him from a different angle. It was unmistakably the sniper. Disgust and rage filled me. I stared at his face. He had sharp features and crescent-shaped brows, which gave him an intelligent look. His skin was tanned, and he had a tight jaw line that enhanced his high cheekbones. His arms were muscular and toned, and he had the physique of an athlete. Had I seen him at the gym or in a restaurant I would never have given a thought about what type of person he was. I would never have marked him as an assassin or murderer.

I stared at him, my mind focused on him completely. A shimmer of light lifted off his skin and the air around him rippled and suddenly his body split into many distinct versions of himself. I counted ten and blinked, trying to refocus. There really were ten, each in a different place and each wearing different clothes. One was sitting in a chair, dressed in black right down to black gloves. As I looked at this black-clad assassin, the world around me changed. The front yard I was crouching in turned into a paved street. Rain was falling heavily. A car appeared around the man's seated form, and buildings appeared on the side of the street. I knew I was again in one of my visions. I was now getting used to the feeling. In a strange way, it felt comfortable—a part of me. It was like the rare occasion when I was dreaming but knew it was a dream.

In this vision, I was crouching, just as I was when I was looking into the window of the sniper, but I was across a narrow street from the car that had formed around the sitting the sniper. Rain poured heavily, but I was not getting wet—it simply went through me just as I had gone through walls and doors in the previous visions. The street was fairly steep and descended down a hill to my right where it crossed a larger street. The man was intently watching a screen from a mobile device resting on the seat next to him in the car. I stood straight and walked toward the car, watching its driver strap on a black face-covering helmet. His gloved hands gripped the steering wheel tightly as he intently looked at the screen. I caught a slight glimpse of the screen as the man put the car in gear and stepped on the gas. It seemed to be some kind of tracking map. The engine roared, and the car sped down the steep hill toward the intersection. I saw the headlights of another car approaching the intersection from the left. The two cars smashed into each other at high speed causing a deafening bang and tearing of metal. The other car, a Lexus, spun and smashed into a building out of my sight. I knew the other car. It was my car—Catherine's car, to be more precise. I was watching the accident that had killed Catherine on our anniversary. This sniper had been the other driver.

I rushed down the hill to the larger street where I could see the cars. The Lexus was smashed in on the right side. Catherine's unmoving body was hanging out of the shattered window. I was slumped unconscious in the driver's seat. The sniper placed the mobile device in his pocket, unstrapped his helmet and pushed his door open. It grated—metal against metal. Anger filled me, and I lunged at the sniper with all my strength, only to fly right through him. Sirens blared in the distance, and the sniper walked to the Lexus, leaning close to examine both of us. Then he turned and jogged away. I watched him in horror. This man had murdered my wife. He had destroyed the person who meant more to me than anyone in this world and did so with no emotion. I looked again at Catherine's motionless body, and tears welled in my eyes. The world of the vision unraveled. The rain and wrecked cars turned to wisps of light which reconstructed themselves into bushes and the street below me transformed into lawn. I was again crouched in front of the sniper's house.

I lost my balance as I fought to contain my emotions and seized one of the bushes. A branch from the bush hit the window. The sniper on the couch—now only the one figure of him in the room—looked sharply toward the window. I continued my fall, hitting the ground on my back and wriggling as far under the bushes as I could get. I looked up through the bushes and saw the sniper walking up to the window. He stood there for a few minutes, scanning the neighborhood. He left the window, but I remained motionless. Seconds later, the front door of the small house opened, and the sniper walked down the porch steps. I froze, not even breathing. He walked past me, almost stepping on my hand, and it took all my concentration to not move. This man could and would kill me if he saw me. He had already killed my wife and had taken three shots at me only hours earlier. I was now on his front lawn without any kind of weapon or defensive skills. If he glanced down, he would see me.

He walked to the side of the house and looked around its corner. He then scanned the neighboring houses as he returned to the porch. Cold sweat was dripping down my forehead as I heard him open the front door and reenter the house. I remained motionless for another few minutes, then relaxed. The bushes jiggled, nearing the window. I froze in panic. The bush did not touch the glass. I remained motionless for another couple minutes, breathing shallowly. Then with painful slowness, I inched out from under the bushes and crawled across the front lawn. As I got to the neighboring house, I looked back. The sniper had returned to the sofa.

As I drove away, I knew I was experiencing reality, but it didn't feel like it. I drove in a blurred numbness for about an hour, feeling so overwhelmed I could barely manage the car. I was drowning in emotion. I finally pulled to the side of the road. The world around me was completely different than I could possibly have imagined. My wife had actually been murdered. The same person was trying to murder me. For some strange reason, I had been seeing visions of events that I couldn't possibly know about, yet they were true, as clear and vivid as life itself. Vanessa had corroborated the vision of the anniversary preparations at the hotel with Cole, Vanessa, and Catherine. The vision of the sniper had led me directly to his house. I had never before seen the sniper; but when I got to his house, I recognized him instantly. Logically, then, the vision of the sniper smashing into my car, killing Catherine, had also happened exactly as I had seen it. It had been devastating to think that an accident had taken Catherine from me, but the knowledge that it was murder destroyed me. I missed Catherine. I missed my life with her, and the simple joy of coming home at night to my family. I was drowning in the emotions of the life I was now living and suffering the loss of the life which had been taken from me. I lost consciousness.

Chapter 6

Maybe it was not really unconsciousness but sleep like a hammer blow from sheer emotional fatigue. In any case, it passed into sleep at some point, though far from refreshing. I kept almost surfacing from the discomfort of sleeping propped up against the window, then drifting back into deeper unconsciousness. My mind and nerves were shattered, circling from one painful point to another throughout the night. In retrospect, I should have been grateful that my anguish did not bring a visitation from the night horrors that were tormenting Sarah.

As the sun rose above the horizon in the morning, consciousness again crept toward me. Hazily, thoughts of a very long and interesting dream settled. I felt as though I was in the process of waking up and would soon be in my comfortable bed with Catherine at my side. I would take her in my arms and whisper how much I loved and appreciated her—how difficult life would be if I had lost her. The haze slowly receded. Confused, I realized I was sitting in my car on the side of the road. As I rubbed the weariness from my eyes, I saw the address and license plate number written on my hand, and the world I was hoping was a dream settled in around me.

Adrenalin and grief washed through me. I forced myself to systematically review the events of the previous day and night. What were my options? What should I do? I was seeing visions of different times and places, but why? If I had suffered brain trauma in the accident that had killed Catherine, Paralight would have never let me fly Stormlight, so rationally, whatever caused this change had happened during the flight. I was transformed into light and then reformed back into my body. As a side effect of that experience, something had happened to change me or somehow unlock my mind. I could see things and life in a different way.

Very well, I accepted that reality. And part of it was that someone was trying to kill me. In my pocket was a bullet that had barely missed me yesterday. Bullet scars marked the gate and the brick wall. I had no evidence connecting the sniper to me other than the vision I had after the shooting. I knew—or at least had seen in a vision or a dream or whatever it was—that the same person who had attempted to murder me had, in fact, murdered Catherine. I had his street address and his car's license number. He could be checked out. I needed to record the information I had and get it investigated to save myself. To do that, I needed help. I needed Vanessa.

Vanessa was very well connected with crime scene units and the police force. I knew she would help me evaluate the scene at the mental hospital and investigate the sniper. I would also need to be discreet and not let anyone know where I was. The sniper had been tracking Catherine's Lexus on a screen in his car. He knew precisely when we would enter the intersection. Then I had a chilling thought. Did my car have a tracking device? If yes, I had led them to Danny at Bonnie's house. And I'd already driven once to Vanessa's office. Furthermore, I was not safe in my own car. I forced myself to think rationally. If they—whoever "they" were—were tracking me, they could have already found me and killed me. So the chances seemed small that my car was bugged. Still, there was no point taking any more chances. I locked my car and started on foot down the street.

Not being an expert at buses I was able to take a taxi into downtown Phoenix. I had the driver drop me off a few blocks from Vanessa's house. I walked down the street behind hers; and when I could see the back of her place, I sneaked through a yard and climbed a fence into her backyard. I crept under the trees planted along the side of her yard and tried the back door. It was locked. At that moment, I heard her garage door opening and dashed down the side of the house. Her car, a silver Infiniti FX50, was pulling out of the garage. I rushed down the walk beside the house, leaped the hedge, yanked open the passenger door, and dove in, clapping my hand over her mouth to stifle her scream as she struggled, killing the engine.

"Vanessa, it's me, Pierce," I said urgently. "Please be quiet. It's not safe."

Her frightened eyes focused on me, then filled with relief. Her stiff body relaxed as I continued, "I couldn't take any chances. Someone tried to kill me last night and I know it's the same person that killed Catherine."

Vanessa put her hand on my wrist and firmly removed my hand from her mouth. She then sat up straight, brushed her hair back, straightened her blouse, and looked squarely at me. "Good morning, Pierce. I slept well, thank you. Looks and sounds as if you probably didn't. That said, I'm not sure this cloak and dagger, hand on the mouth thing is very appropriate. Do you realize how many laws you just…"

"Vanessa, please start the car and drive away. We're not safe," I said urgently.

Vanessa saw the seriousness in my expression, nodded, restarted her car, and backed out of her driveway. I slouched down so that I wasn't visible in the car as she drove past the neighboring homes.

"Someone tried to kill you?"

"Yes, an assassin, a sniper. He shot at me."

"Where?"

"Kensington."

"The mental hospital?"

"Yes."

"This assassin killed Catherine?" she questioned. "He was driving the hit-and-run?"

"Yes."

"He shot at you and missed?"

"Yes."

"Not a great sniper," she snorted skeptically. "If you were shot at by a sniper, why aren't you dead? They don't get paid for missing."

"I ducked."

"You saw the sniper?"

"Not at the time of the shooting. Afterwards. Like when I saw you, Catherine and Cole."

"A dream? You had a dream about the sniper?"

"Yes, but no. More than that. I saw him kill Catherine. He was driving the other car. It was very clear. I was there again.

It was no accident. I went to his house. I saw him. Here's the address, and his car's license plate." I held up my hand with the address and plate number written in ink. "It was just like seeing you, Catherine, and Cole setting up the hotel room on our anniversary. I'm seeing things, Vanessa. I think it has to do with the speed-of-light test flight. Something happened during the flight."

Vanessa looked at the address and plate number written on my hand and said nothing for a moment, absorbing the information I had given her. I could see additional sadness in her eyes as she considered the idea that Catherine's death had not been an accident. "You said you ducked. Coincidence?"

"I was prompted to duck."

"Prompted by whom?"

"I knew to pick up a pen on the street."

"You were prompted to pick up a pen and that made you duck so that the sniper's gunshot missed?"

"Yes."

"Who prompted you to pick up the pen?"

"No one."

"No one? How do you get prompted by no one?"

"I saw the words when I was reading to Danny. They rose off the page of the book and spelled it out for me."

Vanessa looked at me and swerved to the side of the road. She put the car in park and turned to face me, her eyes full on my face: "You were warned by floating words?"

"Yes. They said, 'Get the pen. Don't delay.'"

She looked at me in complete disbelief.

"The floating words said the name of the street, the brick wall and the metal gate where the shooting was going to happen.

It was all there, Vanessa, written in front of me in the air. As I walked to the Kensington Mental Hospital, there was a brick wall around the hospital, parallel to Corrington Street. And a metal gate and a pen. The words told me to pick up the pen. When I picked it up, a bullet hit the gate above me—then again. A third hit the brick wall as I dove out of the line of fire."

A disbelieving laugh jumped from Vanessa, "Please understand my skepticism, Pierce. I couldn't paint a wackier picture than you've just done. Admit it: Your most recent place of residence doesn't speak highly for you. And to top it all off, you're dressed like a superhero. Where's the mask and cape? Come on, Pierce. You can't possibly believe what you are saying, can you?"

I said nothing. She had to believe me.

Her face was angry as she stared at me. "What are you pulling on me? I don't like this joke or prank or whatever it is you're doing."

I pulled the bullet out of my pocket and held it out for Vanessa to see. "I'm not joking, Vanessa. This is no prank. I thought I was crazy, too, so I went back to Kensington and pulled this out of the wall."

Vanessa took the bullet out of my hand and examined it, then looked at me, her face troubled. "This bullet was in the wall?"

"I pulled it from the wall last night. The hole is still there, and I'm sure the other bullets that hit the gate are there, too, although I don't know where they landed. The metal gate is scarred where they hit."

"You really believe you were shot at by a sniper?"

"I do."

"You really believe this sniper killed Catherine?"

"Yes."

"You had a dream that showed this man causing the accident?"

"It was more than a dream, Vanessa. I was there and saw it. I don't know how, but I saw it."

She took a few deep breaths as she considered my story, then said, "Show me the wall."

We drove to Kensington. As we turned onto Corrington Street, the road was blocked halfway down. A construction crew had set up orange cones directing traffic to the lanes on the opposite side of the gate from the mental hospital. Vanessa pulled her car to the side of the road right where the metal gate was supposed to be. A large dumpster was positioned near the curb and rubble from the brick wall was strewn across the sidewalk. Construction workers were throwing the rubble into the dumpster. The entire gate was missing, the wall was smashed in, and workers were busy laying new bricks for the wall. I could not believe it. The gate and the section of the wall where the bullet had struck were gone!

I jumped out of the car and yelled, "What's going on?"

One of the construction workers turned to me and said, "A stolen truck smashed into the gate last night—took out a good section of the wall."

"Where's the gate?"

"Hauled it off a while ago."

"Where's the truck?"

"No idea, we just work here. I'm sure they'll know inside," said the construction worker. He turned away and went back to work. I stood frozen in dismay. This construction crew was cleaning a crime scene. I would have no proof of the shooting if they were allowed to continue. Vanessa had taken longer getting out of the car but was standing at my side.

"They destroyed it, Vanessa," I said. "They destroyed the evidence."

"There'll be a police report. I'll get it," she replied.

"There are two more bullets, they hit the gate. We need to stop the clean up. Can you order it? The police weren't investigating a shooting. They wouldn't look for bullets."

"Pierce, I can't stop this."

"Yes, you can. You're with the district attorney. Please, Vanessa. Stop them," I pleaded. "I need to find out who they are, and why they killed Catherine and why they're after me."

She stared at me for a long moment and muttered, "Your visions better be real." She then turned to the construction crews and with a loud voice said, "Everyone stop working! I'm with the district attorney's office, and this is a crime scene."

The construction workers stopped and looked at one of the men supervising the clean-up. He was a burly man with a tight T-shirt, strong facial features, and darkly tanned skin. He walked up to Vanessa and said, "The police were already here. We run on hourly, lady. You can't stop us."

"I most certainly can; and if you impede the investigation, you'll become part of it," she said firmly.

"You're really going to do this?" he asked.

"I most certainly am," she replied.

"Okay, guys. Paid break," said the burly man with a smile. The workers stopped working.

Vanessa turned to me and said, "I hope you're right." She pulled out her cell phone and dialed a number.

"Thank you," I said as she started a conversation with a police lieutenant. Within minutes, she was delivering a forceful
argument. I was impressed. She obviously had taken charge of
her life and moved forward in her professional career. She demanded that detectives come to the scene, and her instructions
did not allow the officer on the other end to say no.

While we were waiting for the detectives to arrive, she and
I discussed what other steps to take. She would have the bullet
I had given her examined and see what it could tell us. I didn't
know much about sniper rifles, but maybe I could identify the
model from photographs. She would also look up the address
and license plate number and see what name they were registered in and any background information she could uncover on
the sniper. She made it crystal clear that I currently had no case
and considering how I arrived at my conclusions no one in the
world would convict anyone. The bullet could have come from
anywhere, and my dreams or visions would get the case tossed
out of court in the first three minutes.

I was scheduled to go in and resume my position at Paralight. How dangerous would that be? The shooter had somehow
known my schedule when I approached the Kensington Mental
Hospital so it made sense that he would also know about my
scheduled return to work. We decided together that my return to
work should be on my own schedule and not on any predeter-
mined timeline. I called the office from a pay phone, said I was
taking care of family problems and would not be in right away.
The detectives came to examine the area and Vanessa gave them
the bullet I had recovered from the wall. I told them of the shooting and explained that I had retrieved the bullet from the brick
wall before the truck smashed into it. Two other shots had hit the

metal gate which had already been removed from the site. I also explained the shooter had shot from the third-story window of the hotel across the street. One of the detectives, a thick armed man who was wearing a tweed jacket, and introduced himself as Detective Calloway, walked with me to the hotel. The clerk showed us his records—the room had not been occupied the previous day. Calloway marked the room as a crime scene and began a search.

Vanessa took me for an early lunch. We talked about Cole and Catherine and the memories we all had together. Vanessa was beautiful and one of the most comfortable people to be with in the whole world. It was a strange feeling sitting at lunch with her. I had felt such a loss after the death of Catherine and had shunned anything that reminded me of normal life prior to the test flight. After the test I had spent so much time at Kensington trying not to think about anything to avoid the headaches that I had distanced myself from life, reality, and emotions. The last two days had been the most confusing and turbulent days of my life. The comfort I was feeling was odd to me, and tears welled in my eyes. I excused myself and went to the restroom to regain emotional control. I needed Vanessa to see me as strong so she'd believe what I had been telling her. Once the evidence from the crime scenes came back, I was sure we would have a case, the detectives would solve it and all aspects and my life would return to some sense of normalcy.

"Look, Pierce, you've been through a rough time these last five months. I get it. It's been hard on me too," said Vanessa when I returned.

She could see right through me, "You saying I don't need to go to the bathroom to cry?"

She smiled, "No, you can cry with me. Look at my life these past few months. I not only lost Catherine and Cole, I lost you. I went from everything to nothing. I've had my share of wet pillow nights."

"You cried over me?"

A defensive, sly smile slid across her face, "Heavens, no. I chop onions before I go to bed."

I laughed, "Really? They had some onions in the bathroom."

"I know. That's why I brought you here," she smiled.

There are moments in life where you cannot help but smile because your heart is so full. That lunch was one of those moments. I appreciated Vanessa helping me with the crime scenes, but even more, I appreciated being with her. Some of the emptiness in my life was being filled.

After lunch, she took me shopping, insisting I could not return to work as a superhero. With new clothes and a shave in the bathroom at the mall, she dropped me off at a side entrance to Paralight.

"I'll call you as soon as I know anything on the address and license plate," she promised.

"Thanks," I said, leaning in before closing the door. "And thanks for your help today. I didn't have anyone else to turn to."

"I've got some onions in the trunk so if you need to cut more, let me know."

"Take your onions. I think I've moved on to carrots. Fewer eye problems," I said.

"I'll call you," she said before she drove away. I turned toward Paralight and walked through the side doors of the large glass building. I had no idea what a different world I was walking into.

Chapter 7

The side entrance was not as grand as the main foyer, but the marble floors and the brushed chrome and mahogany walls were luxurious. Paralight was a company with money, and the board of directors was not opposed to making the office buildings extravagant. I walked down the corridor toward the main foyer and saw Jonathan, the mentally handicapped janitor, mopping the floor. As I approached, he heard my footsteps, lowered his eyes, and turned toward the wall. It broke my heart to think how Jack had treated him the day before the test flight, and I could not get it out of my mind how enraged I would be if someone were to treat Danny badly because he was mentally handicapped. I wondered how many people at Paralight had treated Jonathan the way Jack had.

"Jonathan," I said, "I have to tell you these floors are incredible."

Jonathan turned back toward me, trepidation on his face. When he saw me, he smiled. "Pierce."

"Yes, you remembered."

"Welcome back," he said with a smile.

"Thank you, Jonathan. It's good to be back. I'm sure I'll be seeing a lot of you." I patted him on the shoulder.

As I touched him, he looked deeper into my eyes and smiled. There was a far-away look in his eyes that again reminded me of Danny. "You are special, Pierce," he said.

"Thank you. You are, too, Jonathan," I said. I walked down the hallway to the main foyer.

The space was extravagant, modern, elaborate, and expansive. I crossed the large open space to the elevators and received some smiles and kind comments from employees passing by which I kindly returned. I took the elevator to the top floor. As I walked down the hallway to Jack's office, his secretary saw me coming through the glass wall and doors, smiled and, as I entered, said, "He's on a call, but wanted to see you as soon as you came in."

Jack looked up from his desk and saw me through his open door. He was talking on the phone but beckoned for me to enter. He wrapped up his phone call as I walked in and grinned at me. "Good to see you standing."

"It's good to be away from the white walls," I said with a smile.

"The board will be happy to know you are back and on the schedule."

"I am happy to be back and to get back to my normal life."

"I have a lot to discuss with you. Things have changed in the past few months, but you're running late and I need you in diagnostics. We need to get you tested." He slid a Scarlet access card to me and called out, "Emily, tell Carter Pierce is on his way." It had not occurred to me that I would need a new access card but perhaps my old card had been deactivated.

While Emily was dialing an extension, Jack looked back at me. "After the diagnostics, report back to me, and I'll put you back in the line-up. The board is planning a second flight, based on your coming out of the coma and progressing quickly to your release from the hospital." With that, he swung abruptly back to his computer.

"I'm on my way," I said, as I picked up the card and left the room. When I got in the elevator I tried my old card and it did nothing. The new card registered, I scanned my finger and the elevator descended to Scarlet.

It was not long before I was in Carter's examination room, running on a treadmill with wires attached all over my body, graphs and charts logging the data from my vital systems. Carter and his assistants were looking at the screens intently, and even the monkeys seemed to be enjoying themselves, jumping and screaming like spectators from the far end of the room.

Carter stood up from his computer and walked over to the treadmill. "This is interesting, Pierce. We're going to speed it up. Just keep running."

"Okay," I said.

"You feeling winded, tired?"

I had not considered it, but I had been running for some time and felt no weariness. In fact, I felt no more fatigued than if I'd been walking. I wasn't even sweating. "No, not at all," I answered. "Feeling fine."

Carter nodded, increased the speed of the treadmill to a sprint and returned to his computer. I matched the speed with ease. In fact, this faster pace had no more effect than my previous running. I was paying acute attention to my body now and was quite pleased with the fact that I was feeling no pain or weariness.

"You okay?" asked Carter.

"Fine," I said, as I continued to sprint.

The lab assistants gathered around Carter's computer, looking with interest at the heart rate and vital signs being recorded. "Can you increase the speed?" asked Carter.

"I don't see why not," I answered.

One of the assistants increased the speed of the treadmill, and my speed increased to match it. I was then in a full-out sprint, running faster than I had ever run in my life. The treadmill read 25.3 miles per hour. "That's fast," said the assistant.

"More?" asked Carter.

"More." I answered.

Carter nodded to the assistant, and he again increased the speed. The digital display on the treadmill rose to 27.8 miles per hour. Again, I picked up the pace.

"That can't be right," said the assistant.

"It is right," retorted Carter.

"How can he sustain it?" the assistant questioned nervously.

"I don't know," answered Carter. "You still okay?" he asked me.

"Challenge me," I replied as I sprinted.

Carter stared at his computer, then abruptly stood up and shut down the treadmill. The lab assistants looked at him in dismay, and I slowed to a stop. "Good job," he said as he began removing the patches that attached the wires to my body, "You're all done."

"Just when it was getting interesting."

"To say the least," he replied as he turned to his assistant, "I need a full diagnostic on him. Schedule a CAT scan, blood samples, bone marrow, EKG. I need to break down everything and evaluate what we have."

"I feel fine. I don't think all that will be necessary," I interrupted.

Carter looked at me, his brow furrowed, "That's my concern. People aren't supposed to be able to do what you just did. Before today the fastest recorded speed of a human being was 26.7 miles per hour, and that speed is unsustainable."

"I broke a record?"

Carter looked me in the eye and nodded. "You are the fastest man in recorded human history."

The idea took a moment to settle, then a smile slid across my face, "I'm the fastest?"

"You're the fastest."

I savored the thought. I had just performed a feat unmatched in recorded human history. I wondered just how fast I could go and how long I could keep it up. I wasn't tired or breathing hard. The only sign of stress was slight moisture on my forehead. I had sustained the sprint for longer than Carter thought humanly possible, and it had hardly affected me.

"It's not you," Carter inserted. "It's the test flight. It must be a side effect or purification that came with the transformation into light and back."

"What you're saying is I'm a superhero," I said with a smile.

Carter looked at me and lifted his eyebrows, "You're a lab rat."

I was about to smile, but Carter's face was serious, "This happened to Cartwright?" I asked.

Carter looked at me and paused for a moment, then furrowed his brow as if annoyed with the question, "No."

"No? Nothing like this?"

"No."

I walked to the cages and looked at the monkey who was my predecessor on the flight. As he jumped in the cage, the nametag on his neck reading "CARTWRIGHT," bounced around, "Why do you think something happened to me and not to Cartwright?" I asked Carter. "You'd think, if the flight had strange consequences on me physically, it would be the same for him."

Carter ignored my question and turned to his computer screen. The monkey stared back at me. As I looked into his eyes, energy lifted from him and the world around him rippled. The nametag on his neck disappeared and wisps of light disassembled, then coalesced, recreating the cages in different positions. I knew instantly that I was in one of my visions and that the room around me had changed. I was getting used to this new ability and was interested in what I would see and learn this time. Did my subconscious mind know more than my conscious mind? Was it somehow guiding me to learn and see what I needed to survive and understand what was happening around me?

I turned away from the monkey with no nametag. The room was in commotion. A monkey was motionless on a table in the center of the room, and Carter was busily attaching electrodes to the body as three assistants set up the computers and workstations to show the readouts. That monkey had the nametag reading, "CARTWRIGHT." Jack was standing back from the technicians, in an expensive business suit pressed with sharp creases running down each leg, his face concerned. I walked toward the table and got a good look at one of the assistants. I did not recognize her. I had not seen her in my previous visits to Carter. I looked at the other two. I didn't know any of them. I looked at their nametags: "Keri," "Howard," and "Raymond."

"We're all up," said Raymond as he looked at one of the computer screens displaying the monkey's vital signs.

"Brainwaves are all over," said Keri.

"He can't die," inserted Jack forcefully.

"Heartbeat normal," said Raymond. A steady pulse pinged on the screen before him.

Carter turned to Howard, "Prepare a sedative for when he wakes." He then looked to Jack, "He seems okay. His vitals are where they should be."

The steady pulse on Raymond's monitor changed, the lines becoming sharp and steep, "Heart fluctuations," said Raymond.

The monkey's hand moved slightly and his face twitched, "He's coming to," said Carter. Jack watched with anticipation.

"His brain waves are scattered. Something's happening," said Keri.

The monkey's eyes opened. It screamed so shrilly that the sound ran through my spine. It sprang from the table, hurdled Carter, and landed on top of a computer monitor which crashed to the floor. Raymond reached for the monkey, but it scratched him, flailing its arms in a rage. It flipped from him to the floor and scampered across the smooth white tiles, the wires attached to its body yanking the other computers over.

"Grab him!" yelled Jack.

Everyone chased the monkey, lunging after it and colliding with the furniture and equipment while the monkey tore between their legs and under chairs. Raymond dove through me and caught the monkey by the leg. Gripping him close, he grabbed the flailing arms and clutched him by the jaw to stop any biting. The monkey screamed and strained in Raymond's arms, then suddenly stopped struggling. Expressions of relief crossed every face in the lab. The monkey's eyes rolled back, it shook as if in a seizure, and then emitted a terrifying screech of mingled fear and agony. The monkey's chest protruded and the muscles strained relentlessly against the convulsion shaking its little body.

"Give him to me," said Carter. He seized the monkey and put him on the table, several electrodes still attached. The assistants quickly pinned down the monkey's legs, arms, and head. Its steady heartbeat still showed on a monitor that had fallen to the floor but had not broken. "I need the sedative," said Carter to Howard. Howard let go of an arm and leg and Jack took his place holding the shaking monkey. The shaking became more severe and foam oozed out of the monkey's mouth.

The monkey gave a last straining arch as its tormented body writhed in pain, then it collapsed motionless on the table. The heart monitor on the floor displayed a flat line and a constant tone. Cartwright had died. My mind flashed to Cole telling me that the monkey had died. I had ignored Catherine as she explained the evidence she and Cole were building. I should have listened, but I hadn't, and now I was watching exactly what had happened to the monkey after the flight. Catherine and Cole were right.

"What happened?" asked Jack.

"I have no idea," answered Carter.

"Out! Everyone out!" ordered Jack. The others looked at him in dismay. "You heard me, out!" said Jack with a firm expression. "Not you, Carter. You stay." Raymond, Howard, and Keri reluctantly left, all three glancing back in bewilderment. "Bring him back," ordered Jack.

Carter sprang into action. He administered CPR, quickly shocked the monkey with a defibrillator, and injected a stimulant directly into the heart, but the line on the monitor remained flat. Finally he stopped, "I cannot bring him back," said Carter, "He's dead."

"This can't happen," Jack said firmly. He looked around the room at the other monkeys, took the nametag off Cartwright's body, and walked to the other monkey cages. He opened a cage, grabbed a screaming monkey, and put Cartwright's nametag around that monkey's neck as it continued to scream. He then put the replacement monkey back in the cage. "This did not happen and will never be spoken of," Jack said, staring directly into Carter's eyes, "The monkey survived and is in perfect condition. You and I brought him back and he is just fine. Do you understand?"

Carter cowered under Jack's glare and nodded shakily.

"Convince me, Carter. Convince me you will never tell anyone about this."

"I won't tell, I swear. I swear on my life."

Jack smiled with the response, but there was no warmth in it. "Let me down," he threatened softly, "and it *will* be your life."

Fear registered on Carter's face. Again he nodded.

"Clean up this mess," instructed Jack. "The test was a success, and the monkey is in perfect condition." Jack shuffled through the clutter in the room, found a box, put the dead monkey's body in it, and sealed it shut.

Carter stood motionless as Jack went through these businesslike movements. "We have an understanding?" Jack demanded, looking again at Carter.

"We have an understanding," said Carter, averting his eyes from Jack's intimidating stare. Jack picked up the box and left the room.

Carter took several deep breaths and, with shaking hands, began picking up the monitors and computer equipment. As I watched him, I felt sorrow for him as well as anger. He struggled with the weight of a monitor, his demeanor exuding fear and weakness. I felt sorrow he would fall in so quickly with Jack's demands and be willing to falsify his records and scientific study based on the will of his employer. I also felt angry because he had allowed me to fly the plane even though the flight had re-sulted in Cartwright's death. I had trusted him and the scientific reports. Everyone had trusted them.

My anger deepened as I thought of Jack. He was the execu-tive in charge of Scarlet, the one responsible for the pilots and the crews I had been working with for years. He was the person who we believed had stood up for us and our safety in all situ-ations and represented us to the board of directors of Paralight. But now I saw him in a new light. He had ordered Carter to cover up the monkey's death and had chosen me as the first hu-man pilot. He did not value my life. What I had thought was a great honor was, instead, an exploitation—a mission which he had every reason to believe would kill me.

As emotions swarmed through my body, energy rippled throughout the room and wisps of light reshaped the walls. I found myself out of the vision and staring again through the bars of the monkey cage at the imposter monkey wearing the collar reading "CARTWRIGHT." I turned around and looked at Carter with new understanding. I felt disgust toward him as I watched him type at his computer terminal. What lies might he be inputting as scientific data? How many other reports had he falsified? And how willing was he to continue in his lies?

I walked toward him.

"Jack is waiting for you," he said, without turning to face me.

"I shouldn't upset Jack, should I, Carter?"

"No, you shouldn't."

"Does he scare you?"

Carter paused from his writing and turned to me, "Scare me?"

"Yes, he's very intimidating."

"We have a good business relationship," said Carter.

"Something more is going on here, Carter. Something happened to me physically as a result of the flight. What I have just done is not humanly possible and the variable is the flight. Wouldn't it also have happened to the monkey?"

"That's what we are studying. I don't have the answers. That's why I want more tests," said Carter as he turned back to his computer.

In Shakespeare's play *Hamlet,* Hamlet arranged for a play to enact the murder of his father while he watched as his uncle, the murderer, reacted to the play. His uncle's reaction confirmed Hamlet's conviction that he was guilty.

Mention of the monkey visibly touched a nerve in Carter. He did not want to look at me. I decided to test him. I pulled up a chair next to him where I could see his face and sat down. I said conversationally, "Cartwright died after the flight. You couldn't revive him. Jack switched the name tag to a new monkey."

His face went pale and froze. His hands began to tremble. His eyes shifted back and forth, attempting to find something on which to focus. He stammered, "Uh…uh…" He could not look at me as he searched for words. I had my answer. He had been confronted with the truth; and just as Hamlet saw in his uncle's face the undeniable expression of guilt, I saw undeniable guilt in Carter's face. I knew the vision I had of Cartwright's death was true.

Carter finally managed to stammer, "I…I…I think you are out of line, Pierce."

Carter was not alone in his guilt. Jack had instigated the cover-up and was ultimately responsible for my taking the flight. I decided to lessen the intensity of my focus on Carter. "Perhaps I am. It's a theory. What do you think?"

"I think," said Carter as his eyes darted to the assistants in the room, "I think anything is possible, though highly unlikely."

"It seems odd that nothing happened to Cartwright."

Carter shivered as he continued, "It seems odd to all of us also. That is science. We need to find out why things work the way they do. That is what we do."

I was amazed at his lie and could not resist another question: "Would you have let me take the flight if Cartwright had died?"

None of the assistants were making any pretense of continuing with their tasks. Carter's hands shook, and he looked from person to person. In a voice that quavered with nerves, he said, "I would never have let you fly if Cartwright had died." He turned immediately to his terminal and continued typing.

"Great," I said, "Thanks for looking out for me."

Eyes glued to the monitor, Carter responded, "That's what we do here."

I walked to the door, then stopped and looked at the assistants in the room, "By the way, good to meet all of you." They smiled automatically and nodded. I turned back to Carter, "Carter? Whatever happened to Keri, Howard, and Raymond?"

Carter stopped his typing again and rubbed his white knuckles, "Uh…uh, I don't believe any of them work here anymore."

"Fired?"

"Something like that."

"All fired? Were they not good at their jobs? All of them?"

The room was deadly silent as the assistants waited to hear the response from Carter. "Jack let them go. Not my decision." Carter did not move his eyes from his terminal. I smiled at the assistants and left the room.

Chapter 8

As I made my way back to Jack's office I methodically outlined my situation. I had seen Jack and Carter cover Cartwright's death, and I was sure the vision had been true, based on Carter's reaction. Jack had chosen me to be the test pilot for the flight, despite the risk that it would kill me. Jack wanted me dead. Catherine had died in a car crash, and I had very good reason to believe it was murder. Now the same man was trying to kill me. I had just made an open accusation against Carter, but now I wondered if I had made a dangerous mistake. What would he do next? Call Jack and tell him about my accusation? He couldn't make such a call in front of his assistants, but his fear of Jack was obviously greater than his loyalty to science or his ethics regarding human safety. Yet it seemed likely that he would remain silent if he thought that I wouldn't press the situation. I decided to be more discreet and learn all I could while not provoking a direct confrontation with Jack. Jack would take action. And if he were connected with Catherine's murder, then he would do anything to cover up that connection—including committing another murder.

I made a firm decision to keep my eyes wide open. I would act as if I knew nothing, interact cautiously with Jack, and seek to learn everything I could to create a case against him. Most important was to find his connection to the man who killed Catherine and had attempted to kill me. This new ability to see visions could be a key to helping me decode their events and motives. I had Vanessa on my side. All I had to do was provide her with information, and we would be able to bring to light the truth behind what was happening.

Jack's secretary again smiled as I walked into the reception area. "He's waiting for you," she said.

I walked into Jack's office, and my body went numb. I felt for a moment I was outside my body and watching the scene as I did in visions. I thought I had prepared myself to confidently walk into Jack's office, but I had not prepared myself for what I saw. Sitting across the desk from Jack was the sniper who had attempted to kill me. He was smiling and stood to meet me with his hand extended. This was the man who had killed Catherine. His smiling face was a horrible dream, and he was standing before me wanting to shake my hand. I was speechless and stood frozen.

"Pierce, this is Don. He's your new flight partner."

"Hi, Pierce," Don said. "I've heard so much about you. You're a living legend around here."

Living, no thanks to you, I thought as I looked this murderer in the eye. Anger filled me. My nerves racked my consciousness to reach out and attack this man and to kill Jack. It was all I could do to hold my hands at my sides. That moment confirmed to me clearly that Jack wanted me dead. He must have hired this assassin to kill Catherine and me. Jack was my enemy. This man was a hired hit man. He had killed in cold blood and was no doubt there at that moment with the intent of finishing me off.

I could see Don's growing discomfort as he stood, his hand extended. I took a deep breath, which helped control my anger slightly. I was determined to keep my resolution to act as if I knew nothing. I grabbed Don's hand and shook it. It was warm though I expected it to be cold and metallic and his face was friendly and accommodating.

"It's good to finally meet you," he said.

Had I not known who he was, I would have perceived him as a decent person. I would have thought no ill of him and most likely would have been excited to get to know him and become his friend. Chills ran down my spine as I contrasted his kindly demeanor with what I knew of him.

"Pierce, I've scheduled time for a review tomorrow. It will be on your calendar. Don will catch you up on anything pressing for today," said Jack. He turned back to his computer, leaving me standing there facing my wife's murderer.

"We're partners," I said finally, the words guttural and forced.

"We are," said Don with a smile, "I have to admit it's a bit intimidating to be lined up with you when I'm so new to the company."

His mask of sincerity was so believable I could scarcely fathom this was the same cold face I had seen on the rainy street, satisfied with his actions upon leaving Catherine dead. I stepped to the side to allow him to leave the office first. He took the lead, and I followed. Jack's secretary smiled as we left, and I walked down the hallway with my new partner. I determined again in my mind I would play this scene out carefully, not saying or doing anything to allow Don or Jack to suspect I knew what they had done. I knew this was the only way I could stay alive. I needed time to think, and it was very hard to do that with Don at my side. "Your name is Don," I confirmed.

"Yes," he answered, "Don Parker."

"How long have you been here?"

"About four months."

"So you know your way around?"

"I'm pretty comfortable."

"I'll meet you in the hangar," I said as we came to the doorway to the stairs.

As I turned away and opened the door to the stairway, he said, "I can help you get your things."

"I assure you, I know my way to the lockers."

"Of course," he said with a smile that caused my stomach to clench.

When the door closed behind me, I leaned against it and took several deep breaths. My heart was beating fast, and I was light-headed. Anger was still streaming through my body, and I needed to let it subside so I could think clearly. As my heart rate slowed, I pulled myself away from the door and descended down the stairs. On the main level, I exited the stairway, entered the elevator, and scanned my new card. The panel under the elevator buttons opened revealing the separate panel with the glass screen. I scanned my index finger on the screen, and the elevator descended. When the doors opened, I passed the hallway to the hangar and went straight to the locker room.

My locker was exactly the same as I had left it. On the door of the locker was my family picture with me, Catherine, and Danny. Pain streaked through my chest as I looked at Catherine.

Her death was unnecessary, and the healing I had experienced since she died seemed to rip right open. How is a person supposed to face the murderer of his wife? She looked so happy in the picture. The loss of her life had immeasurable consequences on our little family. I reemphasized the importance of keeping my mind focused so that I could, in some way, find justice for her death.

Inside the locker, my pressure suit hung alongside my black flight suit. I quickly took my clothes off and put on the flight suit. As I was putting my cell phone into a pocket, it vibrated. I saw Vanessa's name on the caller ID. Seeing her name was a comfort, and I felt stress leave my body, just knowing that I had someone whom I trusted on the other line. I pressed the button.

"Hi, Vanessa," I said with relief.

She broke into her updates, "Nothing yet at Kensington, but the name on the address and license plates is Donald Parker, a pilot from Florida with a clean record. But you won't believe this. He has been working at…"

"Paralight," I said finishing her sentence.

"You know?" she questioned with surprise.

"He's my new flight partner."

"You've got to be joking!" she said.

"Yeah, amazing, huh?" I said flatly as I heard the door to the locker room open.

Don's voice came from the doorway, "Pierce, you in here?" I whispered, "I gotta go. We'll talk later," and shut the phone. I walked down the row of lockers and looked around the corner to see Don standing in the doorway with two cups of coffee. "Weren't we meeting in the hangar?"

"Thought you might like a drink," he said with the sincerity of a long-time friend.

"No, thanks," I replied. I walked past him and headed toward the hangar.

"Come on, Pierce. I insist. Let's start this off right. We're going to spend a lot of time together, and I want to show you I'm a team player."

"A team player?" I said, attempting to mute the shock in my voice.

"Yes, and that means we look out for each other. We have each other's best interests at heart," he said.

My best interests at heart? What are the chances the coffee is poisoned or has some narcotic in it? I was amazed. This man wanted me dead and he was talking about being a team player?

"I insist," he said, as he again held out the cup of coffee. I decided that I didn't need to drink the coffee; but if taking it let him feel he had broken through a barrier in our friendship, it would be okay. I took the cup and he smiled. We continued down the hall in silence.

"You're married?" Don asked.

I looked down at the ring on my finger, "She died."

"I'm sorry," he said with compassion.

"Are you sorry?" I asked with biting firmness. Don was taken aback by my question, and I could tell he was fumbling for words.

He looked at me cautiously and replied, "Of course. If I may ask, how did she die?"

The wounds in my heart were screaming, and anger surged through my veins. I wondered how long I could walk beside him without wrestling him to the ground and choking the life out of him. "A hit," I responded, and I could see a guarded look in his face, "A hit and run. A car crash. The other driver fled the scene on foot. They never found him."

He nodded with a contemplative expression, "Any children?"

I had had enough of his personal questions, and I knew I would not be able to control my words or actions if he continued. I decided to ask the questions, "Jack recruited you?"

"Yes."

"How long have you known him?"

"A few years."

"Have you worked for him before?"

"We've helped each other," he replied.

"What does that mean?"

"I'm an opportunist. A well-paying job comes around, I take it."

I was utterly disgusted with the idea that Catherine's death was a "well-paying job." I did not ask him any more questions and think if I had continued speaking with him I would have lost the ability to refrain from an attack. We were soon in the hangar. A few of the other pilots and technicians welcomed me back, and I made small talk with them. While Don was turned speaking with another person, I discreetly threw the coffee cup in a trash can. It was nice to be among people I knew although I had no idea who I could trust.

Kendall gave me a hug. He introduced me to his new flight partner who was from Texas and had a strong accent to prove it. I did what I could to distance myself from Don, but eventually he walked up behind me and put his hand on my shoulder.

"We're on the simulator," he said. "They should be ready for us now."

I nodded and said quick good-byes. Don was scheduled to go first, and I took the seat in the back. This was the first time I had ever entered the simulation room with a melancholy feeling. This man was destroying everything good in my life. I had thought that it was impossible to dislike anyone more than I already disliked Don; but as we sat in the cockpit and I saw the ramp pull away from the cockpit, I clearly saw that he had tainted the one escape I had from the sorrow and loneliness of my life. The simulator was a place of peace from the sadness of losing Catherine, and now I was in it with her murderer. I secured my seat belt, and Don did the same.

I looked up at the observation booth. Standing next to the technicians was Jack. Don noticed Jack as well and waved to him. Jack nodded, affirming the wave. Jack's presence made me feel awkward. He often watched the simulator runs, but now I felt that this ride was different. I felt danger. The feeling was strong and my hand reached to unbuckle my belt, but I stopped it and convinced myself I was overreacting.

"We're ready," said Don.

The thousands of criss-crossing lights that lined the circular metal mesh of the simulator flared on, and the landscape changed. We were on a runway in a desert. Don ignited the thrust of the plane, and soon we were in the air.

"They tell me your time in here is what gave you the light job," said Don.

"That's what Jack told me," I said.

The plane flew over canyons, "This is my favorite one," said Don as he banked the plane into the canyons. He handled the plane with ease. He was a talented pilot; and as he took a strong curve, he twisted the plane and thrust at the right time to make a smooth transition into the next turn. Had it been any other person in the seat in front of me, I would have complimented him. I could not force myself to say anything good to Don. He then diverted into a canyon seam that was new in the simulator. I had flown this course many times but had never seen this series of tight curves and steep canyons. It was not too disturbing because they were always updating the software and adding to the worlds of the simulators. Generally Kendall and I were the first to test new additions, but I had been gone for some time so there was no cause for concern about a new canyon.

Don again was handling the new canyon with skill. He hit the thrust and the canyon sped past faster. The swerves and g-forces increased and the skin on my face was pulled and pushed with the pressure. There was a steep curve ahead, and I knew there was no way to make it at our current speed but Don did not slow down. He increased the speed and hit the turn. The cockpit swung hard to the left, went through the light wall hologram, and skimmed the metal mesh of the simulator.

"Easy," I said.

"That's nothing," replied Don as he increased the speed even more. The plane swerved through the tight corners and the g-forces smashed me from side to side. He twisted the plane through another curve. The force thrust me upward off my seat, and the seat belt ripped loose from the plane. I grabbed frantically at the side of the cockpit to hold myself inside the plane.

"Don! Stop!" I screamed as I clung with all my strength. Don glanced back at me, increased the speed again, and whipped the plane into another twist. The forces were too strong, and I was thrown into the metal mesh of the simulator. I hit the mesh with my shoulder and the impact broke loose many of the metal bars. I could see the canyons speeding by, and the long mechanical arm that held the cockpit swerved in the air above me. For a brief moment I made eye contact with Don and saw him plunging the cockpit toward me. I pulled myself back under the hologram lights of the simulator and grabbed a bar that had been jarred loose by my impact. I jammed the bar up toward the plunging cockpit, which smashed into the bar, crushed it, and came to a halt a centimeter from my head. Any more pressure and it would have smashed my head into the wall behind the metal mesh.

I remained motionless beneath the cockpit. The simulator lights flickered off. I could hear the doors to the simulator room open and the movement of the mechanical ramp.

"Pierce!" yelled one of the technicians. I heard several technicians jump from the ramp onto the metal mesh.

"Pierce, you okay?" asked Don from the cockpit above me. I ignored his question and waited in silence. My nerves were screaming and my anger was raging. He had increased the speed when he saw that my belt had broken, and he had intentionally swerved the cockpit to smash me on the mesh. He had attempted to kill me again!

"Pierce!" yelled Jack as he approached the cockpit behind the technicians. "Pierce, are you okay?"

"I can't hear any movement," said Don with a worried tone. The hypocrisy of his words and tone stung through my soul.

"I see his legs," said a technician. Several technicians scrambled around the cockpit and one crouched on the metal mesh and touched my foot.

"Pierce, we'll get you out," he said as the others helped Don exit the cockpit. I saw his feet as he stepped onto the metal mesh. The technicians then pulled the cockpit up and off me. I could see their look of relief as they saw that I was conscious.

"That was close," said one of the technicians.

"Thank goodness you're okay," said Don as he stood behind the technicians. Fury welled inside me. My body reacted without my conscious volition. I burst from the mesh and flew toward Don. My fist connected cleanly with Don's cheekbone, and blood spurted from the impact. His head wrenched backward, as though I had knocked it from his body. His body rippled toward the metal mesh. By reflex, he righted himself and twisted to land on his hands, breaking the fall. He pushed off the mesh and flew back toward me with a force that matched my attack. He was a trained fighter, and his first blow knocked me flat on my back. Don pounced on me, his fist cocked to strike into my face. The technicians jumped on Don and pulled him from me. I lunged again at Don, but Jack tackled me and we crashed into the mesh.

"Stop! Stop now!" ordered Jack. His shoulder was under my chin, and I was pinned against the mesh.

"He tried to kill me!" I yelled. "He intentionally slammed it toward me."

"I was following the course!" yelled Don as he wiped blood from a deep cut on his cheekbone.

"Stop!" yelled Jack. I subsided. Jack stood up, extended a hand, and half-pulled me to my feet.

I collected myself and glared at Don. "Check the seat belt for tampering," I said to the technicians. "He set this up. He tried to kill me."

Jack turned to the technicians, "We'll run reports and a full investigation." He then turned his attention to Don and me, "Both of you to visual."

"Everyone to visual," I said.

Jack glared at me; and then as the weight of the eyes of all the technicians hit him, he agreed, "Everyone to visual."

I was relieved with his concession. I did not want to be anywhere alone with Jack and Don. That would have been suicide. They had already proven that they wanted me dead. I was not going to put myself in a position where they could do it easily as long as I had any say in it.

Exiting the simulator was relieving as the large expanse of the Scarlet hangar opened in front of me. We walked along the balcony overlooking Scarlet, but my eyes were on the windows on the left side showing the rows of computers in the Paralight server rooms. *What would the computers show in visual?* I thought. When we got into the visual room, the technicians loaded the simulation we had just finished. We watched as the plane took off from the runway.

"Forward to the crash," instructed Jack. The technician skimmed through the simulation footage to the moment I flew from the cockpit. He then rewound the footage to play the entire scene. I watched as my belt broke and I clung to the cockpit. The plane then twisted through a curve in a perfect display of pilot skill as I fell from the cockpit. The plane continued down the course and into a cavern. In the cavern was a low overhang which the plane skillfully adjusted and shifted to avoid as it swerved into the mesh where it smashed onto my helpless body.

"He followed the course," said Jack with a smug smile.

"He tried to kill me!" I insisted.

"The computers don't lie," said Jack.

"He came at me, Jack. It was intentional," I demanded.

"I followed the course. We're a team, Pierce," added Don, holding his bloodstained shirt to the cut on his face.

I turned to the technicians, "Check the belts. In all the years I've been here, we have never had a problem with a belt in the simulator."

"Perhaps that's why it broke, Pierce," said Jack. "We'll examine everything. You go home, take the day, and come back tomorrow for a briefing."

I decided not to argue but to leave as quickly as possible. I nodded in agreement then reiterated to the technicians, "Check the belts."

As I walked to the exit Don said, "Pierce, let me help you with –"

"You, stay away," I cut in.

"But, Pierce –"

"Stay away," I said firmly. I closed the door behind me and walked past the Paralight servers that whirred behind the wall of glass, telling the lies Jack and Don had programmed into them.

Chapter 9

I hurried down the hallway and turned a corner to the stairway so I could exit Scarlet. The stairwell was concrete, and the walls pressed at me as I climbed. It was as if it were a prison created by Don and Jack, and the breathlessness of claustrophobia set in. I focused my attention on the steps and soon was at the security door, which could be opened only from the direction I was climbing. I pushed the door open, went through, and relaxed slightly as it closed behind me, the lock clicking. The air thinned with the locking of the door. I looked up at a security camera staring down at me and quickly left the stairwell. As I entered the foyer of Paralight, I noticed another security camera. My eyes scanned the foyer. It seemed that security cameras were everywhere. I looked at the floor as I walked through the foyer and made my way to the elevators leading to the underground parking. I thought it strange that I had never really noticed how observed I had been walking though the hallways of Paralight.

The elevator to the parking level also had a camera, and I felt an upsurge of freedom as I entered the underground parking structure. Soon I would be in my car. The feeling vanished as I saw that my car was not parked in my favorite spot. As I looked around, I remembered that Vanessa had dropped me off and I did not have a car.

I would need to leave the facility on foot, which would make things much more dangerous. I ran through the scenario in my mind. No, that option was out of the question. Paralight was on the outskirts of the town and I would be exposed as I walked. I needed a car. Could I steal a car? I rejected the idea. I had no idea how to do it; and if I were to steal keys and take someone's car, I would be on camera and arrested. Would Kendall help? I made the decision to find him and quickly made my way back to the elevator, through the foyer where the cameras watched my every step and into the elevator to Scarlet. I scanned my card and finger and was soon in the hangar. He was on the far side of the hangar flying a hovercraft which resembled a motorcycle and being observed by a tech crew. I walked to the group and said, "Hey, I need a minute with the pilot."

Kendall saw me and powered down the hovercraft. "You miss me?"

"Yeah, having withdrawals," I answered. "I hate the fact I ever met you." Kendall smiled as he exited the hovercraft, and I continued, "Can I steal you for a minute?"

Kendall looked to his flight partner who chimed in, "I hate to get between someone and their addiction."

Kendall looked toward the tech crew and said referring to his Texan partner, "I know he's no good at this but should we give him a try?"

The Texan waved off Kendall and stepped onto the motor-cycle hovercraft. I pulled Kendall to the side and said, "Hey, I hate to ask you this but can I borrow your car? I need to run an errand."

"My car?"

"I know, I know. It's glossy and black and blah, blah, blah…" He smiled and said, "Sure," as he handed me the keys. "It's in the underground, 'C' section."

"Thanks."

"I'll get it back, won't I?"

"I owe you," I smiled and turned away.

"No scratches or dings!" he shouted.

"No promises!" I yelled back.

I knew I had lost too much time. Jack would likely be in his office where he had access to the security cameras in the building. I decided to move casually, being careful to always be near other people. Public areas would increase my chances of survival. I went to the locker room where several other people were hanging around, put on my street clothes, walked calmly to the elevator, and caught it as a couple techs were entering. In the main foyer, I headed down the hallway toward the elevator to the underground garages. Jonathan, the mentally handicapped janitor, was working at the end of the hallway. He saw me and walked toward me. I pressed the button for the elevator as Jonathan reached me, his face a mask of concern.

"Pierce," he said worriedly.

"Jonathan, hello."

"Danger," he said looking me directly in the eyes.

"What?"

"Danger. Do you understand?"

"What are you talking about?" I asked him. Of course, I was in danger but what was he saying exactly? Why was he saying this to me? What did he know? I wondered for a moment if he knew about the attacks on my life or even if he could possibly be a part of them.

"Bad man," said Jonathan.

"Who is a bad man, Jonathan?" I asked.

He looked me in the eyes and grabbed my forearm. As he did, our eyes connected and the warmth of his hand traveled up my arm and to my shoulder. When it reached my neck and face, I saw the rippling of the world around Jonathan that signaled the beginning of one of my visions. A strange sensation wrapped around my mind. Wisps of light disassembled the hallway behind him. The lights above us dimmed, then disappeared. The marble floors and mahogany walls were replaced with concrete, and we were standing in the recess of a stairwell in the underground parking lot of Paralight. Somehow Jonathan had taken me into a vision with him.

Eyes locked on mine, Jonathan repeated, "Bad man." He pulled me around the corner to the elevator doors. There I saw another Jonathan. The second Jonathan must have been the Jonathan who had lived the experience I was witnessing in the past. He was picking up trash in the parking garage. The elevator door opened, and the Jonathan who was picking up trash ducked behind a car to avoid being seen.

Cole exited from the elevator and walked into the garage. I turned to Jonathan, "Cole Trace is a bad man?" Was Cole involved in some way that connected him to Jack and Don?

Jonathan looked at me, "No," he answered. He motioned to the stairway we had just come from. Jack exited from the concrete stairway and I saw fear sweep across Jonathan's face.

"I want the files," Jack said to Cole.

"I can't get them. My partner has them," responded Cole.

"Your sister is dead," said Jack flatly.

Cole's naturally olive skin turned bone-white. His face showed his horror.

"Catherine," I said to Jonathan. He nodded in agreement. The anger I earlier felt returned and was targeted toward Jack.

"There are things in this world worth more than your life, Mr. Trace."

"What are you saying?" asked Cole.

"Your life means nothing to me, and I will take it. Twenty-four hours. That's what I give you. What you do now is your choice."

The words shook Cole, and he stood speechless. I could see triumph in Jack's face. He felt that he had succeeded with his threats as he turned and left Cole standing alone. Cole was stunned and motionless for some time, then got into his car and drove away.

The cement parking lot disappeared with a flash of light ending the vision and I was again standing on the marble floors of the Paralight hallway. Jonathan had let go of my arm but was still looking at me intently. I could see he felt sorrow for me and my situation. "Bad man, danger," he again reiterated.

"You're right," I said. The elevator door had opened during our shared vision. Now it was closing. I put my hand out to keep it open and stepped inside.

"Be careful," said Jonathan.

"I will. Thank you," I said; and as the doors closed, I saw a genuine smile on his face. I was certain I could trust one person at Paralight and it was my friend the janitor. I was amazed at how he had pulled me into his mind and that I was able to clearly see his past. *How did he know I was able to see these visions and how did he pull me into his?*

The elevator doors opened onto the parking level and a sick feeling overcame me. I looked out of the glass doors into the concrete parking structure and saw the stairway I had just visited in the vision with Jonathan. I wondered if Jack would appear from the stairwell as I walked past it. On the far end of the parking lot a couple was walking toward the elevators. I pushed open the glass doors and entered the parking structure. I prepared myself to confront Jack and stared at the stairway. I sped up as I approached the stairway, but it was empty—no Jack. I continued down the row of cars and saw Kendall's black Saab. He was meticulous about caring for it, and it was a beautiful car. I pressed a button on the big key, the locks opened, and the lights flashed. Only a few more steps and I would be in the car.

"Pierce!" I heard a loud voice behind me and jumped. I stopped and turned around fully expecting to see Jack. Instead I saw the security officer from the front desk. "Jack wants to see you."

My heart sank, and my legs lost their strength. I caught myself from falling by gripping the door handle of the Saab. I couldn't take any more of Jack. I was not going back into the building. I refused to. "I already saw him and he told me to go home for the day," I said.

"He just called down. Must be important."

"Can't do it," I said, "Tell him you missed me." I slid into the car and pulled out. He stood watching me. A wave of relief overcame me as I turned a corner, hiding him from view. I pulled out of the underground parking lot, and the sunshine welcomed me. I basked in freedom as I pulled past the outdoor parking lots and drove past Alex in the guard booth. He was on the phone, and I did not look at him for fear he was speaking with Jack. In the rearview mirror I saw Alex put down the phone and step out of the guard booth, waving his arms frantically. I continued to drive as if I had not seen him. The Paralight campus and buildings grew smaller behind me, and the pressures created by my traumatic return to work lessened with each long breath. There was sadness along with the relief. I loved working at Paralight. It was the one joy still remaining in my life. Jack had taken my greatest loves—my wife and my work.

I turned onto a side street as soon as I could to ensure that I was not being followed, waited about five minutes, then pulled out onto the streets again, continuing to check my rearview mirror. As I neared the freeway, I noticed a white BMW some distance behind me. As I angled onto the freeway, the BMW also signaled for the on-ramp and entered the freeway. My heart rate increased, but I attempted to push the paranoia out of my mind. I passed a few exits, and the BMW remained behind me. I decided to test my suspicion. I put my blinker on and moved into the exit-only lane. The BMW slid in behind me. Just before the segmented lines on the freeway turned into solid lines, I moved back onto the freeway. The BMW did the same. The car was following me, and it was accelerating. I kept my speed constant, still hoping that it was a coincidence.

The BMW pulled alongside my car, and I turned to see that the driver was wearing a black, face-covering helmet. It was the same helmet Don had worn on the night he smashed the car into our Lexus, killing Catherine. Don was beside me. I was sure of it. We were speeding toward an overpass and my mind took in the whole scenario at once. If I were to go off the road at the overpass, I would drop thirty feet to the road below and smash into traffic. It was a death trap. The dark helmet turned toward me, and I knew he would smash into my car. Instinctively, I slammed on the brakes, and the Saab skidded along the freeway. The BMW swerved to where my car would have been and braked hard as well. Traffic was fast approaching behind me, so I jammed my foot down on the accelerator. The engine of the Saab roared. I quickly overtook Don and his BMW and sped down the motorway. He pursued me and soon we were swerving in and out of traffic. I knew the man chasing me was an expert killer, and I was nothing close to a Nascar driver. If this chase lasted long, chances were that I would lose. I had to get off the freeway. An exit was coming up on the right, but two eighteen-wheel diesel trucks with trailers were in the right lanes. I sped past the trucks as the off-ramp passed by. As I overtook the second truck, I swerved to the right and pulled my emergency brake. My car spun in front of the truck and screeched to a stop on the shoulder of the freeway facing the opposite direction of traffic.

Don attempted the same maneuver after me; and the eighteen-wheeler, horn blaring, clipped the back of the BMW, sending it smashing into the concrete barricade on the side of the freeway overpass. The back wheel of the BMW bent with the impact, and I was quite sure it would not be able to follow me. I stepped on the gas heading the wrong way on the freeway shoulder, and exited at the off-ramp.

I drove with my knuckles tight on the steering wheel for several minutes, then slowly allowed myself to relax and breathe as I zig-zagged through neighborhoods and commercial areas. Finally I stopped in an alley behind a restaurant. I was safe for the moment, but I was at a loss about what to do. I was being hunted. I knew two of the hunters, but how many more were involved? I needed to take the next steps carefully. They knew the car I was driving. They knew where I lived. They had pursued me after I left work. They wanted me dead, and they wanted it quickly. It was safe for me to assume they somehow had tapped my phone or would be able to zero in on my location if I were to call. I could not use my phone, but my best hope for help was still Vanessa. I needed to get in touch with her, and she could help me put the pieces together. She had connections with the police force, and her career was centered on acquiring evidence needed to charge a person with a crime. Catherine had said she and Cole almost had enough against Paralight to take it to Vanessa so I only needed to continue from where they left off. I opened the console armrest in the Saab and found some change. Leaving the Saab in the alley, I darted out onto the street to find a telephone booth. Tensely, I dialed Vanessa's number.

"This is Vanessa Trace," she answered on the other end of the connection.

"Vanessa, this is Pierce. They're trying to kill me. It happened at work and they made a second attempt just now. There was a crash, two of them. It was Don. They were both him. He's trying to kill me."

"Pierce, slow down. Where are you?"

I realized that I wasn't making much sense. "I'm at a pay phone. For all I know, your line is tapped. I'm sure my cell is. They're out to kill me. I can't go home. They'll go there. I need your help."

"Tell me where you are, and I'll come right away," she said.

"No, I can't risk it. Go to the downtown metro bus station.

Make sure you're alone and not followed." I could see a bus approach the stop on the corner. I ran to the stop as the bus pulled to the curb and asked the driver if he was going downtown. He told me to wait for the next bus—it would go directly where I wanted. I fidgeted anxiously, but within a short while I was on a bus headed for downtown Phoenix.

There was something peaceful about being on the bus. I had time to think. I watched as buildings passed by and people boarded and exited. I did not have to focus on driving or anything else. It was the first extended period of time where I could allow my mind sink into this fantastic ability I had gained after the flight. I had very little understanding about what I could do with my mind and decided to test it.

I looked at an elderly woman across the bus from me. She had a wrinkly, weathered face and looked as though her many years had been difficult. Her clothes were dirty, and she held her purse close to her body. I had gone into my visions at times when I had concentrated on a person or a thing, so I focused my full attention on her, intentionally trying to see into her life. It was the first time I had consciously attempted to take myself into one of my visions. The others had just happened, as though my mind were guiding me. I wanted to be the instigator this time. As I concentrated, a tingling sensation surged through my body. I saw energy lift from her skin and cause ripples in the air around her. Her body split into dozens of versions of her in different outfits and at different ages. One of the images was a beautiful young woman in a wedding dress, laughing. I concentrated on that beautiful young woman and wisps of light rose from the framework of the bus to reform into a beautiful backyard decorated with flowers and white flowing cloth. The young bride was laughing and talking to guests seated at tables while holding the hand of a handsome young man, the groom, who was also laughing.

"Jenna did that. It wasn't me," exclaimed the groom.

"It was your idea," retorted the bride.

"You didn't have to do it," the groom said. "I'm not saying I don't love it, though."

One of the seated guests chimed in, "It's you, though. You have to admit it."

"It is, and I love that she did it," said the groom.

"How does it taste?" asked another of the seated guests.

The young bride beamed, "It's wonderful! Get some quickly. Maybe you can get the cockpit!"

She gestured, and I followed the movement of her hand to the table holding the wedding cake—a three-tiered confection, with its top tier in the shape of a flying saucer. I smiled, wishing I could take a bite. The guests made their way to the flying saucer cake. Two pieces had already been cut out of it, and I assumed that the bride and groom had done that. As I reached out to touch it, my hand, as usual, went through it.

So, the old lady on the bus had once been a beautiful bride, having the time of her life at her wedding. Her husband was an alien fanatic of sorts, and they each seemed to be quite funny. I concentrated on pulling myself out of the vision and watched as light emanated from the beautifully manicured lawn. Finally, it wiped away the scenery, and I was back on the bus. The old woman was sitting across from me, holding tightly to her purse. I looked out the windows and saw that we were approaching the downtown bus station.

I was curious about the lady and wanted to find out if what I had seen were true. "Is Jenna your name?" I asked her.

She instantly looked up, "Yes, it is. Do I know you?"

"I don't think so," I said, "but I may have known your husband."

"My husband?"

"Yes, didn't he like aliens and flying saucers?"

She smiled warmly, "He did."

"You made your wedding cake like a flying saucer."

The lady looked at me with reminiscent wonder. Tears came to her eyes even as she smiled. "That was a great day. He was so surprised and he loved it."

The bus came to a stop and the doors opened. As I stood up to exit I said, "You were a beautiful bride."

"Did you see pictures?" she asked.

"No, I was there," I said, as I stepped off the bus. She looked at me with a very curious expression and then smiled as the doors shut behind me. I was elated. I had gone into a vision of that woman's past and had seen a scene of her life as clearly as if I had been there. What's more, I had returned from the vision when I wanted to. What I had seen had actually happened to that old woman seated across from me. I felt empowered. Energy surged through me, revitalizing the nerves that had been repeatedly shaken from the events of the previous two days. I had an advantage over those trying to kill me. I could know things clearly, and I could control my ability.

I moved through the crowded interior of the bus station and made my way to the street all the while watching for Vanessa's silver Infiniti. The car was not there. I found a comfortable and discreet location at a bakery across the street from the bus station where I could observe all traffic entering and exiting. After about fifteen minutes, I saw the silver car with Vanessa behind the wheel. She drove slowly past the bus station scanning the area. I watched her as she looked for a place to park; and before she could pull up to a parking meter, I opened the passenger door on her car and leaped in.

Vanessa jumped, then smiled. "I don't think I'll get used to you doing that."

"Thanks for coming."

Vanessa nodded and smiled as she continued down the road, "The choice was saving your life or Seinfeld reruns."

"I like Seinfeld."

"Me too, it was a tough choice," she said. She glanced over. "You've got to tell me what's going on, Pierce."

"They want me dead and have tried twice today."

"You said there was a crash, two of them. Tell me about the first."

"At work today I was in the simulator with Don and he somehow rigged the belt so it would break and flipped me out of the cockpit, then smashed the cockpit onto me."

"But you survived. Were there words floating in the air that warned you?" she smiled wryly.

"No, no words hanging in the air," I said calmly pushing aside her jest with a raised eyebrow. "I did it myself this time. I pulled a bar out of the mesh of the simulator and braced it between the simulator cockpit and me. It stopped a hair's breadth from crushing my skull."

"How could he do that at work and get away with it?"

"They rigged the course," I said flatly, "They programmed it somehow; and when we reviewed it, it looked like he was flying the course correctly. They made it look like an accident, just like Catherine's death."

The reference to Catherine stung Vanessa. She was quiet for a few moments, then said, "The second crash?"

"On the freeway when I left Paralight. A car followed me and tried to run me off the road. It crashed just after the off-ramp of the 10 and the 101."

"*It* crashed, not you?"

"Yes, it smashed into the concrete barrier and couldn't follow me."

"So there will be an accident report. I'll get it," she said. "Who was the driver?"

"It must have been Don. I didn't see his face. He was wearing a helmet, but it was the same helmet he wore when he crashed the car into Catherine's car and killed her. He's after me."

"The helmet you saw in a vision of that night?" she said.

"Yes," I answered. There was a pause and I knew Vanessa doubted my story. I could read her face. She was taking in the information, but she was thinking like an attorney. She wanted something she could prove. "Get the accident report," I insisted. "It was a white BMW. They'll come after me again, and we need to stop them."

"Who exactly are they? Don and who?"

"Jack—my boss. Jack ordered it. He hired Don. Cole was right about the monkey."

"What?"

"That's why he's missing. He knew about it."

"About what?"

"It died, and they thought I would die."

"What are you talking about?"

"The test monkey died, and they still put me on that plane."

"How do you know this?"

"I saw it, just like before."

Vanessa took a deep breath, "A vision. That doesn't get you far in court."

"They're more than visions, Vanessa, they're real. The monkey died, and Jack put the dead monkey's tag on a different monkey. I saw him do it."

"I need more than that."

"There were witnesses, three of them—and they all got fired," Her eyes lit up with the thought of actual witnesses—something tangible.

"Names?"

"Keri, Howard, and Raymond."

"Full names?"

"I don't know."

"Why do they want to kill you?" she asked.

"I don't know. Catherine knew, and so did Cole. Some sort of fraud. That's why they're gone, I'm sure of it. I assume they want me dead because Catherine was my wife and was working with Cole to expose them."

"So Paralight is trying to kill you?"

"Yes. Jack is covering up some fraud that Cole knew about and Catherine was helping him."

"I need proof other than visions," she repeated.

"Did they find anything at the gate?"

"Nothing."

"Will you help me?"

"I'd lose all credibility if I told people you have visions and that was the basis for my investigation."

"You think I'm crazy?"

"I don't know."

"Don will go to my house. I know it. He won't stop until I'm dead. Will you help me?"

Vanessa hesitated, then finally said, "If it wasn't you, the answer would be no."

Relief swept over me, and I smiled. I had an advocate. However strange my story, I had someone on my side who could help me. "You think they'll go to your house?"

"I'm sure they will."

Chapter 10

Vanessa had a plan. She was taking a risk and I knew it. As we drove to the police station, she rehearsed with me what I could and could not say about my story. I could not say anything about my visions. She also did not want me to bring up Paralight or the investigation by Cole and Catherine. Cole's disappearance had made the news; and if we were to bring connections to that story, the media would again become involved and the district attorney's office would be inundated with pressures Vanessa did not want to deal with. I should speak only of the shooting at Kensington because Vanessa had already pulled the police into the investigation of an alleged shooting and of the chase on the freeway. Those two experiences could be documented in some manner. She would do the rest of the speaking and ask a favor from a friend of hers.

We walked into the police station and made our way to the second level where many desks, occupied by officers and detectives, filled a large room. "Remember what we discussed," said Vanessa as we made our way to the back of the room. I nodded.

We stopped at a desk near the windows. No one was there, but the name plate read, "Lieutenant Drake."

"Not Johnny Drake?" I said with amusement.

"Not a word," warned Vanessa.

"Box Boy? He's your friend on the police force?" I asked under my breath.

"Quiet," said Vanessa as a burly man strode down the aisle between the desks. It was just as I'd thought—Johnny Drake from high school, built like a box and star-crossed in love with Vanessa. He was stout and solid muscle, but that was not where he got his nickname Box Boy. Schools in Phoenix had the tradition of issuing invitations to dances and proms in interesting ways. When Johnny asked Vanessa to junior prom, couriers wheeled a large cardboard box wrapped in gold paper into her math class. The song "Lost in Love," from Air Supply was playing inside the box. When it got to the lines "You know, you can't fool me, I've been loving you too long..." Johnny burst through the top of the box and sang the rest of the words with Air Supply. At the end he said, "Vanessa, I'm lost in love and will do anything to take you to the prom."

I wasn't in the classroom but Cole was. He said it was the most uncomfortable thing he had ever witnessed. Vanessa's face went scarlet. She was speechless. Johnny stood in the box, and the whole class watched, breathless, for her response. Time ticked by slowly. Vanessa said nothing, and students started to snicker. Johnny's face went red and he added, "Please, Vanessa." Vanessa finally mumbled, "Sure."

She hated being put on the spot that way, but she went with him and staunchly took the position that he was a pleasant boy and she had a good time but there never would be another date.

I didn't think there ever was. Ever since, Cole and I referred to him as Box Boy, a nickname which Vanessa repeatedly and unsuccessfully had attempted to ban.

"You two still dating," I whispered to Vanessa.

"Quiet," she snapped in a harsh whisper, then smiled at Lieutenant Drake. "Hi, Lieutenant." she said respectfully.

"Vanessa, please take a seat," said Lieutenant Drake. "Pierce, it's been a while."

"It has, Johnny. Good to see you." He took my hand and squeezed like a vice. I winced in pain and saw a slight smile cross Vanessa's lips. Johnny noticed the smile too, and I could see that it had an effect on him. He sat down with confidence and looked directly at Vanessa.

"They're still investigating the area around Kensington. There's nothing yet," he said. "I'll let you know if they find anything." As he rubbed his big hands together his eyes covered Vanessa with adoration and I could not help but notice the absence of a wedding ring.

"I need another favor, Johnny," said Vanessa, "and I need to keep this close and quiet for the time being. The shooting was at Pierce, and we believe that the same person who tried to shoot Pierce yesterday tried to run him off the road today. Pierce, would you explain to Lieutenant Drake what happened?"

Well-coached, I pulled my mind from Johnny's affection for Vanessa and promptly responded: "I was driving and noticed a white BMW following me as I pulled onto the 10. It followed me for some time and tried to run me off the road right before the 195th exit. It chased me down the freeway; and at the 101 exchange, I flipped my car to the shoulder of the road. It did the same and smashed into the barricade on the side of the freeway. It bent the axle of the back wheel and I was able to get away."

Vanessa inserted, "As I said, Lieutenant, we think this is the same person who tried to shoot him, and we feel Pierce is in danger of a third attempt. We would like to have you set up a perimeter around his house tonight to watch for and apprehend the person trying to kill him."

Johnny's thick brows furrowed and lines appeared on his forehead as he considered the information. He looked at me. "Why is someone trying to kill you?"

Vanessa cut in, "This is part of a bigger investigation about which I am not allowed to reveal any details. I'm asking you to trust me. I'll give you the details at the appropriate time."

"Vanessa, that's not the way we work around here." Johnny was scowling. "I need to know what I'm involving my men in and I need to know it all."

"I can't tell you, but I need your help," said Vanessa sincerely. "I need to know about the car that crashed on the freeway and I need to set up a perimeter around Pierce's house immediately. I know you can do this. Please do it for me."

Johnny's big hands rubbed his forehead as he thought about the request. I could see his mind brushing aside policy and procedure as he looked at Vanessa and considered helping her. "Okay," he said, "I'm trusting you." With that he stood up and took both of us into a back room furnished with a table, several chairs and a flat screen monitor on the wall. He left the room and five minutes later came back with six detectives and a couple more chairs. We spent the next fifty minutes reviewing my story of the shooting, the chase on the freeway, and the proposed stake out of my house. Whenever anyone asked a question which Vanessa thought I should not answer, she interrupted with her story about the sensitivity of her investigation. Johnny backed up Vanessa and the detectives dropped the questions. They brought up maps of the area on the monitor and assigned the detectives to their various locations. Vanessa added that we wanted to view the events from a safe distance, and they agreed to station us on a ridge that overlooked my neighborhood. Detective Calloway, the detective who had walked with me to the hotel across the street from Kensington during the brick wall clean-up, gave us a camera with a long-range telephoto lens and showed us how to use it. We also were issued encrypted phones which would be used to keep everyone in contact. I was impressed with the professionalism of the detectives and of Johnny.

Vanessa and I left the police station and got into her car. I didn't say anything, although I couldn't help grinning, until we were on the street. Finally I looked at her and said, "Interesting..."

Vanessa tried to ignore the implication I was making, "Think what you'd like."

"So there is something?"

"He's a friend."

"He know that?"

"Yes, he knows that," she said feigning insult.

"I don't think he'd scrap policy for a friend," I said.

"Okay, enough about Box Boy!" she exclaimed, simultaneously realizing that she had called him by the banned nickname. "I mean Johnny Drake."

I started singing, "You know you can't fool me. I've been lovin' you too long. It started so easy, you want to carry on, carry on." She smiled and said nothing as I continued: "Lost in love and I don't know much was I thinking aloud and fell out of touch. But I'm back on my feet and eager to be what you wanted."

"Okay, okay," she said.

"So lift your eyes if you feel you can. Reach for a start and I'll show you a plan. I figured it out, what I needed was Johnny to show me."

"Stop! Okay, stop!" she said while laughing. "If you could sing in tune, I'd let you continue but this is unbearable."

"The cat's out of the bag, Vanessa. You can tell me."

"Our relationship is strictly professional. That's it. What more is there to tell?"

"I'll accept that on your side, but his?"

She glared at me, then said in a softer tone, "Okay. Yes, he's still in love with me."

"And you're using that for your benefit?"

"Actually, I'm using it for *your* benefit," she snapped. "And aren't you doing the exact same thing with me?"

I swallowed the comment I had started to make. She was right. I smiled and said nothing more. She smiled as well, knowing she had put an end to the subject. As we drove in silence, I again remembered the night in the car when she had confessed her love for me. It was still there.

We stopped at a drive-through for a hamburger and with the smell of the food I realized how hungry I was. I was finished with my hamburger and fries before we parked Vanessa's car on the assigned ridge far from my home and had started on her fries. Vanessa ate her food as I secured the camera with the telephoto lens to a tripod that latched to the console of the car. Both of us could lean in and take turns looking through the viewfinder. We were far from my house but through the lens the house loomed up in detail. Johnny had instructed us to take pictures of anything we saw that looked suspicious. We watched the detectives taking up their various positions around the neighborhood. They were discreet and blended in well. One car was several streets from my house, and the remainder of the detectives were in plain clothes and took positions throughout the subdivision doing various activities which were casual and continually changing. The first hour was quite exciting as we took turns scanning the neighborhood and discussing the positioning of each of the detectives and how they hid and blended into the neighborhood; but as two more hours passed, I realized the boredom of a stake out. It was eight thirty and still bright as noon day but with longer shadows. The sun would not set for another hour.

However, it was a good opportunity to catch up on Vanessa and her life. She told me about the intricacies of working at the district attorney's office and general details of her interesting cases. She was too aware of confidentiality requirements to get more detailed. I also asked her about her personal life and she fell back on what she always told us: "I date, but I don't let myself get into any long-term relationships. My work is very demanding, and it would be unfair to get involved with someone when I don't have the time to commit to the relationship."

I sensed from her tone that she was very uncomfortable talking about other men with me. In a sense, I felt flattered. She was an amazing woman, and we still had a strong connection. If Vanessa hadn't done the study-abroad program, if matters hadn't gotten so serious so quickly with Catherine, then Vanessa and I very well could have been a couple. I couldn't resist asking,

"Now, I want the truth. You and Johnny, have you gone on any dates?"

"I have the right to remain silent," she said with a smile. That comment suddenly reminded me of Catherine on the night of our anniversary. It was exactly what she had said right before I lost her. Sadness and loneliness washed through me as I thought of Catherine. My heart hurt as I again considered life without her. I did all I could to not show my feelings on my face and forced a smile at Vanessa to cover my feelings. As I sat in silence, I was amazed how much of Catherine was in Vanessa. They were both strong, they were both beautiful, and although they were not identical twins, their expressions were identical. I longed for Catherine and at the same time I longed for Vanessa next to me. It was one of the most awkward feelings I had experienced in my life. Knowing that Vanessa was beside me soothed the loneliness I was living in and gave me some grounding in my frantic and cold life. I felt guilty about having feelings for Vanessa that were not strictly platonic; however, I *did* have feelings for her and they were strong. I saw someone I loved next to me. I had always loved her. It was a comfort being in the car with her. I felt safe. Warmth emanated from her, and I basked in it, allowing myself to enjoy the moment.

"That's your right," I finally said.

Vanessa leaned over, looked through the viewfinder of the camera, and scanned the area. She did not see anything suspicious; but as she moved the camera around the neighborhood, she focused the lens and a smile came to her face. "The Gallica Rose," she commented. "Take a look."

I looked into the camera and she had focused on a red rose with a beautiful array of petals. "The Red Rose of Lancaster," she continued, "Did Catherine ever get you to read *Richard III*?"

"No, but I'm reading *Hamlet*."

"*Richard III* takes place during the War of the Roses. Richard was defeated and Henry took the throne for Lancaster. That rose is the Red Rose of Lancaster."

I loved listening to her voice and I loved the passion she had for history and learning. It was the same with the whole Trace family. They were all fascinated with Shakespeare and classical literature. Often our discussions would involve characters in history and literature and the events surrounding them. I felt at home with Vanessa at my side. "Did you know Hamlet's story is based on a prince named Amleth?" I asked as I moved the lens of the camera back to center on my house.

"No, who's Amleth?"

"A prince of Denmark. I really don't know much about him, but I think it's cool that you just move the 'H' from the front of Hamlet to the back and you have Amleth."

"Yes, very cool," she said mocking my use of the word 'cool.'

"You have a better word?" I asked. I continued to look through the viewfinder. My backyard backed up to an empty lot, and we had never built a fence separating the yards. There were several tall trees in the lot behind our house, and I saw movement between two of the trees. I adjusted the camera and stared through the viewfinder.

"Interesting, fascinating..." said Vanessa, "There's so much more conveyed with those words than 'cool.'"

"This might be interesting," I said as I panned back to my house and looked through the bushes and trees of the neighboring houses "—I mean 'cool.'"

"What's that?"

"I thought I saw something in the lot behind my house—something in the trees." At the top corner of the lens I saw a blurry figure dressed in black sprint from the last tree to the bushes on the side of my house. "Someone's there," I said, "He's in the bushes on the side of my house."

"Take a picture," said Vanessa. I moved my finger to snap a picture but pushed a button that did nothing. I took my eyes off the viewfinder to look for the shutter release; and as I did so, I saw the black-dressed figure move again. I quickly looked back into the viewfinder, fumbling for the shutter release.

"Hurry," said Vanessa.

The camera was shaking and the focus self adjusted as I moved to see the front of the house. The blurry figure sprinted across the front of my house and smashed through the front door with his shoulder. The door gave way and was immediately shut behind the black figure just as my finger found the shutter release and snapped a picture.

"Did you get him?" she asked.

"I don't think so," I answered, looking up. Vanessa immediately leaned into the viewfinder as I continued, "He's in the house."

"You're sure you saw someone?" she asked.

"Yes. He's in my house. He smashed through the front door."

Vanessa picked up the encrypted phone and said, "Move in. Someone entered the house." In the distance, I saw the detectives move from their positions and head toward the house.

Vanessa watched closely through the viewfinder on the camera, "The first team is at the house right now and waiting for others."

We watched for another couple minutes as the teams gathered around the house. I then saw some police cars driving into the neighborhood, "Johnny called in the black and whites," I said.

Vanessa took her eyes off the viewfinder and followed my line of sight. "They're not taking chances," she said. In a few moments the detectives, with the back-up of two police cars, had all gathered in front of the house. "I want to get down there." Vanessa started the engine and sped down the street.

A few minutes later, we were in front of my house. The police cars had their lights flashing, and several detectives and officers were in positions around the house securing all exits. We exited Vanessa's car and walked toward Johnny who was standing near his unmarked police car. Neighbors were gathering to see what was happening, and Johnny signaled for us to come to him.

An officer exited the front door and said, "Empty, no one inside."

"You've searched everywhere?" asked Johnny.

Several others exited. "Everywhere. Not a soul in the house."

In a loud voice Johnny ordered, "Make a three-block perimeter and hold everyone coming and going."

Officers and detectives rushed in many directions in obedience to the order, and Johnny turned to Vanessa. "Vanessa, you're sure you saw someone enter?"

"I saw him enter," I said, "He was wearing black."

"Then we'll find him," said Johnny confidently.

"Thanks," said Vanessa warmly, and I could see the impact

her appreciation had on Johnny as he turned his focus to the task at hand. Filled with energy, he got into his car and picked up his radio. Vanessa and I returned to her car and watched. Officers were positioned at each intersection in the surrounding blocks, and detectives and officers scoured the neighborhood. As the sun dipped below the horizon, and the perimeter was as secure as Johnny felt it could be, he returned to the house and came to our car.

"Pierce, tell me everything you saw in detail."

"He came through the backyard," I said, "There's an empty lot behind us, and that's where I first saw him."

"Show me," he said.

We walked to my backyard, and I pointed. "He was between these two trees when I first saw him. He then ran across the backyard to that row of bushes along the side of the house." We walked to the bushes. "From here he ran to the front door and broke into the house."

"Broke into the house?" asked Johnny.

"Yeah," I said, "He smashed through the front door with his shoulder."

Johnny walked with me and Vanessa to the front door of my house, "He smashed through with his shoulder? A forced entry? He didn't simply open the door?" questioned Johnny.

"Right," I answered.

Johnny then opened the front door of the house with the door handle and pushed it open. "If he had forced the entry with his shoulder, don't you think the door would have some damage?" I looked at the door. There was nothing wrong with it—no damage, no crack in the wood, and no damage to the door handle or lock. It was in perfect shape. "I saw him smash through the door with his shoulder," I repeated. "I can't explain why there's no damage."

"My men found the front door locked and with no signs of forced entry. We entered through the garage door which was unlocked."

"I swear I saw a man enter my house," I insisted.

"We'll keep looking; and if he came into this house or this neighborhood, we'll find him," assured Johnny. We all returned to our cars. Vanessa and I waited as the officers and detectives did their work.

For the next few hours, the police knocked on doors and searched backyards, garages, and bushes—every conceivable hiding place in my neighborhood and the surrounding blocks. Vanessa and I had both fallen asleep in the car when, about four in the morning, we were startled awake by a knock on Vanessa's window. It was Johnny and Vanessa rolled down her window. Johnny looked at me and said, "There's no one here. Nothing. No forced entry. No trace, no footprints, nothing. The only things sure in my mind are that no one was in your house, no one is in your house, and no one left it. I have to call off the search."

"Thanks for the work, Lieutenant Drake," said Vanessa.

"Now you owe me two," said Johnny with a smile.

"I do," she answered. Johnny walked away and Vanessa rolled up the window. I knew she was thinking I had imagined the man in black. We sat in silence as officers entered cars and left the neighborhood.

"Someone went in there. He smashed through the door with his shoulder," I said.

"The door is intact. No one else saw anything."

"I saw him," I repeated.

"No one left the house."

"He went in my house. I saw it."

"You have to understand, Pierce. In my world, evidence rules. You have to look at the facts. Evidence shows the truth and in this case, no one entered your house. You may have thought you saw someone entering your house, but the evidence shows otherwise."

I felt as if I was talking to Catherine. Catherine was always right, she was smarter than me, and I had to give in for the sake of peace in the house. Frustration built in me because I knew what I saw; but through my life with Catherine, I knew there was a better way than to cause a fight. I had seen a man break into my house. That man was dressed in black. Evidence or no evidence did not change the fact that I had seen him. I took a deep breath and let the frustration flow out of me. Gratitude was the answer that kept peace with Catherine, and I thought that was the best course with Vanessa at that moment. "Thanks for doing all this for me, Vanessa. I really appreciate it."

It disarmed her and she smiled. "Hey, it was this or those Seinfeld reruns," she said as he started the car and pulled away from the curb. "If you'd like, I have a comfortable sofa."

The thought was attractive, but it was already morning and I needed to keep her on my side. To do so, I felt it was important to keep some distance and to bring evidence to back up what I had been telling her. I needed to have some time on my own. "I don't want to make things uncomfortable if Johnny were to show up."

"Right," she laughed, "he's there already—I was just thinking you and he might like to hold hands or cuddle."

I laughed, "All right. You just keep driving. I don't want you doing any more thinking."

"Okay, Albert Einstein, you do the thinking. Where are we headed?"

"Straight, don't turn left or right until I tell you. No thinking."

"Straight ahead," she said with a smile.

I directed her to the alley where I had parked the Saab. While we were driving, we spoke hardly at all, but our silence was not uncomfortable. There were few people I could feel comfortable with in silence. Vanessa was one of them. I felt at peace with her. When we got to the alley where the Saab was parked, I got out and unlocked the Saab.

She rolled down the window and said, "I'll get the police reports about the car that chased you and crashed on the freeway and see what I can find."

"Thanks," I said.

"Where will you be?"

"You need proof, right?"

"I do," she answered.

"I'll be finding some proof."

"Be safe," she said with sincerity.

I nodded as I got into the Saab. She drove away.

Chapter 11

The darkness of the night was fading, and I needed to think. I mentally organized the abilities I had and what I knew I could do. I could actually walk around and investigate past events. The speed of time was variable. After all, I had watched the bullet remove itself from the wall and reenter the barrel of Don's sniper rifle. Most of the visions had come upon me, and I did not necessarily control them; but I hadn't actually tried except for the elderly woman on the bus. In that instance, I had focused my mind and intentionally picked a time in her life. Somehow my mind had shown me the other visions to protect me and to help me understand the reality of the danger I was in. I reasoned that it was a natural protection.

But there was more to the ability. It involved other people like Sarah at the mental hospital and Jonathan at Paralight. When Sarah had touched my arm, I saw the world as she saw it. She had brought me into her world—strange because it was a different world and a different time. When she touched me, day became night, allowing the approach of those strange, cloaked creatures. I wondered if they were somehow real in the world of her mind. In my interpretation of the experience they were monsters that her mind had created. They had haunted her dreams and had become so vivid to her that they became real. That is the only way I could explain what I had seen. After she was taken back to her room and when I saw her through the window in the door I was the able to go back into her mind and see the world as she saw it without touching her arm.

As I thought about Sarah, I focused my attention on her and on the cloaked creatures. I wanted to see if I could go back to that vision and that time. A cold chill ran down my spine and the dashboard of the Saab rippled with rising energy. Wisps of light changed the world around me to the small room at the mental hospital where Sarah lay on her bed. Several cloaked creatures crawled through the window and out from under the bed and scaled the walls around Sarah. It was the same moment I had watched when I stood outside the window. I looked toward the window set in the door and saw myself standing there and watching. I had a dazed look on my face and seemed to be staring into oblivion. I walked past the creatures and sat on the bed where Sarah was lying and from my position on the bed, I could see all of the creatures staring at me. Their eyes were deep and dark, and a chill ran down my spine. The main creature pulled back its cloak revealing a dark, devilish face filled with evil. The creature roared, revealing razor-sharp teeth, and crouched to lunge at me and Sarah. I stepped to the side as it sprang and grabbed Sarah by the wrists, snarling at her while the others jumped from the walls and grabbed her arms and legs. Sarah screamed and closed her eyes as she cried. The creature holding her wrists let out another chilling shriek and ran its sharp teeth ran down her neck. Sarah, with all her might, pulled violently free from the creatures, ran to the door, and banged on the window, screaming, "Let me out! Let me out of here!"

As I watched, my heart broke for Sarah. This nightmare was the world she lived in. Whether the creatures were her imagination or in some way really existed did not matter because for her they existed. I reach out to touch one of them and, as in all of the other visions, my hand passed through the creature without feeling anything. The creatures again crept toward Sarah, but I had seen enough. I thought about the Saab in the alley behind the restaurant. The light of the walls intensified and the world of Sarah's small room began to dematerialize. The creature I had passed my hand through paused as all others continued toward Sarah. Just as the soft threads of light were reconstructing the world of the Saab, the creature turned and looked in my direction, then it was gone, replaced by the steering wheel and dashboard of the Saab and the dark alley behind the restaurant.

Did the creature actually recognize me? I brushed the idea aside. It was a creation of Sarah's mind and did not really exist—at least, not in my world. Besides, the eye sockets were hollow, and it was impossible to tell where it was looking.

My mind moved to my friend, the janitor. Jonathan at Paralight had also pulled me into a vision of his past by touching my arm. He somehow knew I would be able to see his past and had showed me the threat Jack had made to Cole.

As I pondered the abilities I had, I wondered if I could see my own present. It made sense to me that, in my visions, I had gone to a specific time and place and watched it as if it were the present. Why could I not step into the present and see what was around me? I focused on my own hands; and as I did so, the now-familiar feeling which transitioned me into a vision came over me and energy rippled from my skin. My own hands came out of the hands which were on the steering wheel, and I stood up, leaving my body below me. It was the oddest sensation. I stepped through the Saab and looked down through the window of the car at my body sitting in the driver's seat. My eyes were open and staring as if in a daze at the hands on the steering wheel. The dazed look on my face was the same as when I had seen myself outside the door of Sarah's room. I walked around the Saab and looked at my body from all angles. It was strange to be outside my body and looking at it in the present time. I had heard of out-of-body experiences, but I had never thought much about the phenomenon. What I was experiencing was definitely out-of-body. I walked down the alley and looked across the street. The world was moving and progressing just as it normally would. Several cars passed on the street and a man was scurrying down the sidewalk. I stepped through the brick wall of the alley into the restaurant and walked past the tables and chairs of the main eating area, then moved through the wall into the kitchen. The lights were all off, and the place was silent. I couldn't help but smile as I realized I could go anywhere I wanted and no one would be able to see me. I thought this ability should surely help me to find the evidence Vanessa would need to prosecute Jack and Don and to piece together the conspiracy to kill Catherine and me. I focused on closing the vision. A flash of light enveloped the restaurant and rebuilt my hands on the steering wheel.

I was back in my own body or had come back to my own body—I did not know which way to think about it. However you think about it, what I had just experienced was real. I had seen myself in the car and had walked around inside the restaurant while my actual, physical body was sitting in the Saab. I got out of the car and ran down to the end of the alley. The street was just as I had seen it when I had walked there in my vision except the scurrying man was now past the intersection and on the sidewalk of the next block. I looked through the windows of the restaurant and the tables in the main dining room were just as I had seen them when I had walked through the restaurant seconds before. As I walked back to the Saab, in awe of my new abilities, my mind went to the tests at Paralight where I ran faster than any human had run before me. Becoming light did open my mind in an incredible way, but that was not all. It did something to me physically that enabled me to run at superhuman speeds, apparently indefinitely.

I wondered if it also gave me superhuman strength so I thought I would try to lift the Saab. I walked to the side of the Saab, bent down, grabbed the frame, and lifted, fully expecting the car to come off the ground. It did not budge. I tried again, exerting all my strength, but to no avail. I let go, quite disappointed. I reasoned I was probably stronger than I used to be but not a superhero.

I got back into the car and drove toward my house, deciding where to start tracking down evidence to help Vanessa make a case. The sunrise was beautiful and sent streaks of orange and yellow across the sky. The police had cleared out, and the neighborhood was silent. I parked the car in the driveway and again examined the front lock. No damage. I went to my study and searched through everything but could find no trace of the files Catherine and Cole had been working on. Frustrated, I sat at the desk and concentrated on it. With the desk as my focus, I stretched my mind to our anniversary day. Shimmers of energy lifted from the desk top, and soft threads of light transformed the room around me. The room now had the bright colors and vivid clarity of my previous visions. Sunlight streamed in through the windows. Papers, folders, and boxes were scattered across the desk and on the floor. Cole sat in a chair in front of the desk while Catherine, who was standing, wrote on the dry-erase board.

She had listed a series of banks, bank accounts, lists of treasury notes, military contracts, and arrows showing amounts going from one bank to another. Many names were boxed. I tried to make sense of it but could not at first. I sat and listened to the two of them discussing and writing out the case on the board for about forty-five minutes. The amount of information they had gathered was large and their case complex. In essence, Paralight had misused funds from a governmental contract, diverting money from the authorized project to the light plane. Investigations of Paralight were underway by the Securities Exchange Commission and the U.S. military. Cole had been involved in the legal department at Paralight charged with the organization and documentation of the government contracts, and it appeared that Paralight had investors to fund the light plane project but who were waning in their commitment because the plane had not conducted a successful living test flight. The flight with the monkey was the key to the funding. The funds from those investors would replace the government funds. That was the house of cards Cole and Catherine were trying to explain to me. They knew that the monkey had died. For Paralight, the monkey had to survive in order to secure the investment funds to cover the fraudulent use of the U.S. military funds. This case could tear Paralight apart and send its executives to prison. The first to go would be Jack.

Cole read numbers from a series of accounting spreadsheets, and Catherine wrote them on the board. When they finished, Catherine pulled out a calculator and added the numbers.

"They don't add up," she said.

"I know. And when the SEC sees that, they'll shut down Paralight," said Cole. "Marty will get me the Swiss and Denmark accounts. They'll confirm these numbers. That's really all we need."

The two packed up the papers on the floor and put them into organized folders and boxes. I heard someone enter the house.

"Danny! I'm home!" I heard my own voice through the door. Catherine smiled at Cole. "Danny, I was flying today, and I'll take you soon if you'd like. You do any reading today? Janet?"

"Sorry, what?" replied Janet. I walked across the study and through the door. I saw myself in the living room with Janet and Danny.

"Did you and Danny read?" my body said.

"Mr. Brown can moo, can you?" said Janet with a smile, "Danny is having trouble mooing but I think he liked it."

"I can moo, Danny, can you?" said my body as it bent down to kiss Danny. I was getting fairly used to seeing myself from outside my body. "Are Catherine and the bloodsucker in the office?"

"I heard that," answered Catherine, opening the door of the small study behind the living room.

"I thought tonight was our night, not the vampire's," said my body.

"Oh, no, Cole's coming along to dinner and I thought I'd sit by him," quipped Catherine.

Cole said, "One of these days, you'll thank me for what we're doing."

"You're right, I will. Thank you," said my body. Cole smiled. My body turned to Catherine, "You said something about dressing up, right?"

My body and Catherine continued speaking, but I looked at Cole and said, "Thank you, Cole. I wish I had listened."

I knew what else happened that night and did not want to relive the emotions so I pulled myself out of the vision. The room brightened and the soft threads of light reconstructed the present. I was again sitting at the clean desk in my study. I turned on my computer and, for the next hour or so, wrote down all the information I could remember about the case against Paralight, emailed it to myself and printed out a hard copy. It ended up being ten pages. I put the print-out into an envelope to take with me. I decided I needed to find Marty in accounting and learn of the accounts he had been discussing with Cole but also knew I needed to have my mind working at full capacity. I looked at the clock and it read 6:30 am. The sun was up and I had slept only briefly in the car with Vanessa. My eyelids were heavy and my eyes were coated with the dryness of exhaustion. I thought of Don and realized I was in danger being in my own home. I went to the kitchen, opened the refrigerator and rummaged through the well-stocked items left by Rick from Paralight. I took two apples, two bananas and a bottle of juice and quickly threw together two deli sandwiches. The bag I put them in was stuffed.

I scanned the neighborhood through my front window before leaving the house then rushed to the car and was soon out of my neighborhood. When I had sufficiently distanced myself from my house I parked the car on a quiet side street and devoured my thrown-together meal. It was refreshing but my eyes burned and the comfort of closing them was overwhelming. I convinced myself a power nap would be beneficial and closed my eyes to give them a rest only to be overcome with the blackness of exhaustion.

When I woke, sweat was running down the side of my face and the car clock read 10:15 a.m. I was frustrated I had slept so long. I rolled down the windows to let in some fresh air and drove until I saw a pay phone. I called Paralight, and, when the operator answered, said, "Hi, Marty in accounting, please. What's his last name?"

"There is no Marty in accounting."

"Could you put me through to the accounting office?" I asked.

"Please hold."

Another voice came on the line: "Accounting."

"Yes, Marty used to work in accounting, and I've forgotten his last name. Could you tell it to me?"

"Sobisky."

"How do you spell that?"

"S-O-B-I-S-K-Y"

"And do you have contact information for him?"

"No and we can't give out any personal information over the phone."

"Listen, this is Pierce Black from Paralight. I'm not some stranger. I need to talk to Marty about some accounting work he did for me. Please just give me his number and address so I don't have to come upstairs."

"Oh, Mr. Black, I'm sorry, just a minute." A few minutes later I had an address and phone number. I called the number, but there was no answer. I got back into the Saab and drove to the address. I knocked, but there was no answer. I looked into the window and could not see anyone inside. I tried the door handle—locked. I thought this was a good time to use my new ability so I looked down and concentrated, just as I had while I was sitting in the Saab in the alley.

Ripples of energy lifted from my skin and I stepped out of my body. I walked through the front door and into the house. It was very silent. I walked through the entryway and into the kitchen. On the refrigerator, I saw happy family pictures—Marty, his wife, and two children, a boy and a girl. His family had an aura of goodness and I immediately felt a kinship with them. In one family photo, they were standing near a river, each holding up a fish. The enjoyment in their faces was contagious. I went to the family room where I saw more family pictures. The next room was a study, its shelves filled with books. On the desk was a computer, scattered papers, and photocopies on many colors of paper, each with Marty's face on it. Across the top was written "MISSING!" Under the photo was a detailed description: age 43, last seen wearing a red T-shirt and jeans, missing since March 3. Two days after my test flight. My heart sank. He was missing—just like Cole and for approximately the same amount of time. I saw movement at the front door, glanced out the window to see what it was and saw a woman walking around my body, trying to get my attention. She was shaking my shoulder and yelling at me. I quickly ended the vision, light engulfed me, and I was back in my body.

"Hello in there!" yelled the woman. I looked at her, and she jumped.

"I'm sorry," I said, "Sometimes I kind of go out."

"I'd say," she replied. "You ought to get yourself checked out."

"Right. You're right. I ought to," I said. "Are you Mrs. Sobisky?"

"I am," she replied.

"I was wondering if you could tell me a little about your husband. My brother-in-law has been missing since about the same time."

"Cole Trace?"

"Yes," I answered.

"I am sorry about your loss," she said as she put her key in the door, "You can come in if you'd like."

I went in with Mrs. Sobisky; and as we walked into the living room, she asked, "Can I get you anything? A drink?"

"Thank you, but no, I'm okay," I answered.

She motioned for me to take a seat on a sofa and sat down in a comfortable chair, "I know about Cole, and I feel for you and your family. I lost my Marty at about the same time."

"I am sorry about Marty," I said. "I just wanted to get in touch with you and find out more about him and his disappearance."

She looked at me with the pain of loss and said, "The short version of the story is that he went to Florida and never returned. We don't know much else. I've been in close contact with the Missing Persons Department of the police for months and have been to Miami many times. I know Vanessa Trace very well. She and I coordinated our searches for several months, hoping that the two cases had a link. After all, Cole and Marty both worked for Paralight Technologies but that led nowhere. Our case centered in Florida and hers was here in Arizona."

"Did Marty and Cole know each other?" I asked.

"I really don't know," she said sheepishly, "I feel horrible saying it, but I didn't know much about his work or the people he associated with at work. When he got the job at Paralight, he had to sign confidentiality agreements that didn't allow him to talk about his work outside the office. We separated our family life from his work. He loved his job; but near the time he was laid off, he seemed more distant than he previously had been." Her mind wandered for a moment and then she continued, "I do wish I had known Cole. From what Vanessa said of him, he was a wonderful man."

"He was," I said. "We all hope we find him and that he is okay. What was Marty doing in Florida?"

"He went there for a job interview. Paralight had laid him off, just as they did your brother-in-law, and he was job hunting. He had flown out a day early to go fishing off the coast, and the company he was interviewing with said he never came to his scheduled interview. That's about all I know. The airport records show that he was on the plane, but he never checked into his hotel." Mrs. Sobisky looked at a photo of her family on the wall, and tears welled in her eyes, "Not knowing is the worst part of it. I don't know if he is dead or just left us. I know I shouldn't think this way, but as time goes by I wonder if he is still there and just doesn't want me to find him. Maybe he was distant because he did not love me anymore. I just don't know." She wiped a tear from her cheek and breathed in deeply. "I'm sorry. I shouldn't have said that."

"No. It's okay," I said with empathy. "If it's any consolation, I do understand the not knowing. I would love to know where Cole is or what happened to him, and I do know it is different when it is your spouse." I paused for a moment, wondering if I should continue, but I felt it would help her to feel she was not alone in her sorrow, "I lost my wife shortly before Cole went missing."

"Your wife is Catherine, of course, Vanessa told me. I'm sorry. You've been through a lot also. Thank you for listening to me."

"You're sweet and Marty is a lucky man. I can feel the goodness in your home."

She smiled warmly and looked again at the photo of her family, "We have a good family, and we have had a good life."

"Mrs. Sobisky, I am very interested in Marty and Cole, and I am working to put the pieces together the best I can. May I have a photograph of Marty?"

"Of course," she said. She stood up and left the room, returning in a few moments with a photograph of Marty. I stood to leave.

"Thank you for inviting me into your home," I said. She watched me walk to the Saab and waved as I started it. After a couple of blocks, I pulled over to the side of the road and looked at the photograph. Marty was sitting in his family room, looking happy. I needed to know what had happened to him, so I focused my attention on the photo and, in my mind, formed the idea of seeing the last moments of his life.

The picture rippled with energy. His face came alive. His hair blew in a slight breeze. Behind him were blue skies and the wide expanse of the ocean. The energy inside the photo rippled through the world around me, and I was on the deck of a deep-sea fishing boat. I could not see land or other boats on the whole horizon. Marty was sitting on a fishing seat, which was bolted to the deck in the stern, a fishing pole clenched in his hands with the ocean breeze blowing his hair and T-shirt. I turned from Marty to the captain's seat. A man was hunched over, picking up something under the seat—a set of handcuffs. The man glanced toward Marty in the stern. It was Don. He was going to kill Marty, and I was going to witness it. Without thinking I yelled, "Marty! Look behind you, Marty!" He, of course, could not hear me but continued innocently fishing, his face radiating enjoyment. How had Don arranged to captain the boat? Horror clogged my throat for Marty.

Don quietly walked toward the fishing seat, a cold emptiness in his eyes. It was horrid that a human being could be so callous. It was business to him. He was an "opportunist" and this was a "well-paying job"—just like Catherine. He quietly walked behind Marty, reached over his shoulders, and snapped the handcuffs onto Marty, who jerked in shock and confusion.

"What are you doing?" Marty demanded. He tried to stand up, but he was buckled in.

Don, without a word, pulled the fishing pole from Marty's hands, unbuckled the seatbelt, and yanked him to the deck. Marty yelled in pain. With uncanny speed and strength, Don grabbed the rope next to the fishing seat and knotted it around Marty's legs. Marty bucked and strained against Don, but without any hope of winning, "What's going on?!" yelled Marty, "What are you doing to me?"

With Marty's hands cuffed and his legs secured with rope, Don coldly said, "Someone doesn't want you around anymore."

"What do you mean? Who doesn't want me around?" asked Marty in horror.

"It doesn't much matter," answered Don. He secured the

other end of the rope to a large cement weight on the side of the deck.

Marty screamed, "Don't do this. Please, don't do this."

My heart was in pain, I felt horrible sadness and compassion for Marty, and my anger and disgust toward the cold murderer was unequalled. I wanted with all my might to secure him to the weight and throw him overboard.

As Marty begged for his life, Don picked up the weight and threw it overboard. The rope secured to Marty's legs dragged him to the edge of the boat. He struggled to brace himself inside, but Don picked him up bodily and threw him overboard.

"Noooooo!" was the last word out of Marty's horrified mouth. He splashed into the deep blue ocean and disappeared below the surface. Don watched coldly, then mechanically went to the captain's chair, picked up cleaning materials and methodically cleaned the deck, fishing seat, and fishing equipment. It was just work for Don, a common job.

I pulled myself out of the vision and, with a flash of light, was again sitting in the Saab. My heart was hammering, and anger toward Don consumed me. I rested back in my seat to regain my senses and evaluate my next course of action. Marty was dead. That was clear. I was tempted to drive back to Mrs. Sobisky and tell her what I had seen to give her some closure on her husband's disappearance, but realized I had no proof. Until I could make a case against Paralight that would implicate Don, anything I would say would sound as if it came from a crazy man.

I knew what I needed to do next and drove to Cole's house to search for the files he and Catherine had gathered. I needed the evidence, and I needed to know what happened to Cole.

His house was in a suburb not far from my place and I had not seen Jackie, Cole's wife, for months. I knocked on the door and Jackie answered wearing a waitress's uniform, carrying a crying toddler and looking ready to cry herself. She was beautiful but looked tired and much older than when I had last seen her.

Cole had met Jackie when he was in law school at UCLA, and they had instantly been attracted to each other. Jackie was four years younger than Cole, just beginning her junior year and still undecided on her major, when Cole passed the bar. When Cole was offered the position at Paralight as an in-house attorney he asked Jackie to come back to Phoenix with him. She was elated, and the two were soon married. Jackie enrolled at Arizona State University but, after one year, found she was pregnant and decided to focus on raising their daughter. They now had four children and the loss of Cole was written in the dark circles under her eyes and the unrestrained grief in her countenance. She smiled when she saw me, but it did not lift the anxiety and stress from her face.

"Pierce? Vanessa mentioned you were out," she said as she bounced the toddler on her hip.

"Yeah, they decided I'm not a danger to anyone," I said as the boy cried even louder.

"Sethie, please," she said, as she looked to the sky for help.

"Hey, little man," I said. I took the child from her arms and snuggled him in close, "What has she been doing?" I asked the little man as he cried, "I know, I know. Sometimes moms are heartless but uncles—that's another story." Before the flight, Seth was seven months old and he had grown a lot. I looked at Jackie and said, "He's huge!"

"I know and he has the lungs of a tuba. Come in."

I stepped into the house. Jackie's mother was in the small kitchen cooking lunch for two of the other children. I smiled at her and she smiled back as she continued her work at the stove. I bounced Seth around and soon got him to quiet down.

"Sorry about Cole. Vanessa told me," I said to Jackie.

Jackie's eyes became watery and she could not talk. Seth started to cry again. Jackie took him from me, held him close, and said, "If he could stop crying for one minute, I could think." She rocked him, stroked his hair, and hummed a tune in desperation. Soon the little boy stopped crying, "Thank heaven," she said. Her mother came across the kitchen, took little Seth and put him in a baby chair. Jackie then turned to me and said, "Throw me off a cliff, please."

"Jackie, can I look around in Cole's study?" I asked.

"Sure. The night he went missing we were robbed. Not much left."

Of course, I thought. Jack would ensure everything was cleaned up and taken care of including all the paperwork gathered for the case against Paralight. "I didn't know that," I said, "Sorry."

"That's okay, unless it was you, but I figure you have as good an alibi as anyone."

"Right," I said as I left the kitchen and walked down the hall to Cole's study. A chill streamed through my body as I walked down the hall. I was still weak from the shock of watching Marty die, and I knew I would be able to see what happened to Cole with an item from his study. My legs were rubbery as I reached the door. I felt nauseated. I knew Don's coldness. I had watched him kill Catherine, try to shoot me, and throw Marty into the ocean. Now I was going to find out what he did to Cole. I tried to tell myself that Cole could still be alive and that I would learn a clue about his location, but my body did not believe it. My arms and legs were numb, and tears welled up in my eyes. I closed my eyes for a moment and leaned forward taking deep breaths to battle the wave of emotion I was swimming through. I put my mind back on task and felt strength return to my legs. I entered the study and saw a photo of Cole, Jackie and their children on the desk. I quickly searched the filing cabinet and desk drawers. Nothing. None of the files Catherine and Cole had compiled—nothing resembling the case against Paralight.

I sat at the desk, did what I could to prepare myself emotionally, then focused on the picture of Cole sitting with his family. Ripples streamed across the photo. The image went black. The world around me turned dark, and I was standing on a road over water by the trunk of a car. I looked around and saw boats in the distance and knew where I was—Lake Pleasant. The boats in the distance were at Pleasant Harbor Marina. This was a beautiful lake north of Phoenix where I had come often to rent jet-skis and spend the day in the sun. I was on a cement road, Scorpion Point Road, that led to a platform extending off the dam out over the lake. The car, a white BMW, had its lights off and was a few feet from me. The driver's door opened and Don stepped out, his expression the same as when he was on the boat—cold and heartless.

Don opened the trunk. Inside, Cole was lying on his side with his hands and feet tied. He moaned groggily as he struggled to focus on Don, who yanked him up bodily and dropped him on the concrete road. Cole landed with a thud and gasped in pain, then turned over quickly in an attempt to get his bearings. Don was hovering above him, "Please," Cole gasped, "you've got all the documents. He has all the proof. Please don't. I have a wife and kids."

Don, ignoring Cole's pleas, hefted a heavy concrete block with a metal loop at its top out of the trunk.

He's doing the same thing, I thought in horror. I had just witnessed Marty thrown overboard into the ocean and now I was watching this soulless man do the same thing with my best friend. I loved Cole and felt horribly guilty I had not listened to him as he begged me to understand what Paralight was doing. Could I have helped avoid this dreadful scene if I had listened?

"Please don't do this," begged Cole again.

Don kicked Cole in the stomach, and Cole doubled over in pain. Don took a roll of duct tape from the trunk of the car and wrapped it around Cole's head several times, covering his mouth. He attached a bracket from the rope on Cole's feet to the loop on the concrete block. Cole screamed through the tape but without conscience Don picked up the concrete block and threw it over the edge of the road. The force yanked Cole across the ground until he smashed against the shoulder of the road. Don picked up Cole and threw him over the edge. His body sailed down and splashed into the water twenty feet below.

"No! No, no, no!" I yelled. The nausea returned, and blood pounded my temples. Sweat streamed down my face, a light flashed brightly, and the darkness of Lake Pleasant vanished. I was again sitting at the desk in Cole's study.

Jackie was leaning over the desk, shaking me, and yelling, "Pierce! Pierce! Are you okay?!"

"AAAAAHHHHHH!" I screamed as I lurched backward in the chair, sucking in a deep breath of air.

"You're awake," she said with relief, "Are you okay?"

I did not know what to think. Sweat dripped down my forehead, and tears brimmed over in my eyes. The pressure inside my head was excruciating, and I was gasping to breathe.

"What can I do?" she begged, "How can I help?"

I cupped my numbed hands over my eyes and let the tears flow. I couldn't speak. I hunched over and fell to the floor, still gasping. Jackie knelt beside me and picked me up in her arms. She stroked my hair as she had tried to soothe Seth when he had cried. Even in my haze, I felt comfort and realized my lungs could hold the air. The panic slowly dissolved. My heart rate slowed, and feeling returned to my limbs, but the image of Cole falling was distinct in my mind.

"No, no, no," I mumbled as my vocal cords allowed words to come again. I felt the pain of loss tear my heart from my body and screamed, "No!"

"Pierce, it's me—Jackie," she said shaking my shoulder. I pulled my hands away from my face and looked into her eyes. I saw caring and concern. "What happened?" she asked. She wanted to comfort me and help. But I had just seen her husband die. How could I inflict this terrible news on her? But how could I withhold it? I could not throw her frantic life into more chaos when I was emotionally torn apart myself. I needed to get out of the house. I felt suffocation returning and stood up.

"I've gotta go, Jackie," I said. "I've gotta go." I rushed out of the room and down the hallway.

Jackie followed me out the front door, "Are you okay? What happened?"

"I'll come by later," I said. I quickly got into the Saab and left her standing on the front step as I pulled away, still trying to suck enough air into my lungs.

Chapter 12

I drove down the street and around the corner where I swerved to the curb. The world pressed against me. I still felt suffocated. I searched my mind for comforting thoughts and focused on Vanessa. I felt warmth as I thought of her. She was my advocate. She was helping me. I had someone I could trust. Calm returned and with it, easier breathing. I started the car again and drove to the nearest pay phone. I needed to talk to Vanessa.

I dialed her office number, and she picked up. "Vanessa Trace."

"Vanessa, this is Pierce."

"Pierce, we've got to talk."

"You're right. I have a lot to talk about," I said.

"There was no crash on the freeway. No report. Nothing." Her tone was steady and professional, almost clinical. She had changed since the last time we had spoken.

"There was a crash, Vanessa."

"It didn't happen, Pierce," she said. "The detectives at the mental hospital came up with nothing. There was nothing there, Pierce. None of it is real."

"We need to talk. Can you meet me?"

"I spoke to your doctor, Pierce—Dr. Reed," she said, now her voice sympathetic. "He told me about you, about your situation."

"You talked to Dr. Reed?" I asked.

"Yes, I went to his office. It's not real, Pierce. None of it is real."

"I'm coming to your office," I said and hung up.

If I did not have Vanessa, I was dead. They would get me. I needed Vanessa. I knew there would be evidence of the white BMW on the freeway. I drove to the freeway, entered on Avondale, and went to the location where the white BMW had smashed into the cement barricade. I pulled to the shoulder of the freeway, took out my cell phone, and turned it on. I could use my phone camera to take proof back to Vanessa. I saw the skid marks Kendall's Saab had made on the freeway and snapped a photo. I then walked further down the freeway, inspecting the cement barriers where the BMW's back end had hit. There would be impact marks and perhaps fragments of the tail light. Cars zipped past as I walked slowly along, scrutinizing the barrier. There were sporadic scuff marks all the way along it but no white paint, no tail light fragments. I walked all the way across the bridge, growing more anxious and frustrated. I turned around and walked back. I noticed that the shoulder of the freeway was particularly clean. A sweeper must have run along the bridge since the accident. I felt trapped in an insane world. Once again, my search for evidence had been thwarted. I knew it had happened. I knew I needed to keep Vanessa on my side.

"It didn't happen, Pierce." Those words stabbed at me. *"It's not real, Pierce. None of it is real."* I felt desperate, frantic at being let down, but I calmed myself.

When I got to Vanessa's office, I knew I needed to approach her in the right manner, not hysterical and demanding. Vanessa was very factual. She saw things as clear-cut, right and wrong, black and white. That is why Cole and Catherine had taken the time to organize their case before they took it to Vanessa. They knew Vanessa would tear through the evidence. If it did not prove the point they were trying to make, she would not take the case. She had gone on the line for me because she cared about me, but I knew from the phone call she had drawn a line and was disassociating herself. I needed to know what Dr. Reed had said to her so I could counter his perspective and change her mind.

When I pulled into her parking garage, I knew what I was going to do. I concentrated on my hands on the steering wheel, energy rippled off my skin, and again I stepped out of my body as I had in the alley and at Marty's house. It was easier this time. I was getting used to it. It felt almost natural. I walked through the parking lot and into the building. I went up the stairs and walked through the claustrophobic, stuffy hallway to the door with the frosted window and "Vanessa Trace—Assistant District Attorney" stenciled on it in black letters. I stepped through the door and saw Vanessa at her desk. She was leaning over a legal book with file folders strewn across her messy desk. I watched her study the book for a few moments and was mesmerized by her beauty. She was a work of art. The sun from the window softly rested on her smooth skin, and the shadows outlined the perfect lines of her face. As I looked at her, I knew I needed her.

I didn't need just her legal skills. I needed her as a person, as a woman. My life without her held only emptiness.

I focused on her face, and energy rippled off her body. I saw dozens of versions of her in different outfits and positions. I then focused on Dr. Reed and the world around one of the images of Vanessa expanded into a new setting—Dr. Reed's office. Vanessa was sitting in the chair across from his desk where I had spent many hours.

"I am about the closest person Pierce has to family and I need to understand what happened to him," she was saying.

Dr. Reed nodded. "His mind suffered a severe trauma in the flight; and after the coma, he needed the time here to heal. That's what he did."

"So in your opinion he's fine?" she asked.

"In my opinion, he is okay to continue his life."

"So he's not fine?" she pressed. "He has problems?"

"He suffered a trauma."

"What were the effects of the trauma? What was wrong with him?"

"Do you have daydreams, Miss Trace? Do you ever look out your window at your office and fantasize?"

"I do."

"Then what was wrong with him is not much different than you or me, just enhanced. He simply would see things that were not there—daydreams. However, his were slightly more complex."

"Complex in what way?"

"It seemed he formed new images based on people or events around him. What you and I would recognize as a daydream, he would actually see—would believe it existed in the real world. The distinctions between reality and fantasy were gone."

"And you feel he is over this?"

"Once you have an injury, there are always scars. He has a strong mind and has shown me that he is able to distinguish between reality and the complexities his mind creates."

"What do you mean by scars?"

"I would expect him to have recurrences. It would only be natural. He will see things which, in reality, do not exist. I feel he has a strong enough mind that he will be able to live his life fairly well, despite the scars."

Vanessa considered, then nodded and said, "Thank you, Dr. Reed." As she stood up, I pulled out of the vision in a flash of white light and was again in the Saab. So, as I suspected, she did not believe I could tell the difference between reality and my own mental projections. I needed to give her evidence. I had none and I had no idea of how to find any.

Am I crazy? I thought. I looked at the situation from her point of view, and the answer was a resounding yes. I would think I was crazy if I had been asked to listen to myself explain the previous few months of my life. If I had not lived through these experiences, I would not have believed them, especially given the absence of any physical proof. *Were the attacks on me real?* I wondered. I felt doubt creep in. I felt humiliation for the absurdity of the claims I had made. *What if I had created them in my head? What if the sniper shots at the gates of Kensington were not real? What if I had created them just as Sarah had created the creatures in her world?* I believed that Sarah believed they were real, but I didn't. What if I had created this whole conspiracy around Paralight, Don, and Jack. *How could I know if my view of events was true?* Even though I had seen the creatures in Sarah's rendition of the real world twice, I knew in my mind that she was crazy. Was I replicating her madness with a more sophisticated form of monsters? *What is madness?* I wondered. *Am I mad?*

I thought of Hamlet and his doubts as he struggled to make a decision. He had wondered if the apparition of his father was real and if he could trust its information. He had continued to hesitate and, as a result, people had died. He lost his love, and his life became a tragedy. He lost everything. I decided I had hesitated enough in my life. Hesitation, in most cases, leads to destruction. My hesitation in listening to Cole and Catherine had probably led to their deaths. I did not want to lose any more. I was not going to be Hamlet. Sarah was living in her world, Hamlet had lived in his, and I was living in mine.

"Mad or not, this is my world and I am going to live in it," I said out loud. I opened the Saab door and picked up my envelope with the notes about the Paralight case with a determination to see things through. I would move forward. All I could trust was what I had seen, evidence or no evidence.

Within moments, I had climbed the stairs, breezed past an empty receptionist desk, walked down the stuffy hallway, and rapped on Vanessa's door.

"I know what happened to Cole," I said with confidence, the instant I stepped through the door. "It was horrible."

"Pierce, stop. Please stop," she said as if my words were causing her head to ache, "I talked to Dr. Reed."

"And he told you I see things which in reality do not exist," I cut in.

"Yes, you're creating this, Pierce."

"I'm not creating it."

"There was no accident reported on the freeway."

"There was an accident. It just wasn't reported," I retorted.

"There was no one in the house. No one anywhere near the house. No tracks, no broken lock, nothing," she said sternly. "There were no bullets at the gate."

"I've created it? You think I've created it?"

She nodded her head in a sympathetic way, "You've see the movie *A Beautiful Mind?*" she asked.

I nodded. "Yes, great movie." In that movie Russell Crowe played a brilliant mathematician whose mind took him on adventures that were vivid and real to him, but which did not exist in reality. He literally saw people and interacted with them, but they were not real. Eventually he learned to live in peace with the world his mind created around him, and true reality.

"That's it, Pierce," she said, "That's what you're doing. It's not real. I want to help you and I sincerely care about you more than anyone I know, but going forward with this is not helping you. Supporting you in this fantasy is the worst thing I can do for you. I hope you understand. I can't spend more time on this. Please don't ask me to."

"I didn't create it, Vanessa. Cole's been killed. He's not missing. They killed him. They killed Catherine. I wrote down what I know," I said as I put the envelope on her desk.

"I can't do this, Pierce," she restated, pushing the envelope back.

"Vanessa, you need to help me," I said, almost begging. I heard the desperation in my voice and knew she did also.

"I am. It's over, Pierce." She looked down at the book on her desk. "Please close the door on your way out."

A frigid wave ran through my body. I was being rejected, told to leave. I now knew what she must have felt that night, sitting in my car, when I told her I was marrying Catherine—the night I had rejected her. She had looked as if her life had been sucked from her. I felt the same.

"No, you can't do this. They killed Cole and Catherine!" I yelled.

She looked up from the book with empathy. "I know it's been hard." She looked directly at me, and I could see she had made up her mind. There was nothing I could say to change it. That was a characteristic of the whole Trace family. "I've helped all I can, and I would appreciate your understanding that I am very busy."

I was helpless. "So that's it? You think it's my imagination and you're finished?"

Vanessa nodded, her expression pained but determined. "Please take the envelope."

I picked up the envelope, turned and walked to her door, but stopped as I reached for the knob. I could not leave. Only emptiness, loneliness, and death waited on the other side of the door. I was determined to live in my world, but I had to take Vanessa with me. I turned back to her, walked to Vanessa's side, knelt beside her, put the envelope on her desk and wrapped my fingers around her forearm. I looked Vanessa directly in the eye. Despite her surprise, she looked directly back at me.

I focused all the attention of my mind to the night on Scorpion Point Road when Cole had been murdered by Don. I could feel energy and warmth leaving my hand and entering her arm. The world around us shimmered and went dark. The light from the window retracted, and the walls dissolved into threads of light that formed a long concrete road. She looked to the right where the white BMW was parked.

"Lake Pleasant," I said. Don opened the car door, and walked to the trunk. "That's Don," I told her.

Vanessa stepped forward, staring in shock at Cole. "Cole?" she called. "Cole, can you hear me?"

"They can't hear you. It already happened. We're watching the past," I explained.

She looked at me in amazement, then back to Don as he yanked Cole from the trunk and dropped him to the ground. Vanessa winced at Cole's pain. It was excruciating for me to witness this scene a second time as Cole begged. I couldn't even bear to see how Vanessa was processing the dreadful scene.

"No!" screamed Vanessa, "Cole! No! Don't do this!"

Don attached the bracket from the rope on Cole's feet to the loop on the concrete block. Cole let out muffled screams through the tape.

Vanessa turned to me in horror, "Stop him, Pierce. Stop him!" I put my arm around her. As the weight of the falling concrete block pulled Cole to the shoulder, Vanessa broke from me and lunged forward. She screamed again as her hands went through Cole and Don threw him over the edge. "No! Cole! No!" she yelled.

I pulled us both out of the vision. In a flash of light, the darkness of Lake Pleasant was replaced with the soft light of Vanessa's office. Vanessa sat before me, pale-faced, with tears streaming down her cheeks. I let go of her arm and watched as her mind wrapped around what she had just seen. Her eyes softened, and she leaned forward, her arms going around my neck. I pulled her against my shoulder as she sobbed. She had just lost her brother for good. Holding her close brought peace and comfort back into my emptiness. Her weeping slowed and she relaxed in my arms soaking in my warmth. Finally, she pulled back, looked me in the eye, and in a determined tone said, "I will have divers search Lake Pleasant. We'll find him."

"Thank you," I said and the desperation in my voice was gone.

Chapter 13

Vanessa was a different person as she sat back in her chair. "How do you comment on that?" she said with a breath of astonishment.

"I don't know," I replied as I sat in the chair across her desk, "I've been trying to figure it out myself."

She looked me in the eyes and smiled, "I believe you. I believe it all." The abrasiveness and formality learned in law school and through years as a prosecutor had melted away. "Now we need to put it all together and make our case," she said as she pulled out a yellow pad of lined paper, "I want it all. Tell me everything you know."

I started with Cole and his being fired from Paralight. I continued through everything I knew about the case. There was calmness in her demeanor as I recounted my visions. She viewed it all as fact and truth. There was no doubt in her mind I was telling the truth. To her my visions were expressions of reality—they had become fact. I opened the envelope and handed her the notes I had written about the case Cole and Catherine had put together. She scanned through it quickly, asked question after question, took meticulous notes, and organized her thoughts into a lawyer's brief. As we spoke, I felt as though she were a part of me. The comfort of having her in my world was the piece missing. The emptiness in my life was eclipsed with Vanessa.

After about two hours in her office, we went our separate ways. She headed to get Johnny to assign a dive team to Lake Pleasant, and I set out for Paralight to gather as much physical evidence as possible. My goals were to find paper evidence of the investment group funding the light plane and its demand to have a successful flight. We also needed documentation about accounts for the military contract. If we could make the same connections that Cole and Catherine had discovered, we would have motive; and the case for murder, attempted murder, and fraud would be solid. Jack and Don would be central in the case, and through discovery we would learn how many others in the leadership of Paralight were involved.

As I pulled out of the parking structure, I felt confident about our approach. Vanessa had thoroughly explained the legal particulars required to make prosecution possible. This case was extremely significant because Paralight was well financed and well protected. It had political connections in Arizona and nationally. It employed thousands of people. The documents and evidence gathered by Catherine and Cole were precisely what we needed. If they had compiled it once, we should be able to compile it again. Jack couldn't shred something stored on bank computers outside Paralight. It is getting them, putting them in the correct order, and presenting a convincing case for fraudulent use of funds, the investments used to cover the fraud, and the murders committed to cover the trail. I also needed to get the full names and contact information for the assistants in Carter's lab who had seen Cartwright die. Cole had told me that they would be willing to testify so he must have already contacted them.

Suddenly, red and blue lights flashed in my rearview mirror. I looked back to see a police car behind me. I had been so absorbed in thinking about the case that I had been speeding. My heart sank. A quick squawk of the siren followed, then the police car's blinker turned on, telling me to pull to the side of the road. My first instinct was to step on the accelerator and make a run for it, but I knew that would be a bad decision. I slowed and pulled to the side of the road.

As the Saab came to a stop, I focused on my hands again and I stepped out of my body. Leaving my physical body in the Saab I rushed to the police car. The officer was entering the license plate into his computer. The read-out informed him that the car had been reported stolen. I focused on the date and time of Kendall's report and projected myself to the police call center at the time of the report. The world again changed and before me, a woman with a headset sat at a computer. Kendall's call was coming in.

"I need to report my car stolen," said the voice.

"What is your name?" she asked.

"Kendall Vest," said the voice, but I recognized it. Don. The woman went through her list of questions, typing in the answers. When she asked if he knew who had taken the car, Don said he didn't. I had heard enough and pulled myself out of the vision and with a flash of light I was again in my body and looking at my hands on the steering wheel of the Saab.

I looked in the rearview mirror and saw the police officer opening his car door. I quickly realized that I could not follow through on my plan with Vanessa if I were incarcerated. Don had not mentioned my name, but I was sure he had a way of scanning the police frequencies and would know it had been spotted. I had to stay free both from the officer and from Don who would soon be on my trail again.

Try to catch me, I thought. I swung the door open and bolted.

"Stop right there!" yelled the police officer. "Hey you! Stop!"

I blazed down the wide downtown sidewalk in a full-out sprint. *Who said you can't run from your problems?* I thought with a wide grin on my face. It was freeing to know that I was the fastest human on the earth.

"Stop him!" yelled the police officer to the people on the street. At the next intersection, the light was against me but traffic was moving slowly. I dashed through the intersection and down the next block. I looked back and saw the police officer lagging, obviously winded from the sprint. I laughed. It felt good to run. Somehow the very act of deciding to take complete control of my situation freed my soul. I raced another four blocks, changing directions at each intersection to make sure I was out of the officer's sight, then slowed and walked into a shopping center. I was not winded at all. I had sprinted at full speed for six city blocks and felt only elation.

I discreetly found a restroom area, entered, and sat in a stall. I pulled out of my body and concentrated my mind on the image of the police officer. The world around me rippled and changed to the streets of Phoenix and the officer who was walking back toward his car—sweat streaming down his face. I actually felt sorry for him. He was just doing his job and I had outrun him. It would be hard for him to report that the criminal got away. However, I was not a criminal.

I focused my mind on Don. The world again rippled, and the streets changed around me. I was still in downtown Phoenix. A silver car was parked at the side of the street. Don was at the wheel, his eyes focused across the street on the police car behind Kendall's black Saab. I had been right. As soon as the officer had radioed in the sighting, he had come to the site. Chills went through me. I needed to be extremely careful.

I pulled out of the vision with a flash of white light, left the restroom, and made my way out onto the street. I watched carefully for Don's silver car and caught a bus. It was headed away from downtown, and the driver told which buses would get me closest to Paralight. After three transfers I could see the Paralight buildings. If I were to go past the gate, Alex would either notify Jack that I was in the building or Jack would see me on the gateway's surveillance camera.

I needed to go to the Human Resources Department and find out all I could about Carter's three assistants who had been fired, then the accounting office, and finally the legal offices. The building north of Paralight was owned by a company called Syndeo that created sporting apparel and equipment. The Syndeo complex also included a series of warehouses. I walked into its unguarded parking lot and strolled past the factory to the warehouses, which extended almost to the fence separating Syndeo and Paralight. The landscaping along the fence line on the Paralight side was carefully groomed with a row of trees growing close enough together to block the view of the warehouses. When no one was present, I rushed from beside a warehouse, quickly scaled the fence, and dropped into the protection of Paralight's trees and landscaping.

Making sure I was well hidden from view, I sat down, and pulled myself out of my body. It was getting easier with practice. I ran into the building and hurried up to the top floor. I walked past Jack's secretary and through the door into his office. He was not at his desk. This was a relief. Away from his computer, he would most likely not be watching the perimeter cameras. I pulled myself out of this vision with a flash of light and was again sitting under the trees on the north side of Paralight. I stood up and casually walked into the building.

I was sure that my being hunted was not general knowledge throughout Paralight so I acted the way I normally would, stepping into the elevator with several other people and punching the button for the third floor where the Human Resources Department was located. The Human Resources executive over Scarlet was Rick, the small man who had come to my house to help me when I first came home from Kensington and had stocked my refrigerator, but I did not know if Carter's lab was under his jurisdiction. I pushed open the double doors and asked the receptionist, "Is Rick in?"

"One minute," she said. She dialed a number on her phone system, then asked, "Your name?"

"Pierce Black."

"Pierce Black is here to see you." She smiled and said, "You can go right back."

I walked down the hallway and stepped into Rick's office. He was all smiles and cheerfully asked what I needed.

"It's not really about me," I said, "but I had some friends who no longer work here and I need to get in touch with them. They worked in Carter's lab as assistants. Their first names were

Keri, Howard, and Raymond. They all left Paralight several months ago at about the same time."

Rick hummed as he turned to his computer. Within a few minutes, he was handing me print-outs with contact information for Keri Reynolds, Howard Hunt, and Raymond Kent. "Anything else?" he asked.

I smiled and told him that was pretty much everything. I walked out, feeling elated. It had been so easy. Now I just needed to make contact with the three witnesses to the monkey's death, and part of the case against Paralight would be covered.

"Pierce," I heard a voice behind me—Jack's voice. The air inside me deflated as if a vice had tightened around my chest and numbness engulfed me. I turned and saw his tall, suited figure walking toward me. "I've been trying to reach you," he continued, "You didn't come in today as we had discussed."

I was too stunned to make a response, and my mind stretched for options. *How had he found me so quickly?* I felt the impulse to flee but heard another voice behind me: "Hi, Pierce." I knew that voice also. Disgust and despair hit me simultaneously. I turned away from Jack to see the face I loathed more than any other smiling brightly at me. Don put his hand on my shoulder and continued, "We've missed you, partner." I was trapped.

Don had been downtown in the silver car; and when I entered Paralight, Jack had not been in his office. It was reasonable that Don would get back to Paralight before me because I had taken the bus, but I was surprised by their efficiency. Obviously the two were focusing their full attention on apprehending me.

"What did you want in H.R.?" questioned Jack. His voice was casual but he twitched the papers from my hand, scanned the names, and told Don: "It seems we have an investigator."

Don took my arm in a vice-like grip, and they pulled me toward the stairs. My nerves were screaming. Don was Jack's hired killer. I was being taken to my execution. The hallway was empty, but I yelled, "Rick!"

Don cupped his hands around my throat, collapsed my windpipe, and pulled me around the corner. Jack leaned in close and said in a harsh whisper, "One more word, and I will kill you and your son." The secretary stuck her head out the doorway and Jack strode back into the hallway and calmly turned to her. "We have everything under control. Tell Rick thanks."

"Okay, Mr. Jones," she said, turning back into her office.

Jack stepped back around the corner and said, "Not wise, Pierce."

Don released my neck, and I gasped for air.

"You make a sound to anyone, and we will kill your son, the little girl that watches him, the pretty attorney and everyone else that means something to you," said Jack. "Tell me you understand."

The world moved in slow motion as I looked into Jack's cold eyes. He would do what he said. It was not only my life he would take, it was also Danny, Janet and Vanessa. I looked at Don, and the grip on my arm tightened.

"Tell me you understand," repeated Jack.

I looked back at him and knew I had lost. "I understand," I said.

Jack stared at me for another moment, then brushed past me. Don swung me around and we followed behind. As we walked down the hallway, a woman exited an office, saw us, and smiled.

"Hi, Mr. Jones," she said.

"How are you, Melody?" he asked.

"I'm great, and you?" she answered.

"Today's a great day," he said with a smile.

"It is," she said returning his smile.

As she walked by, the slow motion of the world continued and I saw the cloth on her shirt flow with the movements of her arm. The shadow below her slowly moved forward as she passed the light in the hall above her and dissipated as she approached the next light. My shadow did the same in the opposite direction. I remained silent although I wanted to scream.

As soon as she had passed, Jack opened the doorway to the stairs. Don pushed me through into the cold, concrete stairwell. Still gripping my arm, he shoved me ahead of him down the stairs. The echo of our footsteps brought the world back to normal motion again. Within moments we were in the underground parking, and Jack unlocked a supply room door near the stairwell exit. When the door closed behind me, Don shoved me to the other side of the room. The two stood by the door, and Don pulled a gun from a shoulder holster. He screwed a silencer to the end barrel.

"Turn around and get on your knees," said Don flatly.

To this point I had not said a word. I looked at Jack and began, "Jack, you don't want to do this."

"You don't need to say anything. Just turn around," was his quick reply.

"Jack, listen, you don't want to do this," I repeated as a revelation came to me. I had a way to win in this situation, to save my life. He was guilty of orchestrating murder, and I could use that against him. He was, in my mind, the ultimate deceiver, and his life was about advantage—whatever was best for him. I decided to play on that. I organized my next moves quickly in my mind.

"The problem is I have wanted to do this for some time now," said Jack as he turned away and moved toward the exit.

Don stepped forward with his gun leveled at me, "Turn around, on your knees." His eyes were cold and distant. No emotion. No heart.

"Jack, I have something very important to you," I said, ignoring Don. "You threatened Cole Trace just before you had him killed. He was wearing a wire." Jack stopped. "I have the tape." It was a lie, but he didn't know that.

"You have nothing," said Jack, then to Don, "Kill him."

Don shoved me to my knees. I said, "You told him his sister was dead. You then said 'There are things in this world worth more than your life, Mr. Trace. Your life means nothing to me and I will take it. Twenty-four hours. That's what I give you. What you do now is your choice.'" I quoted it perfectly and I saw Jack turn around. I continued, "The police have now found the body at Lake Pleasant off Scorpion Point Road. The tape links you to the murder."

Jack stared at me, his face expressionless. "Where's the tape?"

"I've given it to someone. If I go missing, it goes public. They don't know what is on the tape, just to mail it if they don't hear from me."

"Who?"

"I'll never tell. That's my key to freedom. Yours also," I stared back at him, my eyes as hard as his own.

The silence was deadening. "What do you propose?" he finally asked.

"You resign. Don resigns. You both relocate and no one will ever know. Your secret dies. You back off. I back off."

"I don't work this way," he said.

"The police have the body. You have no choice."

Don glanced at Jack, then back at me. Jack looked me deep in the eyes and asked, "How can I know I can trust you?"

"You don't. But you have no choice," I said. "Your life is already over if I do not walk out of here. Give me my life back, and I will protect you."

Jack looked away then, weighing his options. I saw something change in his face. "It seems I have no choice. Give me your word. Nothing goes out. You remain silent, and I will do as you ask."

"I give you my word," I promised.

"You have your life," said Jack. Don looked at him with surprise. Jack motioned for Don to put the gun away, and Don obeyed like a puppet. "You won't need these," said Jack, holding out the contact information sheets for Keri, Howard and Raymond.

"I won't," I answered as I stood up.

The two walked out of the room leaving me alone. I took a few deep breaths, relieved I was alive. I had survived and Jack had agreed to resign and take his hit-man with him. I considered the deal I had made. The deal gave me my life. He would certainly check to see if the police divers had found the body, but once it was in the morgue, my story was solid. As I walked out of the small room, I felt freedom.

I took the elevator from the parking structure back up into Paralight. I still did not trust using my cell phone so I stepped into an office on the main level and borrowed a phone to call Vanessa.

"Pierce, they found the body. It was right there. It's being transported right now, and they'll confirm his identity through dental records. It's Cole, Pierce. He was wearing the same clothes we saw when he was thrown over, and the duct tape." Her voice was breaking and fragile, "It's Cole." She stopped and I could hear the pain in her voice.

"Can you pick me up? Not at Paralight but Syndeo, the building north of Paralight."

"I'll be right there." She hung up, and I walked out of the building streaked to the bushes I had used as cover when I entered Paralight, climbed the fence and made my way to the parking area in front of Syndeo where I sat down at the curb. Images of Cole falling from Scorpion Point Road circled in my mind. Cole's death had already been real to me, but now the reality was solid—a body. I watched people walk into and out of Syndeo and marveled that their lives were so simple. After what seemed an eternity, Vanessa's car entered the parking area. I stood up and waved. She swung to the curb, and a wave of warmth engulfed me as I climbed in, but I could not feel comfort.

Her face was sober, and she looked at me with concern. "You okay?"

"No," I replied.

"Cole?"

"Yeah," I answered, "And everything else."

As she pulled out of the parking lot, she said, "They want us to go to the morgue. Are you up to it?"

"If Johnny is our host, I'm all for it," I said.

She smiled, "He made the invitation."

We did not speak for several minutes, and I watched neighborhoods pass by. I was alive, and Cole was dead. I was driving to see his dead body directly after making a deal with the man who had him killed. I broke the silence by saying, "I'm sorry, Vanessa."

"You're sorry about what?"

"Catherine and Cole," I replied.

Tears welled in Vanessa's eyes. She glanced at me, and I could see the loss digging inside her. Her brother and sister were both gone. This new emptiness was making her very unsure. When she had lost Catherine, she was devastated. The disappearance of Cole was different. She had still hoped to find him despite the months of fruitless searching. That hope was now cut off. "They loved you, Pierce. They both did."

"I know they did," I said, as I fumbled through my thoughts. Jack's face came to my mind. *You have your life,* he had said in the storage room after our deal. The words seared across my mind. It was a comforting thought and I wanted my life, but at what cost? Allowing Jack to get away with murdering Catherine and Cole? Would Jack honor the deal? Would I? I was disgusted with Jack and myself. "I don't know what to do, Vanessa. Can you pull over?"

Vanessa nodded and turned into a parking lot.

"What is it?" she asked.

"It's easier to show you," I said. I leaned forward and took her hand in mine. I looked into her eyes, and she smiled. Warmth emanated from my hand, and she glanced down curiously. Ripples rose in the air around her skin, and the car around us dissipated into soft threads of light that rebuilt the storage room in the underground parking at Paralight. I was still holding her hand as the vision took form. Vanessa looked around the room to get her bearings, then turned to see another version of me standing across from Don and Jack as Don screwed the silencer to the front of his gun.

"This was a few minutes ago," I said.

"They caught you?"

"Yeah," I answered, "Just watch."

She stared as the image of me was shoved to its knees and negotiated with Jack for my life. As Jack agreed to my demands, told me I had my life, and led Don out of the room, she turned to me and said, "You were brilliant."

"A brilliant liar."

"You did what it took," she said. The cement storage room disappeared in a flash of light and we were back in her car. "Thank you for staying alive," she said with wide eyes and hugged me.

"You're welcome," I said as I absorbed her affection. "There has definitely been enough dying."

She sat back and digested the vision. "You have him cornered," she said.

"Do you think he'll keep the deal?"

She thought for a moment and said slowly, "He's trapped for now. But if he finds any advantage, he'll take it. We won't give it to him."

"He knows about you. That's an advantage. He threatened to kill Danny, Janet, you, and anyone important to me before the deal."

"Nice to know I'm in good company," she said wryly.

"I never should have got you involved."

"We're in this together. Right now we have the advantage,"

she said. "We play our cards right and we'll get him. Besides, what do I have to fear? I have you."

"You do have me."

"We'll figure this out," she said confidently. She put her car in gear and drove back onto the street.

When we got to the morgue, Johnny took us to see the body after warning me that it was not a pleasant sight. He was right. Cole's flesh was decomposing, but he was wearing the same clothes we had both seen in the vision. We explained to Johnny that we believed they were Cole's clothes on the body.

Outside in the hall, Johnny said, "We need to go over some questions regarding the body. Will you meet me at the station?"

At the police station, we followed Johnny into a small conference room and sat at a table across from a two-way mirror. Another detective with thick arms and a tweed jacket entered the room. I recognized him from the stake-out at my house.

"You remember Detective Calloway?" asked Johnny.

"Good to see you again," I said.

Calloway nodded.

"Either of you want something to drink?" asked Johnny.

I shook my head, and Vanessa said, "No thank you."

Calloway said, "We'll video this conversation through a camera behind that mirror."

"Why do you need this recorded?" I asked.

"Do you have something to hide?" demanded Johnny.

I'll admit that I had a grudge against Johnny merely because he was so attracted to Vanessa but up to this point I had appreciated his help on the case. From his intonation it was clear he did not like me and my dislike intensified. I did not trust him. I turned to Vanessa, "Do we need to let them record this?"

"No, we don't," she answered clearly.

"No recording," I reiterated.

Johnny looked into the mirror and said, "Turn off the camera." Detective Calloway opened the door to the conference room, looked around the corner, nodded, and returned to his seat, "No recording."

Johnny looked directly at me, "Pierce, as you understand, we have found a body, which you believe is Cole Trace because the clothes appear to be his, and we are currently running tests to confirm the identity."

"Yes," I said.

"We found the body through a lead given by you."

"Yes."

"You knew Cole Trace had been murdered and told Vanessa the location of the body?" said Johnny, his tone communicating suspicion.

"I did."

"How did you know?"

I looked at Vanessa. I didn't know how much I should tell him. She looked at me and nodded. "I saw it in a dream."

"You dreamed about the exact location of the body?"

"That's correct."

"Who would want to kill Cole Trace?"

I couldn't say Jack Jones and Don Parker. If I breached the agreement, then they would have no reason to keep us alive. Finally I said, "I don't want to get involved in this."

"You're already involved."

I turned to Vanessa, "I don't have to answer any questions, do I?"

"No, you don't," she answered.

"You're the only person we have on this murder," stated Johnny flatly.

Was he accusing me of murdering Cole? "What do you mean by that?" I demanded.

"We have a dead body and we have you," he said.

I was appalled, "You don't think that I…" I stopped.

"What would you think?" asked Johnny.

"I'm done here," I said flatly.

"You're only making it hard on yourself."

"Look, I've just been released from a mental institution and I dreamed about my friend."

"Was it a dream or did you do it?" he asked directly.

Vanessa perked up at this point, "Don't go there unless you're ready to charge him," she warned Johnny.

"It's just a question," he said, throwing up his hands in the air as if to say it was innocent.

I stood up, "I'm leaving."

"No, you stay right here," he ordered.

Vanessa turned to me. "Pierce?"

I was not going to stay in that room and be accused of murdering Cole. I knew the feeling of freedom, and this man had nothing against me. I had a solid alibi. I had been in a coma when the murder took place. Johnny had a vendetta against me because the woman he loved was attracted to me. I knew what was going on in his high-testosterone body. "I'm through. Can they hold me?"

"You're making this much worse for yourself," he said, pushing his chair back and standing.

Vanessa jumped to her feet. "His alibi is rock solid. He was in a coma when Cole went missing."

"He knows about the murder, and he will not speak."

"I know where this is going and you have no evidence," she insisted. "Charge him and you'll lose. You have nothing."

"You're withholding also," said Johnny in what I thought was a surprising attack against Vanessa.

I could see fury in Vanessa's eyes, "So charge me," she challenged.

Johnny looked at both of us and lifted his hands in a disgusted gesture of surrender. Vanessa and I walked out.

Chapter 14

Outside the station, I again felt freedom. I was tired of running for my life. I was tired of people around me dying. The accusations from Johnny were shattering—he had been helping but was now against me. Vanessa did not speak until we were in her car. Then she said, "That could have gone better."

"Drake was coming after me, Vanessa. He was ready to charge me with Cole's murder."

"He has nothing."

"He was ready to charge *you*."

"A fact that will probably influence my next decision to go on a date with him," she said with a wry smile.

"What do we do?"

"We get Jack," she said plainly.

"It's that simple?" I asked.

She thought for a moment, "Yeah, it is. We turn the tables. We stalk them. You're some sort of super brain. We use it, and we make them believe you will keep the deal. We find the evidence and we put them away."

"You're not going home tonight," I said. "They kill without hesitation, and now you're on the list."

"You're not going home either," she said.

"Interesting situation," I said.

"Yeah, interesting," she agreed. "What do you propose?"

"I'm some sort of super brain so I suggest we get a hotel."

"I'm with you, super brain," she said, her smile dimpling.

She stopped at a bank and withdrew several thousand dollars in cash. We checked into a hotel room in downtown Phoenix using false names and paying cash. We went to our room, and Vanessa laid her briefcase on one of the two queen-sized beds. "You hungry?" she asked.

The sun was setting when we took our seats in the hotel restaurant. It was nice to sit down and eat, and I could feel myself relaxing; but Vanessa could not get her mind off the case. She wanted me to take her into a series of visions related to the case and investigation Cole and Catherine had created against Paralight. We quickly ate and returned to the room. We sat on the bed and held hands. As I looked into her eyes warmth, emanated from both of us. The world around us rippled, and the wisps of soft light deconstructed the hotel room and rebuilt the study at my house on the day of our anniversary. Cole and Catherine were in the room discussing the case and Vanessa listened intently, examining the documents carefully. She noted times, locations, banks, transactions and many details I had missed in my brief overview of the case contained on the ten pages I had given her. When we were satisfied with the information from the vision, I focused on returning us to the hotel room. In a flash of white light, the study disappeared and we were again holding hands on the bed. She asked me to take her to Cole's study, and I did.

We also visited Marty Sobisky at work at Paralight and skipped through time until he was meeting with Cole. Marty had printed out documents on international bank transactions, and Vanessa added them to her notes. When we returned to the hotel room, I could see exhaustion in Vanessa's face. She was pale, and her eyes streaked with red. She wrote down the bank information, then rubbed her heavy eyes.

"Are you okay?" I asked.

"Sorry. I can't keep my eyes open," she said.

"Lie down," I insisted, "Get some sleep and we'll figure things out in the morning."

She nodded. I think she was asleep before her head touched the pillow. I pulled her shoes off, slipped her limp body under the blankets and sat in the chair next to the bed. I watched her for some time before my own eyes sagged. I longed to lie next to Vanessa, but knew I should not. I stroked the hair from her face, and her skin was smooth and warm. I kissed her on the forehead, stripped down to my t-shirt and boxers, brushed my teeth, then pulled back the covers of the other bed, climbed in, and felt sleep overcome me.

I woke and showered before Vanessa stirred out of her deep slumber. She must have been exhausted from the mental strain of the visions I had brought her into, confirming my impression that I was more used to it. I ordered breakfast from room service and the waiter's knock on the door woke her. I paid for the food and brought it to her bed where she was propping herself up against the headboard.

"Good morning," I said.

"Good morning," she replied taking a drink of her orange juice. "Thank you for breakfast."

"You're welcome. It was nice spending the night with you."

"Likewise, although I can't remember a thing," she said. She put the glass down on the nightstand.

"You weren't too talkative after the visions. I rather liked you that way. You should try it more often," I teased.

She threw a pillow at me, "As if talking to you is entertaining!"

"I didn't say talking to you isn't entertaining. It's just more entertaining not talking to you."

"Why, you!" she said in comic exasperation as she threw another pillow, then jumped from the bed to ensure that one would hit me.

"Okay, you're entertaining!" I said, laughing under a bombardment of pillow attacks.

"And you remember it!" she said with resoluteness as she made her way back to her breakfast. I had not seen that side of Vanessa for years. Cole, Catherine, Vanessa, and I had mock-fought and played in that manner all through high school and into college, but much of the rough-housing had ended when Catherine and I had become engaged. Vanessa had become much more reserved, professional. I liked seeing the fun side of her. It felt like home.

We finished our breakfast and decided that the best course of action was for me to return to Paralight and act as if I were fulfilling my side of the commitment to Jack. We would stay in close contact and gather the evidence necessary to convict Jack, Don, and any other people at Paralight connected to the deaths of Catherine and Cole. We checked out of the hotel, and Vanessa drove me to the street where I had left my car.

The old Pontiac Grand Am was a welcome sight. As I looked

at my car, I saw the scratch on the right fender where I'd parked too close to a light post when Catherine and I had taken Danny to Kiddie Gym when he was two. Catherine and I were broke, and there wasn't any way to get it fixed. Both of us felt like crying, but we had laughed instead. The dent and scrapes on the car were comforting.

I stepped out of Vanessa's car and got into mine. I had bought the Grand Am when Catherine and I were just married because it was the only thing on the lot where I traded in my broken-down car. My old car had had to be pulled to the lot by a tow truck, and I had no way to drive it off the lot or to pay for the repairs. I had to take the trade-in value they gave me, and my choices were limited to what was on their used car lot. But I soon really liked my Pontiac.

I twisted the key, and the engine turned over, but did not catch. That was normal. It started when it felt like it—part of the relationship I had with the car. I looked at Vanessa, and she smiled. She knew the car also. I had left the lights on several times, and the battery was close to dead, but I had not made a priority of getting a new one. Usually it would start, but sometimes I would need to get a jump-start from Catherine or whoever was nearby.

Vanessa's window rolled down, "You want me to pop the hood?"

I held up my finger and sat still for the count of ten to let the battery rest and then tried again. This time it started. "She's a beauty," I said.

"She is," Vanessa confirmed.

"We'll meet here at five-thirty," I confirmed.

"Five-thirty," she nodded in agreement.

"You're not going in to work," I stated.

"I'm sick," she said.

"You are," I confirmed.

She gave me an exaggerated scowl, then replied "Stay safe," with sincerity.

"I will. You, too."

She rolled up her window and pulled away. As I drove to Paralight, I felt as though I was back in high school after the first time I had gone to the movies with Cole, Catherine, and Vanessa. I felt the comfort of belonging, and I was elated. I turned on the radio and scanned through the channels, stopping on a news station. I listened for several minutes, then the reporter told about the discovery of Cole's body. "Cole Trace was last seen as he left his home on the evening of March 6th this year. Police inform us that evidence from the scene clearly indicates he was murdered, and they are following all leads. Anyone with information regarding the death of Cole Trace is asked to contact the Phoenix police immediately."

I felt nausea, and the street ahead of me wavered like heat waves rising off a desert road. I parked on the side of the street to clear my mind. I missed Cole. The images of his murder and his body in the morgue flashed clearly in front of me. I became more determined than ever to make Jack and Don pay for the murders. I would stick to the plans Vanessa and I had made, and I would find the evidence we needed. I pushed thoughts of Cole's murder out of my mind, gearing myself up mentally to face Paralight and Jack. As I drove through the Paralight gates, I waved to Alex in the guard booth and he waved back. In the underground parking garage, my favorite spot was available.

Inside the building, I walked down the hallway to the foyer

and thought how odd it was that the same building could represent completely different things based on experience. Before the loss of Catherine, I viewed this building as a playground and working there as the highlight in my life. The previous day when I had come seeking evidence, the building was my enemy. I was there to find evidence against it. The building now represented an advocate in my attack against Jack—a step toward my ultimate goal of freedom. I felt uneasy as I walked into Jack's office, but I was determined. His secretary told me to go in and I did, closing the door behind me. I sat down across from him without speaking. Jack looked at me, waiting. Catherine had told me, in discussing negotiation skills, "He who speaks first, loses." It was an interesting thought because if the other person speaks first, you can position yourself according to their words, tone, confidence, and body language.

"They found the body," said Jack finally.

I nodded and remained silent. He wanted me to speak. I could see it in his eyes. He wanted to hear what I had to say. I refused to give him what he wanted. Before the flight, I had trusted Jack and thought of him as my advocate. He had always complimented me and had given me every opportunity to shine. I had sat across from him at his desk many times discussing different projects and their potential impact on the world. In many instances, my life had been in his hands, and I had trusted that he had done everything in his power to protect me. Each new project brought inherent dangers, of course; but with Jack leading Scarlet and ensuring that everything had been thought of, I had always felt safe. Now things were different. The trust was gone. He wanted me dead. The only reason I was alive was because

I was blackmailing him, and ironically, I was blackmailing him with a lie. Yet he was showing trust in me by sparing my life.

"I'll keep my agreement," he finally said. "Check in down in Scarlet. Kendall will be your partner again. Don is no longer with Paralight."

I nodded again and, without speaking, stood up.

"You know Lieutenant Drake?"

I was immediately curious yet remained silent, merely nodding.

"He was asking about you," Jack continued. "I trust you will keep your side of the agreement as will the pretty attorney. Nothing is to be said."

"We will," I said, wondering about the conversation he had had with Johnny and how much he knew about Vanessa.

"You have your life back," he added.

I nodded and continued to the door.

"You can go get your kid from Bonnie Hatch."

I stopped cold. He knew where Danny was. He knew Bonnie's name. I slowly turned back to him, and his eyes were intent on my face. He was looking for weakness. The slight squint with the upturn of his lips sent the message that he was in control. He was looking for a break in me, but I refused to give it to him. "I'll do that," I responded, then turned and exited, closing the door behind me.

I felt dirtier walking out of his office than when I had entered. I had just extended another promise to work with Jack—a promise to keep my side of the deal. I never would keep the deal, and I wondered if he saw that in me. He was searching my face and I shuddered at the thought that he could see through my facade. Did I believe I would keep my side of the bargain, or had I let my face show my true intentions? I forced myself to believe he saw a firm determination to remain silent. I was still alive, and that was an indication he still believed I was keeping our bargain.

I went into Scarlet and found Kendall. After about twenty minutes of ribbing for stealing his car, we got to work. He told me the police had called him, saying that they had retrieved his stolen car, but he had never reported it stolen. I did not mention Don's call to report the car. It did not seem necessary, and I had already involved too many people. At this point Kendall was an innocent bystander, and the less he knew, the better. I was able to laugh with Kendall, relax, and act like myself. It helped relieve some of the tension I felt from my encounter with Jack, but my curiosity about exactly what Jack was doing and my determination to assemble our case remained unswerving.

It was Wednesday. A second test of the speed of light plane was scheduled for the following Friday with Kendall as the pilot. Paralight had also scheduled a press conference for the same day to present the results of the first speed of light test flight to the world. This was a momentous occasion for Paralight, and I was scheduled to be on a panel and answer questions about the first flight. Basically, I was the face for the speed of light technology. I would become famous, an icon in history. It was what I had been longing for, yet now it was hollow. I wanted meaning in my life and I had learned clearly with the loss of Catherine and Cole that meaning comes from the people surrounding you. What are accomplishments without someone to share them with? Catherine and Cole had brought meaning to my life and they were now gone. Vanessa and Danny were still in my life but if I made the wrong moves, I would lose them also. I was determined to

keep them alive and would play the chess pieces of my life carefully.

In preparation for the press conference, on Thursday morning, I was to give the board of directors a detailed briefing on
the mental effects I had experienced as a result of the test and
Carter was to report on the physical tests he had conducted. Kendall and I tested the progress of the X1 on the flat desert behind
the hangars of Paralight, and it handled much better than it had
previously. The technicians had solved the problems with cornering, and it was much more stable. Upon returning to Scarlet,
Kendall was called away for scheduled physical examinations,
and I needed to prepare my report for the board. I retired to my
small office adjacent to the locker room, shut the door, locked it,
and sat at the computer determined to know more about Jack and
his meeting with Johnny Drake.

I focused on my hands, and the ripples of energy lifted from
my skin as my hands came out of my body. I stood up, leaving
my body at the computer, rushed through the door and was soon
to Jack's office. He was sitting at his computer reviewing video
footage of the speed of light plane test. I sat across from him
for several minutes. He was casual, relaxed. A call came in, and
he answered pleasantly, responded to several questions, made a
few witty comments, and ended the conversation. I was struck
with the reality that you never really know what is behind the
pretense a person creates for the public. How would the person
on the other end of the line know he had just spoken with a murderer?

I focused my attention on Jack; and a shimmer of light lifted
off his skin, the air around him rippled, and suddenly his body
split into many distinct versions of himself. The versions ranged

in the position of his body and colors of suits. I was amazed at the number of different designer suits Jack possessed, each fitted to perfection. I focused my mind on Johnny Drake, expecting to see a vision of the two of them talking; but as I did so and looked at the different versions of Jack, the versions slowly dissipated until they were all gone and Jack again sat alone in his office, reviewing the video presentation. I was at a loss. Had Jack *not* met Johnny? Why then had he mentioned him to me?

I again focused on Jack and the idea of a police officer. As I did so light again shimmered from his skin, and his body again spilt into many versions of him. One of the versions stood out to me. I was immediately drawn to it, and the walls of Jack's office wavered. Soft threads of light deconstructed them, then reconstructed a restaurant where that version of Jack sat alone in a booth, eating a meal. A heavy-set man wearing a tweed jacket and jeans, sat down next to him. I recognized him—Calloway, the detective who had been in the interrogation room when Johnny accused me of murdering Cole. He had also been with Johnny and the other detectives on the night we had staked out my house.

"The body was Cole Trace," said Calloway.

"You're on the investigation?" asked Jack.

"I am. Drake is leading it," he answered.

"What are the leads?"

"There are no leads," answered Calloway. "Pierce Black is the only connection. Vanessa Trace gave the location to Drake; and when we questioned Black about it, he said he dreamed it."

"He said he dreamed it?" Jack smiled wryly. "He didn't mention any names?"

"No, and Drake pressed him, even threatened charging him with the murder."

"Why didn't he?"

"No motive and a strong alibi. He was in a coma when the death occurred," answered Calloway.

"He could have hired the killer," said Jack.

"Still no motive," answered Calloway.

"Stay with Drake," ordered Jack, and Calloway nodded. Jack put a twenty dollar bill on the table, then stood up and left.

Calloway discreetly picked up an envelope that Jack had left on the bench and slipped it into his inside pocket. Calloway stayed at the table for several minutes, then left. I followed him down the sidewalk and into an alley where he entered a car, pulled the envelope out, and looked at a thick sheaf of bills. He smiled and put it back in his pocket. *So Calloway is also an opportunist,* I thought. I pulled myself out of the vision. With a flash of light, I was back in my small office at Paralight.

Jack had no reason to doubt my determination to keep the deal. Calloway had given him answers that protected me. I had Jack trapped. I spent the next several hours preparing the board report, determined to assure Jack that I was returning to my normal life and that he was safe. At the end of the day, I was called back to do a final run in the X1 with Kendall. The courses prepared were simple; and again, it handled with precision. With my day at Paralight finished, I showered in the locker room, wrote up my log for the day, and went to my car. Although I was confident that Jack believed I would keep my side of the deal, I felt uneasy driving out of the underground parking and across the campus of Paralight. Would Don be waiting somewhere to attack me? Nothing happened. I drove past the guard gate, and

Alex again waved at me. I drove down the street; and as I considered precautions to ensure I was not being followed, I thought of Jack's comment just before I left his office. *You can go get your kid from Bonnie Hatch.*

The only way he would have known about Bonnie is if he had placed a tracking device on my Pontiac like the one on Catherine's Lexus. I had driven it to Bonnie's house and then abandoned it on the side of the road. I stopped at a gas station to test my theory. I closed my eyes and created the image of Jack in my mind, focused my attention to the present time, and felt the energy surge through my body. I opened my eyes to see the wisps of light creating Jack's office with Jack sitting at his desk. I walked around his desk to see the two large, flat-panel monitors in front of him. In a window on the left-hand monitor was a GPS map with an arrowhead icon at the exact location I had stopped my car. Jack was tracking me. He was watching my every move. He was watching to see if I would betray our agreement. In a flash of light, I was back in my car. For me to stay alive and to protect Danny and Vanessa, I needed to keep Jack believing that I would not betray him.

I was scheduled to meet Vanessa on the street in Laveen near Bonnie's house so I drove in that direction. As I pulled around the corner in the quaint neighborhood, I could not see Vanessa's car. I stopped on the side of the street. Was Jack tracking her, too? I saw Vanessa's car turn onto the street several blocks ahead of me, closed my eyes and again created the image of Jack in the present time. He was still watching the GPS monitor. The arrowhead icon in the exact position, pointing the same direction as my car in Laveen, but it was the only icon on the monitor. He was not tracking Vanessa's car. With a flash of light, I was again in my car and Vanessa had stopped in front of me.

I climbed out of my Pontiac with my finger to my lips. Vanessa looked at me oddly, waiting until I climbed in. I closed the door, then told her, "Jack has a tracking device on my car. I assume it's also bugged. Your car is clean."

"That's good to know," said Vanessa.

"Detective Calloway is a crooked cop. Jack pays him. Calloway told Jack we kept silent when Drake grilled us on the murder. Jack believes we're keeping the deal."

"We, not you?"

"Jack is watching you, too. He told me that you needed to stay quiet, and I told him you would. He also told me to pick up Danny from Bonnie's house."

"He knew about Bonnie?"

"We need to play our cards right, Vanessa," I said.

Vanessa was quick. "We need to keep up the façade."

"Life has to look normal. That means bringing Danny home and also having Janet return, but I don't want to involve Janet or anyone else."

"He already threatened to kill her, didn't he?"

"He did. She was on the list of people I care about."

"She is safer if life returns to normal," said Vanessa.

I agreed. "Will you follow me to Bonnie's house?"

"I will," she said.

Vanessa followed me to Bonnie's house; and during the drive, I turned on my cell phone and called Janet. I was sure Jack would listen in.

"Hello?" answered Janet in monotone.

"Janet, this is Mr. Black"

"Hi, Mr. Black," her tone was suddenly enthusiastic.

"Danny is coming home and I was wondering if we can go back to normal."

"Really!" she was thrilled.

"Really."

"Oh, you don't know how badly I want out of my house! Thank you! Thank you!"

"Can you come tomorrow morning?" I asked.

"I'll make breakfast. Thank you, Mr. Black," she said.

"You're welcome and thank *you*."

"See you in the morning," she said and hung up.

As the line went dead, I knew Jack got a clear message; however, I felt deceitful for involving Janet without telling her the danger. But telling her would actually decrease the chances that any of us would survive.

When I stopped at Bonnie's house, Vanessa walked with me to the porch. Bonnie answered the door and, with a big smile, gave me a hug. She turned to Vanessa and said inquisitively, "I've met you before, haven't I?"

"Bonnie," I said, "this is Vanessa. She's Catherine's sister."

"Then I saw you at their wedding," she said, "Come in, come in, both of you. Danny and I have just finished dinner, and I was about to sit down and read with him."

We sat in her front room. Danny was in a chair and staring at a wall. I had missed him sorely. When I saw him, it almost brought tears to my eyes. I crouched down in front of him and said, "Danny, are you ready to come home?" His expression remained the same. I turned to Vanessa and Bonnie and said, "That means he's ecstatic." They both smiled.

"You're taking him home?" questioned Bonnie.

"Yes, and thank you so much for taking him these past few days. You will never really understand how much it means to me."

"It was nothing, and I'll take him again in a heartbeat," she said. I could see in her eyes she meant it. She did all she could to try and keep us in her house, and we talked and looked at pictures for a short while. As we left, I could not help but think the world we lived in would be a utopia if everyone were a Bonnie.

After I had buckled Danny in my car, I walked Vanessa to hers and she asked, "You hungry?"

"You asking me on a date?"

"We have to act normal, don't we? Normal people eat," she said in a subdued tone and with a charming smile. "Besides, my choices are you, Johnny, Jack or Don."

"Tough competition."

"It is. You rank somewhere near the top."

"I'm starving."

"So what do you want?"

"I'm not sure," I said.

"Thai food! Green curry is what you've been craving. I agree! I'll head to a place I know. You and Danny follow." Thai curry was always her favorite, and she never tired of it.

The evening was great. We were at the restaurant for several hours. I loved being with Vanessa and having Danny at my side. The conversation was comforting and fun as well as serious and sober. She explained that her parents, who had retired in San Diego, were flying in for Cole's burial a week from Friday. Cole's death was a tender subject, and tears welled in her eyes. Still, she said, it was better now because she could get some closure. Her parents felt the same. Knowing the truth outweighed a false hope. Taking in a deep breath, she changed the subject: "You're reading *Hamlet* to Danny, right?"

"Yes, I was. I finished it on my own."

"You finished it on your own?" she asked with a raised eyebrow.

"I read books," I retorted.

"Technically it's not a book. It's a play," she said.

"I read plays," I confirmed.

"Really? Which other ones? Which ones have you read yourself?" she questioned playfully. "And I don't mean Catherine reading them and discussing them with you."

I had to think. In fact, I couldn't remember having read any other play from cover to cover on my own. Generally I would read portions of a play or book with Catherine, she would tell me the plot line and themes of the play, and we would discuss the challenges of the characters.

"Let me help you," she said, "I can see the question clogged up the gears you have inside that head of yours so you don't need to answer. I got you a present."

"A present?"

She pulled a book out of her purse and said, "The War of the Roses to commemorate our night watching your house." It was Shakespeare's *Richard III*. "Shopping—that's what a woman does on sick days off from work."

I smiled. "Soon I'll be able to tell you I've read two plays on my own." She pulled cash out of her purse to leave on the table and I said, "Wait, this is on me. I have some cash."

"I asked you on a date, right?" she said. "The person doing the asking pays." She looked at me firmly as she put the money on the table.

"Thank you," I said. "And Danny thanks you."

"You're welcome, both of you."

"I've been thinking this through. You can't go to your house. It's too dangerous. I think we need to be together as much as possible until this situation is taken care of. I will not accept a 'no' answer. You will sleep at our house. You can have my room, and I will sleep with Danny."

"You will not accept 'no'?"

"No."

"Do I have any other options?"

"No."

"I guess that means okay," she smiled.

I turned to Danny, "Danny, when you get what you want, you move fast before minds change. Let's go."

The sun was setting with beautiful streaks of orange, red, and yellow across the scattered thin clouds in the Arizona sky as we drove back to my house. Vanessa took Danny's arm and helped me guide him to the house. Before we reached the door, I said under my breath, "I have to assume that the house is bugged also. We can't say anything about Jack or Paralight while we're here." Vanessa nodded.

We took Danny to his room and tucked him into his bed. I got Vanessa a t-shirt and shorts to wear for the night and threw on a pair of sweats. I found an unopened toothbrush in our bathroom supply box and after we brushed our teeth I said, "We read at night, and I have a good book." I held up *Richard III*. "Do you want to read with us?"

"I'd love to," she replied.

We went back to Danny's room. I sat in the comfortable chair beside his bed, and Vanessa sat on the bed next to Danny, propping a pillow behind her. I began reading. Richard was not a good man. He rose to power through treachery and murder. I instantly saw Jack in Richard. As I read on, I pictured Jack playing the part and the fit was great. Richard looked at people as objects, and he would use them for his gain with no thought of their value as human beings.

My eyes got heavy, but I kept reading late into the night. As I was looking at the type on the page, I saw it shimmer as it had when I was reading *Hamlet*. I instantly recognized the movement and was fully awake. I sat up straighter, and letters rose from the page. They formed a sentence in front of me: "Dad, I have wanted to talk to you for so long but you wouldn't see." I was stunned. I looked at Danny. He was lying still, looking straight up at the ceiling. Vanessa had fallen asleep, but the world around me had the crisp, vivid colors of a vision. As I focused on Danny, his body turned into two images of the same person. One image sat up and looked at me while the other remained motionless, looking at the ceiling. The Danny who sat up looked directly at me and smiled.

"Danny, can you see me?" I asked.

"Yes, I can, Dad. I've always been able to. You just wouldn't see me."

I stood up to approach Danny and realized I had already split from my body as well. My body was asleep on the chair with the book on my chest. However, the words that Danny had spelled out were still hanging in the air. I went to Danny and cupped his face in my hands, "Do you know how much I love you?"

Danny smiled, "Yes, Dad, I do. You have always loved me and so did Mom." I hugged him, and he wrapped his arms around me. As he did, an understanding of his world came to me.

I understood without words the feelings he had toward me—that he had always been with me, that he understood everything I had done in my life and appreciated the time and care I had given to him. It was a feeling beyond the physical experience of embracing, and the best way for me to describe it was intelligence shared through contact. His world opened up for me, and I realized there was much more to the world around me than I had ever before imagined. I saw that he had also helped me and had guided and directed me when my mind began its journey to this level of existence. He had been with me and helped me though the coma and recovery in the mental hospital. He had helped me to control my mind and focus my attention when I was not able to do so on my own. He also helped me when I came home from the mental hospital. I was washed with emotion and warmth, and my chest burned. I felt healing in the wounded emptiness that had ravaged my heart since the loss of Catherine.

"You've been helping me. You're the one who wrote with the letters from the *Hamlet* book," I exclaimed. "You told me about Corrington, the brick wall, the gate?"

"I knew that man would try to shoot you and told you to get the pen. I wanted you to know the truth about Mom."

"You saw the future?" I asked.

"I knew their plans and the past. The past is clear," he said, "the future blurry."

My son had saved my life and had directed my mind to give me an understanding of the truth of Catherine's death and the people responsible for it. "The future is clear for us now. We have each other," I said.

"I love you, Daddy."

"I love you too, Danny."

My eyes opened. I was again sitting in the chair with *Richard III* open on my chest. Danny's eyes were closed. He had fallen asleep. There was a joy in my soul that I had never felt in my life. I knew my son from a level impossible to fully explain. I understood his feelings and his appreciation for me as a father. I went to his side and gently touched his sleeping face. There was a depth to our relationship that had not previously existed. I used to feel alone with Danny. I had always loved him, but now I knew he understood me. My efforts and attention had not been unappreciated. His mind was on a higher level than the minds of everyone around him, and he comprehended much more than I had ever imagined. I would never again feel alone when I was with Danny. I had Danny, and he had me. My greatest wish was that Catherine had known the wonderful person she was raising. She had loved him and devoted her life to him, but I now knew him in a way she never had. I wished Catherine had been able to feel the love and connection I now felt with Danny. She had been robbed of that privilege when Don took her life.

I picked up Vanessa and softly carried her to my bed. Her eyes opened when I laid her on the soft mattress.

"I fell asleep?"

I nodded, "I met Danny tonight."

She looked at me quizzically, trying to make sense of my statement in her drowsy state, "Pardon me?"

"I spoke with Danny."

She smiled, oblivious to the real meaning of what I was saying, and commented, "He's a wonderful boy." She slipped under the blankets, her eyes closed and her head sank into the pillow.

"He is a wonderful boy," I said, echoing her statement.

Chapter 15

The next morning I woke Vanessa before sunrise and held my finger to my lips. Silently, we left the house for a walk. The red-orange wash of light from the sun rising above the horizon coated the white walls of the homes on the street. Vanessa's olive skin glowed in the warmth of the colors. When we were a good distance away, I said, "Thank you for being with me on this."

"Hey, you only live once, right?"

"That's what I want to talk about," I said soberly. She looked at me with concern. I continued, "I might die, Vanessa. They may kill me."

"You're *not* going to die," she insisted.

"I'm not planning on it, and I'm not so much concerned about me as I am Danny. Right now, if I die, Paralight has full legal authority over him. I signed papers before the flight that allowed them to arrange for his needs if anything were to happen to me. Those papers supersede my will. That means Jack cares for Danny. I can't live with that," I said resolutely. "If they kill me, will you take care of Danny?"

She took both of my hands and looked directly into my eyes, "You're not going to die, and, yes, I would love to take care of Danny. You don't need to worry."

"Can you make the legal documents that will ensure you get him?"

"I'll make them today," she confirmed.

"And if they do kill me, please promise me you will take him and leave here. Go as far away from Jack as possible. He *will* kill you, too. I can handle my dying, but not you and Danny."

She embraced me, and I felt the warmth of her affection flow through my body. "I promise," she assured me. Time passed, and still we clung to each other. We were standing on an ordinary street, but there was no other place in the world I wanted to be. My eyes closed, and I felt the softness of her skin under my finger tips and the gentleness of her caress on my shoulders. I opened my eyes and marked the spot where we were standing. This was our spot. A palm tree on the side of the road cast a shadow across the paving stone where we were standing. That was our tree. I do not know how long we stood in our embrace; but when we pulled apart the colors of the sunrise were gone. However, the beauty of the moment would never leave.

As we walked back to my house, we discussed our plans to gather the evidence for our case. We both agreed that we would be cautious and move forward only if we were absolutely sure that Jack was not privy to our actions. I would make my way around Paralight only if I knew precisely where Jack was, and Vanessa would not make any definite moves at the District Attorney's office.

Janet came over early and prepared breakfast for Danny, Vanessa, and me. She was excited to be out of her house and gave Danny four hugs while he ate. I left for work, confident that Danny was safe in her hands, and she promised she would read to him and not spend the whole day watching television. "I don't promise I won't watch *New Moon* again but TV is out," she said, as Vanessa and I were leaving.

"Sounds fair," I said as I pulled the front door shut.

I drove to Paralight, wondering if Jack was sitting in front of his computer watching my progress. I met Kendall in the locker room, and the two of us reported to the board meeting. Jack started the meeting with two high intensity films, a short and flashy opener for the conference and a longer, more thorough presentation about the speed of light technology and the human test flight with animation and visual effects that rivaled Hollywood films. The productions were to impress the reporters invited to the press conference, and the board was thrilled. I followed him with my presentation on the speed of light test flight, the mental effects of the flight, and my stay at the mental hospital. I explained that my dreams were more vivid and that sometimes I had had difficulty distinguishing dreams from reality, but that now I was fine. Mr. Turnbow asked how I felt another person would respond to a test flight. I grinned, cleared my throat portentously, and announced, "I'm sure Kendall can't handle it. If you want a real test pilot, I'm willing to go again."

They laughed; and after my presentation, Carter gave a report that showed my post-flight heightened physical capabilities. He attributed the heightened abilities to the cleansing process of having my physical body transformed completely into light. When my physical body was rebuilt, it was rebuilt without the impurities. He displayed charts and diagrams showing the tests he had conducted both before and after the test flight. Carter explained that I had run on the treadmill faster than any recorded human and that I was able to sustain the speed longer than we believed physically possible for human beings.

Mr. Turnbow, who sat at the head of the table, turned to me and quipped, "If you decide to go into professional sports, we will demand royalties."

I smiled, "I've just been hoping for a public setting with witnesses where I can arm-wrestle Kendall."

Board members around the large mahogany table smiled, and Kendall replied, "Impurities or not, I can beat him."

Mr. Turnbow looked at me as if I were his own son and said, "Tomorrow will be an entry into a new phase for Paralight, and you will become a very popular man. I will be proud to sit next to you at the press conference."

The meeting ended after a few more comments about the video presentations, and Mr. Turnbow thanked us for coming. Jack followed Kendall and me out of the board meeting and thanked both of us for being there. Later in the day, Jack called me to his office and told me he would be submitting his resignation following the second test flight. He would need to work with the company to get a replacement up to speed but assured me he would fulfill his part of our agreement. I left his office with a steely taste in my mouth, feeling disgusted. I knew I could not trust him, but I believed I had put him into a position where he must live up to his deal, and the proof was plainly being laid out in front of me. I felt more secure that our plan was working.

That evening Janet cooked a meal that was far from edible. She had fried frozen chicken, not realizing that she had to first thaw the meat. When we stuck our forks into it they scraped against ice; and after a few awkward looks across the table, we all laughed and ordered pizza. After we put Danny to bed, Vanessa and I stayed up talking about everything except Paralight. While we were reminiscing about a flight I had taken her on in high school, she pulled legal documents out of her briefcase and gave me a pen. Without mentioning the documents out loud, I signed them and was relieved to know that Jack and Paralight no longer had any authority over my son.

The next morning, I felt anxious during my drive to Paralight, wondering if Jack still believed I would continue in the deal. I could not park in my favorite space because Kendall had taken it with his Saab. I parked, went to Scarlet without encountering anything untoward, and changed into my flight suit. I spoke briefly with Kendall, but he soon left for an array of physical tests. I was scheduled for the simulator; and as I entered the large, circular room, I felt strangely at peace. The anxiety had subsided. The enthusiasm I had for the room was cracking through the walls I had built against it; and as I fastened my seatbelt, knowing that Don was nowhere near, I allowed myself to relax. I pulled the helmet on, and the readouts on the visor lit up as the small bridge to the cockpit retracted. The thousands of lights sprang up, creating a runway in front of me that extended along an oceanic paradise. Palm trees blew in the wind and the lush hills of Hawaii appeared.

"Jack wants to see you in the lobby," said one of the technicians through the speakers in the helmet.

"In the lobby?" I questioned as the lights dimmed and the holographic paradise around me faded.

"Yeah, ride's over. He said to shut it down."

"It didn't start," I insisted as the small bridge returned to the cockpit and I removed the helmet.

"Sorry," was the response.

I exited the simulator, walked along the balcony to the stairs leading to the exit from Scarlet where I entered the elevator. As the elevator doors opened to the lobby, I saw Jack standing with Lieutenant Johnny Drake. My nervous system sent a shock wave through my body, telling me this was a dangerous situation. I felt the muscles in my legs give way a little. I had no idea what to expect. I breathed as evenly as I could to keep my emotions in check as I walked to the front of the foyer where the two stood waiting for me.

Jack was the first to speak, "Pierce, Lieutenant Drake is investigating the case of Cole Trace and has asked me to get you and Don Parker up for questioning. I told him that Parker is no longer with the company, but that you were here."

"Hi, Johnny," I said.

"Why don't we go to a conference room?" suggested Jack.

"That'd be great," said Johnny.

In the conference room near Jack's office, Jack closed the doors behind us, and we sat at the table.

"Lieutenant, ask your questions," said Jack.

"First, Jack, thank you for offering your help in the investigation of the murder of Cole Trace. Perhaps you will not know some of the answers, but I would like to start with you."

Offering his help? I thought. *Did Jack set up this meeting?*

"Yes," said Jack.

"Cole worked here and was laid off as I understand."

"Yes, he was," answered Jack.

"When was he laid off and for what reason?"

"He was in the Legal Department, not my department. For that information, you will need to go to the Legal Department."

"Great," said Johnny, "After we're finished here, if you wouldn't mind accompanying me to the Legal Department, I would appreciate it."

"No problem," said Jack.

"Tell me about Don Parker," Johnny said to Jack.

"A test pilot we hired for a time."

"Did you hire him?"

"I did."

"Did you know him before you hired him?"

"I did not," answered Jack. I knew that was a lie.

"How did you know about him?"

"I review resumes and applications all the time, Lieutenant Drake. His was among them, and I interviewed and hired him. All that information will be in the HR files. Those files also have records of all communication between executives and employees."

Unless Jack deletes the information, I thought.

"You fired him?"

"We recently let him go," confirmed Jack.

"Why?"

"I cannot say," answered Jack.

Johnny rubbed his brow, then looked at Jack under his large hand, "I can make one call and have a warrant faxed to me in twenty minutes."

"You aren't my worry. I'm willing to cooperate with your investigation and release all information you need. However, we do not discuss confidential employee information in front of other employees," said Jack motioning toward me.

Johnny nodded in understanding.

Jack then asked, "Why are you so interested in Don Parker?"

"I have a dead body, and it was a murder. The hands and feet were tied, and the body was attached to a weight in the bottom of Lake Pleasant. I'm following all leads."

"You have a lead pointing at Don Parker?" questioned Jack.

"That's why I am here to talk to Pierce," Johnny said.

"By all means," agreed Jack.

"Pierce, you asked Vanessa Trace to run a license plate number for you and a home address a few days ago, right?"

I felt the accusation in Johnny's stare, and my defenses rose, "Just tell me where this is going," I demanded.

"Can you simply answer the question?" asked Johnny.

"We already talked," I said.

"We didn't talk. You refused to talk," he said back.

"I don't have anything else to say," I said.

"Then I'll need to take you down to the station," said Johnny.

"You have to charge me to do that," I said.

"I will," said Johnny, his eyes firm. "This is a clear murder, Pierce; and right now, in my mind, you orchestrated it."

I could see he would take me to the station and I finally said, "Yes, I asked Vanessa to run the license plate number and address."

Johnny continued, "How did you get the license plate number and home address of Don Parker?"

"I dreamed it," I said.

"You dreamed it?" he said with brow furrowed and frustration in his voice.

"Yes," I said, "That's the truth."

"Just like you dreamed the location of the body?" questioned Johnny.

"Yes."

"Did someone shoot at you at the gates of the mental hospital?" he asked.

"I thought someone did," I said. "Your detectives never found anything so that leads to the conclusion I dreamed that also."

I could see him getting frustrated. "Vanessa also asked me to run reports on a car crash on the freeway. What happened there?"

"I went there the following day and could find no evidence of the crash," I said. "You tell me what's real or not."

"A murdered man who used to work for this company is what is real," said Johnny emphatically.

"He is my brother-in-law," I said. "You think I don't want the killers to pay?" Jack shifted in his seat when I spoke those words, and Johnny relaxed a little.

"You dreamed it all?" Johnny said, almost to himself. He sat back in his chair, rubbed his forehead, and took a few breaths as he organized his thoughts; then he looked back at me, "I'll have more questions for you later." He looked to Jack and said, "I'd like to visit Legal."

Jack stood up, "I'll take you there now." The two left, but I stayed at the table with an uneasy feeling. Jack was orchestrating something, and I wanted to know what it was. I got up, and entered the elevator. I punched the button for 3, the level for the Human Resources and Legal Departments. As I walked down the hallway, the image of Jack and Don trapping me came to mind as the HR doorway approached. I passed the doorway and cautiously continued down the hall to peer into the archway leading to the Legal Department. Its reception area is a large room with black marble floors and brushed chrome pillars. A sleek, modern reception desk stood in front, with custom-built cubicles for paralegals and assistants in the next rank. Beyond them was a row of executive offices with glass walls. To the far right I could see Johnny and Jack in the large office of Cody Berkshire, the head of the Legal Department.

The receptionist lifted her head, and I stepped back. I turned and walked back down the hall to the Human Resources Department. Counting on Jack being distracted, I asked the secretary, "Is Rick in? I need to speak with him again."

"He is. Just a minute," she pushed a button on her console, "Pierce Black to see you." She looked back at me, "You can go right back."

I walked down the hallway and stepped into his office. I shuddered with the memory of facing Jack and Don right after my first meeting with Rick. "You gave me a printout last week with the contact info for Raymond Kent, Keri Reynolds, and Howard Hunt. Could you pull that up for me again?"

"Sure," said Rick. He hummed as he tapped his computer keys. "That's strange."

"What's strange?"

"I don't have the authority to view his information." He typed a bit more. "Same with the others."

"How's that? You just printed them up for me."

"I don't know," he said, "Could be a glitch. It happens sometimes. You could go to Jack—he'd have authority—or you might just try the phone book," he said with a smile.

"Thanks," I said. I walked down the hallway to the elevator where I used my card and descended to Scarlet. I went to my small office, locked the door behind me, and focused on my hands. The shimmers of energy rippled through the air as my hands came out. I stood out of my body. The room had the vivid brightness of being in a vision. I ran up the stairs to the third floor, down the hall to the Legal Department, past the cubicles, and into Berkshire's office. Berkshire was gray haired with high cheekbones, light blue eyes, and the deep wrinkles of a thinker. He was summarizing a monologue on facts and opinions: "Facts therefore, not opinions, are the basis for all employment decisions made in the Legal Department."

"And Cole Trace was a problem for you?" asked Johnny.

"A problem for the company," said Berkshire.

"That an opinion?"

"A fact," answered the attorney, "He returned repeatedly after he was fired—a clear breach of policy."

"Why was he returning?"

"I have no facts," answered Berkshire.

"There must have been a reason," said Johnny.

"Others have said it was for a case against the company," said Berkshire. "That he was copying documents. I have no knowledge of that."

"He was bitter," inserted Jack, "We get it a lot from employees who are let go. Pierce Black told me that Trace, who, as you know, was his brother-in-law, was preparing a lawsuit against Paralight and his actions were adding heavily to Pierce's already miserable marriage."

"Miserable marriage?" mumbled Johnny under his breath.

My miserable marriage? I thought.

"Yes, Pierce's wife was pulled into the case with her brother, and Pierce hated it," continued Jack.

I could see what Jack was creating—motive. And Johnny was taking it in.

Johnny looked back at Berkshire, "The fact is you fired Cole Trace for sloppy documents," said Johnny.

"I did," answered Berkshire.

"And you have copies of those documents?"

"I do," he answered.

"Can I get copies?"

"Of course you can." Berkshire picked up his phone and pressed a button, "Emily, would you come in for a moment?"

A young paralegal entered the office and Berkshire gave her instructions to retrieve several files and copy them. I looked at Jack, dismayed and angry. I needed to immediately gather evidence that would support a case against him before Johnny accepted that I had a motive for murdering Cole. With a flash of white light, I was sitting again in my body at my desk in my small office.

I needed to find those witnesses. I did not have a phone book in my office, but I went to Kendall's. He was out. As I sat at his desk, I saw the keys to his Saab next to the telephone. I found a phone book in his desk drawer and found three Raymond Kents, four Howard Hunts, and one K. Reynolds who may have been Keri. The first Raymond number had been disconnected; but I got an answer on the second.

"Hello," said a gruff male voice.

"Is this Raymond Kent?" I asked.

"It is," was the reply, followed by a hacking cough—the rough voice sounding much older than the assistant I had seen in Carter's lab with Cartwright the monkey.

"Are you the Raymond who worked at Paralight Technologies?"

"That would be my son."

"I'm a friend of his from Paralight and was hoping to get in touch with him again."

"I don't see much of him, but I can give you his mother's number."

He told me her name was Hannah and gave me the number. That number had also been disconnected, but I looked up the name and found an address in Mesa, east of Phoenix. The clock on the wall read 10:15 a.m. and the press conference didn't start until 1:30 p.m. I had time to get to Mesa and I had access to Kendall's Saab. If I left my car in the underground parking, Jack wouldn't know I'd left the building. In the locker room, I changed into street clothes and pulled on a baseball cap. As I walked through the building, I lowered my head as I passed each camera and walked directly to the Saab that was parked in my favorite spot. It took almost an hour to get to Mesa. The home was vacant and had a foreclosure sign on the door. After asking the neighbors, I found another number for Hannah.

I dialed the number from a phone booth, and a woman answered, "Hello?"

"Hi, is this Hannah Kent?" I asked.

"It is."

"I'm a friend of your son, Raymond, and need to get in touch with him right away. Would you give me his number?"

"He's at work and can't take calls."

"Would you tell me where he works?"

"A restaurant called the Desert Sun."

"Downtown, near the stadium?" I asked.

"Yes, that's it."

"Thank you very much." I knew exactly where the restaurant was and pulled into the restaurant parking lot just after noon. The place was packed. The floors were marble and the atmosphere modern. Flat-screen televisions were hung so that every table had a view of at least one. The main seating area was a media wonderland with a large projection screen, flanked by many smaller flat-screen televisions. What was on the screens varied greatly—most of them were sports channels, but some were of animals and others of history.

The hostess looked at me and said, "Just one today?"

"I'm actually not here to eat. I need to speak with Raymond Kent and I understand he works here."

"Could you come back in an hour? Right now is our busiest time." She looked behind me to the next customer.

Frustrated, I stepped into her line of sight, "I can't really. It is very important that I speak to him now."

"It is our policy that we don't allow servers personal time during the lunch hour."

"It's a police matter, and I don't have much time. It involves a murder case."

She looked closely at me, and her face turned to stone. Fear crept into her eyes. My words sank in, and she stumbled over her words, "You... I... I'll go... I'll go get him."

She disappeared into the crowded restaurant, and I waited as others were seated by another hostess. I was pleased that she had immediately changed her mind and decided to help, but the fear in her eyes bothered me. Was it the mention of police or her closer look at me that had triggered the fear?

A constant flow of customers were seated and leaving. A digital clock on the wall read 12:13. I had been waiting for more than eight minutes with no sign of the hostess. The press conference at Paralight was scheduled for 1:30, and it was a thirty-minute drive from downtown Phoenix. My eyes jumped from one television screen to another. In the central eating area, one of the games was interrupted by a news report. I recognized the reporter as a local anchorwoman but couldn't hear anything she was saying. A small photo appeared in the top right corner of the screen. I couldn't fully make out who it was, but it eerily resembled me. I walked into the main dining area to get a closer look. The picture had disappeared but images of Catherine and Cole followed. There was no sound on, but I'd seen enough.

A woman at a nearby table looked at me, then quickly focused on her food. The man across from her did the same, and the nervous tension of being hunted returned. A hand tapped my shoulder, and I spun around to see the young man I had seen in Carter's lab—Raymond Kent.

"Can I help you?" said Raymond, the hostess standing behind him.

My mind flashed to him chasing the monkey in the lab as the wires pulled computer equipment to the floor. It took me a moment to regain my composure. "Yes, yes, you most definitely can," I replied as the hostess returned to the reservation desk. "Can we take a seat?"

"I don't have time," he said with trepidation, "I have six tables and they're all waiting on me."

"I'll make this quick," I said. "You knew Cole Trace?"

"I did," he said. "I knew him from my last job."

"Right," I said. "I'm Pierce Black, his brother-in-law, and I work at Paralight."

"Okay," he said slowly. He was scanning the restaurant, not looking at me. He seemed to be looking out the windows.

"Cole was building a case against them and he told me you were willing to testify that you saw the monkey die."

"I...I met with Cole several times, but I don't want to get involved," he said, glancing toward the entry. I followed his glance and saw two uniformed police officers talking to the hostess. They looked in my direction, and the pieces came together in my mind. "Are they here for me?" I asked Raymond.

Panic formed on Raymond's face, and slowly he nodded.

My muscles tightened. Johnny Drake was behind this as well as Jack. I was sure of it. But I would not allow myself to be incarcerated. I needed options, and I looked down at my hands. A wave of warmth surged through me; I watched as the shimmer of energy emerged from my body and sinews of light lifted from my skin. My hands pulled out from my physical hands, and I stepped out of my body and rushed through the tables immediately beside me, the booths near the windows, and the restaurant wall.

Detective Calloway and another plain-clothes detective were jogging to the back doors. A black and white police car and an unmarked car were parked in front of the entryway to the restaurant, and a second black and white police car had just pulled in next to them. The officers from the third car slammed doors behind them as they sprinted to the front entry. *Jack is definitely involved,* I thought as Calloway, Jack's paid henchman in the police station, entered the back doors of the restaurant. I closed my eyes and with a flash of white light returned to my body.

I looked up. Raymond had stepped aside. A tall, fit officer with chiseled features, whose face was only inches from mine, pulled back slightly as I opened my eyes and looked at him. "Pierce Black?" he asked, his hand on his gun.

I nodded, "Is there a problem, officer?"

"You are under arrest for the murders of Cole Trace and Catherine Black," he said as he grabbed my arm with his free hand. "Please turn around."

The phrase reminded me of Don ordering me to turn around and my knowledge that Don would kill me. The same feelings overwhelmed me. I was under arrest for the murder of my wife and my brother-in-law. They must have enough evidence to charge me—evidence from Jack.

"Mr. Black, please turn around, and we won't make a scene."

"I didn't kill my wife," I said, my mind racing. His grip tightened on my arm, and he twisted, forcing me to turn around. I saw Calloway and the other officer approaching from the rear entrance. Claustrophobia engulfed me as I realized I was completely trapped and would soon find myself in a jail cell at the downtown Phoenix police station. From the cell, I would be dependent upon others to prove my innocence. The world would believe I had killed Catherine and Cole, and Jack would hide all contrary evidence. My freedom for the rest of my life depended on the seconds before the chisel-faced officer handcuffed me. I could see his free hand moving from his gun to his handcuffs. This was not my plan. My plan had been to make Jack and Don pay for the murders of Catherine and Cole. I would bring them to justice. *This is not justice,* I thought as the pressure built inside me.

"You have the right to remain silent," he said, and I made my move. I twisted and yanked my hand from his grasp. At the same time, I pulled the back of the chair of a man eating next to us. He shrieked and fell backward between me and the officer. The man's arms flailed and he grabbed the officer's shirt, ripping a button off and pulling Chisel Face down with him.

"Stop!" I heard in stereo from Calloway, approaching from the rear and the officer behind Chisel Face. I leaped onto the table of the man who was falling to the floor with Chisel Face. The other two diners at the table screamed. I jumped to the booths, brought my arms to my face and threw my body full-force through one of the large windows. It shattered. I squeezed my eyes shut and felt a rip in my shoulder. My body flew through the darkness, and I felt a stab of pain as my ribs hit the ground with a thud. I opened my eyes and saw a tear in the fabric at my shoulder and several nicks in my hands and forearms that were welling with blood. I rolled, sprang to my feet, sprinted across the small grass area, leaped across the hood of one of the police cars, and dashed through the packed parking lot to the Saab. As I ran, I pulled the keys from my pocket and frantically felt for the unlock button on the key chain. I found it and unlocked the doors just as I reached the car.

"Pierce! Stop!" It was Calloway as he and the others rushed through the parking lot.

I pulled the Saab door open and jumped in. As I slammed it shut, relief swept over me. The officers would have to run back to their cars, giving me a significant head start. I stabbed the key at the steering column, the location of the ignition on every car except a Saab. Naturally, I fumbled and dropped the keys. In a Saab, the ignition is on the console between the driver and passenger seats and I should have been used to it. The officers were approaching fast. I hit the door lock and groped below my legs.

"Open the door!" ordered Calloway, his hands slamming against the driver's side window. The four others yelled a chorus of orders as they banged on the other windows and tried the other doors. "Open it now!" Calloway ordered again, emphasizing the order with several more hard blows to the window.

Calloway pulled a nightstick from the belt of the uniformed officer next to him and cocked his arm to hit my window.

"The ignition is in the console!" I yelled.

He paused his swing, "What?"

"It's a foreign car!" I yelled as I found the keys. "The ignition is in the console." I continued more calmly as I shrugged my shoulders innocently.

He was not amused. "Open the door or I'll break the window," he threatened, glaring, as Chisel Face shoved through on the passenger side.

"Open it now!" ordered Chisel Face.

I twisted the key, and the engine roared to life, just as Calloway's nightstick shattered the window at my side. His big fist grabbed my blood-soaked shoulder. I slammed the car in gear and screeched backwards, ripping his hand loose, tearing my shirt even more. The other officers jumped back. Shifting the car into drive, I screeched forward and barreled out of the parking lot. Looking back, I saw Calloway nursing his arm and yelling frantically, while the others sprinted back through the parking lot to their cars.

I hit the brakes. The street was jammed, and I had been accelerating into a line of stopped cars. The Saab screeched toward the back of a compact car with two startled little girls in the backseat who swung their heads toward me, fear on their faces as I skidded toward them. Somehow the Saab came to a halt inches from the back of theirs. After a couple seconds of frozen eye-to-eye contact, the small girls turned to each other and laughed. I waved at them, then turned to see the parking lot behind me. The two black-and-white police cars barreled toward the parking lot exit with lights flashing and sirens blaring. Calloway's unmarked car was speeding through the parking lot. I reversed a little and swerved the Saab up onto the sidewalk. The few pedestrians immediately ran for the cover of the store doorways. I accelerated down the sidewalk and around the corner. The two police cars followed me down the sidewalk.

The next block was also packed with cars. I sped down the sidewalk, blasting on the horn. I stayed on the sidewalk around another screeching and honking corner; and half way down the following block, a woman with two small children yelled for her children to run. One child ran in her direction, but the other ran directly in front of the Saab. I swerved to the left to miss the child, scraped the side of a parked car, and swung onto the street where I saw the shiny grill of a large Dodge truck headed right toward me. I stepped on the gas, but the acceleration was not enough. The large, solid bumper clipped the back of the Saab, causing me to spin to the other side of the road where I came to a stop facing the oncoming traffic.

The car headed right toward me was Calloway's car with Calloway in the passenger seat. I slammed the Saab into reverse, tires squealing. I smashed into something with a loud crash, and my head jerked back against the head rest. I turned to see one of the other police cars. It had managed to get behind me after the truck had passed. Calloway's car stopped in front of me, and we had a moment of staring at each other. Then the other police car stopped to the right of the Saab. The sirens stopped, but lights kept flashing. I glanced quickly to the right, then looked back at Calloway. He held up his hand, signaling me to not move, and slowly opened his door. I could see blood dripping from his injured forearm as he pulled his gun from his holster and leveled it at me. "Out of the car, Pierce," he ordered.

In my rearview mirror, I could see Chisel Face step out of the car behind me. Again, I was trapped. The muscles in my throat tightened against the suffocation of claustrophobia. The muscles in my fingers twitched as they strained to hold tighter to the steering wheel. I could feel blood running down my arm from the cut in my shoulder and could hear my heartbeat accelerate. I looked again at Calloway, and my losses came crashing down on me. Catherine. Cole. The career of my dreams. My family. That world was gone, and I was facing the barrel of a detective's gun and the potential of spending the rest of my life in prison while my loved ones' murderers walked free. I could feel the pulse beating in my temples. My vision blurred from a flush of heat over my face. I was not going to live that life. My jaw locked with the strain and pressure. I looked to my left. The entrance to a parking structure was directly on my left, but Calloway's car was too close to mine to make the turn. Calloway looked at the parking entrance, then back at me as Chisel Face approached from behind. Calloway could see I was going to try for the entrance.

"Don't do it," he said forcefully, as his knuckles whitened on the hand holding the gun and his finger tightened on the trigger. The pressure that had built inside me released in a loud scream. I stepped on the gas, and the Saab lunged forward, clipping the bumper of Calloway's car, shoving it into his legs. His gun discharged, and the bullet hit my windshield directly in line with my head. Cracks spread across the windshield, but they moved slowly, like a time-lapse film of a plant growing. I saw the bullet penetrate the glass and punch its way through. Miniscule crystals of glass covered the nose of the bullet and slowly fell to the sides of the rounded tip as it came toward me. I thought of the time I had seen the bullet from Don's sniper rifle hanging in the air, and this moment was strangely similar. Specks of glass trailed behind the bullet in a wake of crystals that spun rhythmically. I could see a rainbow of colors made by the light coursing through the crystal dust. As the bullet slowly approached my face, I tipped my head to the side and watched it pass my cheek. The motion of its passing pressed against my skin as if warm, soft fingers touched my cheek, then time sped back to normal.

The crack of the bullet being fired sounded in my ears. So did the smashing of metal on metal from the collision of the two cars. The force sent Calloway toppling onto the hood of his car, and the Saab broke free from the trap. I heard another yell from Chisel Face as I accelerated into the parking structure.

Calloway ran after me, and the sirens from the police cars began again. As I made my way down the first row of cars and took the first corner, I saw the three police cars pursuing. I turned the corner to rise to the next level; and from the hood of a parked car, Calloway jumped and landed on my hood.

"Stop the car!" he demanded. He slammed the butt of his gun into the windshield, creating more webs of cracks. "Stop now!"

He raised his gun again, and I could see in his eyes that he was willing to kill me. I slammed my foot on the brakes, and the force sent him tumbling backward onto the hard surface of the parking garage. The two police cars and the unmarked car pulled around the corner behind me and accelerated as Calloway rolled and stood up in front of me, lifting his pistol. I stepped on the gas and accelerated toward him. In my mind, it became his life or mine, and I was fighting to survive. Calloway fired again, again hitting the windshield, but he was diving sideways to avoid being run down. I accelerated through the next turn and felt the car slide. The wheels spun and thrust me up the next rising aisle. I could see the downtown buildings outside the parking structure rising to the skies, and I realized that I was heading into another trap. At the top, I would be cornered. My options would be to jump to my death or to be taken into custody. I rejected both.

Another level passed at high speed with sirens and lights behind me, and then I saw the glass doors leading into the office building. Through them, I could see the parking elevators with another set of glass doors leading to elaborate elevators for the executive offices. Past them were large ornate doors leading to the reception area for a high-end company.

Without thinking, I made the decision. My muscles acted. I accelerated. Metal twisted, glass shattered, and the doors caved in from the impact of the Saab. The shattered glass sprayed past the parking elevators and hit the second set of glass doors at the same time the car smashed through them. Again the wrenching sound of metal tearing and glass crunching roared in my ears. I braced myself for a third impact. The large, ornate doors leading into the executive offices rushed toward me and caved in over my head as the car smashed through them.

The Saab slid to a halt in a large open reception area with a desk on the far side. Two secretaries were sitting behind it, their faces astonished. The sirens cut out as the falling debris of my attack on this innocent company settled. I looked back through the gaping wreckage I had left behind me leading to the parking structure. Chisel Face was running past the first set of smashed glass doors, followed by the other officers.

In front of me and to the left of the desk were two hallways that led to executive offices. Several businessmen in suits stuck their heads out of their offices and looked at the Saab and the settling debris with puzzlement. Behind me, to the right of the desk was a large open area housing cubicles. Through the large glass windows beyond them, I could see the mirrored glass of the neighboring skyscraper; and as I scanned the open area, I could see the buildings across the street and, in the distance, blue skies. I longed for the freedom of the skies but felt only the pressure of the approaching officers. Chisel Face had made it past the second set of smashed doors, and I knew I had to make the next decision.

I turned to one of the secretaries. "Would you tell me the best way out of here?"

Her eyebrows raised, and she answered, "The elevators."

Chisel Face, gun drawn and backed up by four other officers, was passing the executive elevators, "Hands in the air and out of the car!" he demanded.

"The elevators are out of the question," I said. I put the car in reverse and stepped on the accelerator. The wheels squealed as they spun on the marble floors. The car accelerated into the open area and cubicles zipped past. I held my breath, hoping that I would live more than the next few seconds. By the time, the bumper of the Saab passed through the windows on the far side of the open area, I was going fast enough that the cubicles and frightened employees were merely blurs. Another deafening crash roared in my ears, and again shattered glass rained around the car, some fragments streaming through the broken window at my side and spraying across my cheek. Sunlight hit my hands. The mirrored windows of the building I was leaving stretched across my view and I could see the street to my right as I sailed through the air. I braced myself for an impact, closed my eyes, and heard another crash as the back bumper crashed into the windows of the other skyscraper. I was smashed into the back of my seat, which gave way from the force of the impact, and I lay pinned by pressure seeing dust and debris engulf the car. The car slid backward along a floor and smashed through two sheetrock walls, coming to a stop halfway into a second office.

Through the crashing, I heard a loud, high-pitched scream. I was on my back looking through the heavy dust at the fabric of the ceiling of the car when a yell echoed, "What in this great earth!"

I felt a wave of panic. I was alive, but *had I killed anyone in this building?* My heart stopped with the thought. I moved my head slightly to see if I had broken my neck. It seemed fine. My fingers also worked. I moved my legs and felt assured that I had survived the jump intact. I sat up and, through the dust, saw a woman sitting at a desk behind the cracked rear window.

"Who are you and what are you doing in my office?" she exclaimed.

I unbuckled my seatbelt and climbed through the side window of the Saab. She was pinned against the wall behind her by her desk, which rested against the back bumper of the Saab. "You okay?" I asked as I moved toward her.

"Do I look okay?" she demanded.

"Are you hurt, anything broken?"

"I'm not comfortable," she said, looking at the desk pressing against her stomach. Another six inches and she would have been cut in two.

"Looks like you made it," I said. I looked at the complete destruction of the office across the hall from her, "Anyone in that office?"

"He's out of town," she said and the weight of taking an innocent life lifted slightly.

"Lucky day," I said as the dust dissipated enough that I could see there were no bodies in the debris.

"What just happened?" she pressed. "Who are you?"

"You'll be hearing about me on the news," I said as I rushed into the debris and looked through the gaping hole at the other side of the destroyed office. Officers were standing at the cavernous hole in the other office tower up one story from where I stood. Chisel Face and I stared at each other. His head shook in disbelief, and he raised his radio to his mouth.

Seconds—that's all I had. Police would swarm into the building, and I needed to get out. I ran from the office, turned down the hallway, and emerged from the settling dust and debris into a crowd of cautious, well-dressed businessmen and women.

"Who are you?" questioned one of the men.

"Very crowded on the streets. You mind parking it for me?" I asked as I handed him the keys. He looked at me astonished as

I pushed past him. "Whatever you do, don't scratch it!" I yelled back as I pulled open a doorway marked Stairs.

I leaped down the stairs as quickly as my legs would carry me and was soon on the main level. I brushed as much of the debris off my shoulders and shirt as I could and stepped into the foyer of the office building. The well-dressed people waiting for the elevators looked at me with surprise. I saw my reflection in the glass of a coffee shop near the elevators and shook my head. I looked like an injured construction worker in a sea of fashion models. I was a walking disaster. My shirt was torn and red with blood near my shoulder, small scrapes and cuts marred my exposed skin and face, and I was covered with a layer of white dust. As I walked toward the security desk to the right of the entry doors, the blue-suited guard, who was on his phone, eyed me suspiciously and replaced the handset.

"Excuse me, sir," said the guard. Outside the glass doors, a police car came to a stop. Two officers jumped out and ran toward the building, eyes fixed on me through the glass doors. There was no mistaking that they knew who I was. The guard was now on his feet. "Sir, can I speak with you a moment?"

I turned and ran the other way, past the elevators and down a long hallway, hoping to find another exit. An exit sign pointed down a hallway to the right, and I sped in that direction. I saw doors with the same sign above them and burst through them into the alley behind the glass tower. A police car was driving down the alley toward me and immediately hit the siren and lights. I ran away from the accelerating car. Heat swept over my body, and time again slowed down. I pulled away from the pursuing police car, and the walls of the alley sped by faster. A glow emanated from my body and I could see ripples in the air around my skin, much like the ripples I would see when I was entering a vision—but I was not leaving my body. I reached the end of the alley much faster than I had expected; and when I looked forward, it was too late to change direction. A large diesel truck with a double trailer was passing by directly in front of the alley, and I was going to smash into it. I raised my arms to protect my face from the impact, the glow from my skin intensified, and instinctively I jumped. I sailed into the opening between the two trailers. To the right and left of me were trailers; and below me, I saw the heavy bars connecting the two. I fended off the rear trailer, pushing away from it and sailed out between the two trailers, high above the ground. I had plenty of time to shift my weight, preparing for a landing on the opposite sidewalk. I safely rolled into the alley between two other buildings and leaped up, sprinting, my skin still glowing. Near the end of the second alley, I slowed my pace and the world gradually sped up. The glow faded, and the ripples in the air around my skin disappeared.

I walked onto the crowded street and saw a bus with "Mesa Express" on the front read-out. I pulled out my cell phone, turned it on, and jammed the phone into the bus's back bumper as it pulled away from the curb. Then I sprinted across the street into a hotel.

I heard police sirens coming from several directions, and I knew they were all looking for me. I found a pay phone in the lobby, dropped in a quarter, and dialed my cell. Johnny Drake would trace the call, I was sure of it. When the voicemail picked up, I set the handset on the shelf in the phone booth, grabbed a green jacket left on a chair near a fireplace, and ducked into a bathroom.

I turned on the faucet and stared at my reflection. Dried specks of blood flecked my cheek where sprays of shattered glass had torn the skin, and my shoulder was caked with blood. I cupped my hands in the cold water and splashed it on my face. The dried-up blood came off easily, but below it I could see no trace of the cuts that made the blood. I stared in disbelief at my unscathed skin. It was smooth and clean. I scooped up another handful of water and carefully washed my shoulder. It was the same. The deep gash from my dive through the window at the Desert Sun restaurant was gone. Somehow the wounds had healed. I fingered my shoulder, confused. My body had healed itself as I had run. I pulled off my torn and bloodstained shirt, washed the blood from the sleeve, and wrung it out. The red-stained water swirled down the drain. I finished washing my shoulder, splashed water on my hair, finger-combed it, and dried myself as best I could with paper towels. I put my shirt back on and buttoned the green jacket over it. I looked almost presentable. I took a deep breath and exited the restroom.

Chapter 16

I made my way through the hotel and out a back exit into another alley. The sounds of the police sirens were fading to the east—heading toward Mesa. I grinned as I thought of the scene when they caught up with the bus. I walked down the alley and onto the sidewalk fronting the street, then entered the shopping mall, avoiding eye contact. My nerves were still on edge, but I felt safe. I had escaped the chase. I was no longer trapped. I thought about Danny. *Would the police go after him?* I stepped into an electronics store, purchased a pre-paid cell phone, and dialed Janet's cell.

"Hello?" said Janet.

"Janet, this is Pierce. Is everything okay?"

"Yeah, everything's great," she answered.

"Danny okay?"

"We're both okay," she said in her typical, distracted way.

"Anyone come to the house?"

"Nope, pretty dead here," her nonchalant attitude told me she was watching some video and was oblivious to the news reports about me.

"I've got a new phone. Program this number. If you need me, call me here. Call me if anyone comes to the house."

"Is someone coming?" she asked, still distracted.

"No, but the police may come. If they do, call me."

"The police?" She sounded suddenly alert.

"Don't worry. If they come it will be to help us," I lied. I did not want her to worry. "Just call me if anyone comes."

Next I dialed Vanessa's number.

"This is Vanessa Trace," Vanessa's voice was comforting.

"Vanessa, it's me," I said.

"Pierce, you're all over the news. Are you okay?"

"I'm okay, but I don't know why they're after me. Drake let me walk away this morning."

"A judge issued a warrant for your arrest after Drake showed him daily logs at Paralight detailing your stress and distaste with Catherine and Cole previous to their deaths," said Vanessa. "Did you write daily logs at Paralight?"

"I did," I said. "Every day and sent them to Jack, but they were never anything personal, never anything about Catherine and Cole."

"It was incriminating, Pierce, approaching psychotic. He also had emails connecting you with Don Parker."

"Jack is changing the originals," I said. No surprise there.

"They have motive, and your running has made it worse. They have a strong case. Without opposing evidence, you could be convicted. They think you orchestrated the murders." She paused, thinking. "If he changed the logs, there will be proof. What can prove it?"

I flashed on Jack's face, smiling smugly, just as he had when we were in visual looking at Don's attack in the simulator. *The computers don't lie,* he had said after watching Don come within inches of taking my life. I remembered my anger as I had left visual and walked down the hall past the Scarlet servers. Then I had an idea. "If he changed the logs, the database will display the changes, but the servers register the dates and times keystrokes are entered. The server discs would show times and dates Jack made the changes to my logs."

"Do you know where the servers are?"

"I walk past them every time I go to visual."

"Get to those server discs before he destroys them or has them altered," she said. "They could prove your innocence."

I disconnected the line and was soon on the street again where I waved down an approaching taxi.

"Head west on the 10," I said. The driver nodded and made his way west.

I slouched in the seat and let my nerves calm, but my mind was replaying the events of the last hour. I had watched a bullet come through the windshield at me and had avoided it by tipping my head sideways. I had driven a car from one office building to the next one. I had effortlessly outrun a police car and jumped the four lanes span of a city street. My wounds had healed. I again felt my shoulder. The skin was smooth, without so much as a scratch, even though the shirt was still damp and torn.

"Where to?" questioned the taxi driver as he took the on-ramp of the I-10.

"I'll tell you when to exit," I said.

I directed him toward Paralight; and as we approached the building, I asked him to drive slowly. I saw several press and television vans in the visitors' parking area. A police car was there also. I looked at my watch. 1:36. The press conference was already underway.

"Stop at the next building," I said to the taxi driver, indicating Syndeo, the company to the north of Paralight. I paid the driver, ran past the main building of Syndeo, and climbed the fence to Paralight in my usual place. Under the cover of the bushes and landscaping along the fence of Paralight property, I took several long, controlled breaths to slow my heart rate and to focus my thoughts. I needed to know what I would be facing in Paralight. The press conference was in the Scarlet hangar and so were the servers. Most of the company would be there, so entry would be easy; but my primary concern was the police car. Were the officers there for press conference security or to arrest me?

I pushed aside a branch so I could see the police car, and I focused my attention on it. Ripples appeared around me, and the bushes flickered away into streams of light that rebuilt the parking lot around me. The police car came to a stop in front of me. I stood up in the clear and vivid world of a vision that I felt was only slightly in the past. Two tall officers stepped out of the car and walked toward the Paralight entry. I looked at the watch that one of them was wearing. 1:28. They had arrived only minutes before me. Johnny was covering all bases. As some officers were pursuing my phone, he had sent others to Paralight. I followed them through the doors to the front reception desk. The stairway leading down to Scarlet was open. Rick from Human Resources and a security guard stood next to a sign reading Press Conference.

"We're looking for Pierce Black," said one of the police officers.

"He should be at the press conference down the stairs," said the receptionist. "Are you here for the conference?"

"No, just for Mr. Black."

"Let me make a few calls. I'm sure we can get permission to take you down so you can speak with him."

"That would be great," said the officer.

The receptionist picked up her phone and dialed an extension. I had seen enough—the officers were there to arrest me. I pulled myself out of the vision, and the colors of the foyer melted away into a bright, white light.

I looked at my watch. 1:42. Twelve minutes into the conference. The conference was supposed to start with the one-minute opener video, after which Mr. Turnbow would speak. Jack would then speak and play the longer media presentation displaying the speed of light plane and explaining the scientific research behind the speed of light technology. Following that it would be my turn to answer questions from the media. During the media presentation would be the best time for me to make my way to the balcony and into the server room without being noticed. Mr. Turnbow was a man of few words, and I wondered how long Jack would speak. I needed to move quickly. I stood up, crossed to the side entry of Paralight, and opened the door. The hallway was empty. When I came to the corner leading to the main foyer, I peered around it. The receptionist was the only one I could see. I continued down the hall and entered the foyer to see Rick and the security guard by the stairway.

"Rick," I said, "you don't get to see the show?"

Rick smiled. "No, that's the drawback of my position." His expression then changed to worry, "You're on the panel, and it's already started."

"I know," I said, walking by him. The doorway to the stairs was closed, and I did not want to use my card. "Will you open it for me?"

"Sure," he said with his overly wide smile.

I descended the concrete stairway, cracked open the door to Scarlet, and checked the hallway. It was empty except for a thin technician who was standing near the entry to the hangar as an usher. He looked at me in surprise. I instantly laid my finger on my lips. Without speaking, he walked toward me. As I moved forward, I could hear Jack's voice over the speakers coming from the hangar.

"Everyone's been looking for you," the technician whispered. His name tag read "Ted."

"I know," I responded in hushed tones. "They haven't started the presentation?"

"No, but the opener was mind-blowing!" he said—his voice rising with excitement.

"Shhhh," I said, again putting my finger to my lips.

"Oh, right," he whispered. "How cool to be the one who flew that plane." His face was that of a comic-book-collecting, star-struck techie.

"Some police came to meet me. Did you see them?" I asked.

"Yeah, they're right around the corner."

"I want to talk to them after the show, not before. Could you help me get by them and to the balcony when the presentation starts?"

"Like covert?" said Ted, his smile widening.

"Yeah, covert," I answered. "I need to get to the server room before my turn on the panel. Can you come with me?"

"Sure," he smiled.

"When the lights go out, we'll walk past the hangar opening, you on my right."

"You've got it."

I could hear Jack wrapping up his speech: "…this is a day, years in the making. I present to you the speed of light."

The lights turned off, and I grabbed Ted's arm, pulling him along on my right as we passed the opening to the crowded hangar. I pressed forward to the stairs and was soon on the balcony. An explosion of light appeared on a screen on the far side of Scarlet, and footage of Stormlight flying raced across the screen. I saw the crowd of about thirty television crews with cameras and reporters hugging the stage, built directly under the balcony where I was standing. On the stage was the table where Mr. Turnbow, Jack, Kendall, Carter, and three members of the board of directors sat. Eight seats total, and seven people occupying them. My seat, between Jack and Mr. Turnbow was conspicuously empty. Behind the press were hundreds of folding chairs filled by employees of Paralight. Against the hangar's far wall was an impressive display of hovercrafts, surrounding the company gem, the sleek speed of light plane, Stormlight.

"Ooohs" and "Ahhhs," emanated from the audience as the presentation continued.

With all attention on the presentation, I made my way to the door of the server room. "Ted, will you open it for me?"

"Uh…" he hesitated. "You know we're not supposed to use our cards for others..."

"My card's in the locker room," I said.

"Uh, okay," he said, "For you I'll do it." Again the sci-fi-lover's smile lit his face.

I nodded, and he swiped his card. The door opened and we entered. The stacks of machines were labeled. I had been in the room about a year ago when one of the technicians was having trouble with the programming for one of the hovercrafts and had had to retrieve some information from the discs. I had had nothing better to do, so I had accompanied him. He had pulled the discs from the RAID (Redundant Array of Independent Disks), which is the core of the servers for each department. The rack containing all of the machines for Scarlet was about halfway through the room and clearly labeled Scarlet. I quickly found the rack and pulled open the first disc chamber. It was empty. I pulled open the next. Empty. I quickly pulled open all the chambers—all empty. Jack had taken them all. I thought of Rick, searching fruitlessly for information. Jack had tightened all permissions from accessing server data from the Scarlet servers because he had removed the discs. He had doctored my logs, and the police had obtained a warrant for my arrest. Then he had removed all the discs that would prove he had made changes.

It was as if a chasm in the earth had opened, and I was falling through the air. I was helpless. The ground was approaching, and I had no way to brace for the crash. The claustrophobia of a prison cell engulfed me as I fell. It was only a matter of time before the police caught me, and a jury would be listening to the evidence that I had hated my wife and my brother-in-law. They had motive. I had known the location of Cole's body. I had no contrary evidence other than my crazy visions. Jack had connected me to Don and set us up as co-conspirators. From far away, I heard a phone ring. It was not the ring I was used to. The sound got louder. It was coming from my pocket—the new cell phone. The caller ID showed Janet's number.

"Janet?"

I heard sobs, then, "He's gone!" She choked on her sobs and struggled to speak. "He took him. I couldn't stop him. He broke through the door, hit me, and took Danny."

My heart sank, and I sputtered, "Who took Danny? Was it the police?"

"No. He was wearing a black mask. He was all black. He took Danny. He's gone... Danny is gone," Janet continued to sob.

"Is everything okay, Pierce?" asked Ted.

I looked at him, "No, it's not. Nothing is okay." The lights in the hangar outside again turned on to applause. I felt sick. My son had been taken—kidnapped, and people were applauding.

"I'm sorry, Mr. Black," Janet sobbed.

"Janet, I'll take care of this," I said. I pocketed the phone, brushed past Ted, and hurried to the exit. Jack was responsible for kidnapping Danny, and Don was the kidnapper. Danny's life became all that mattered.

Jack's voice again filled the hangar, "The flight was a success. Traveling the speed of light is no longer fiction, but a reality. A human being has traveled the speed of light, and Paralight Technologies is the company that created the technology." Applause followed. I looked over the balcony and could see the two police officers near the entrance. Some of the reporters were standing, waving to get Jack's attention. Jack pointed to one of them.

"Is the Pierce Black, who is being charged with murdering his wife and his brother-in-law, the pilot of the speed of light plane?" asked the man.

"He is," answered Jack. "Life has its unfortunate twists"—he paused effectively and added, "We are cooperating with the investigation; and although the evidence has led the police to press charges, our prayers are with him and his son."

Ice coursed through my veins, and anger at Jack seared against the ice. He had created evidence to lead to a warrant for my arrest and ordered the kidnapping of my son, then claimed he was praying for us! I had no more control than an avalanche storming down a mountainside. My legs took me from the doorway of the server room to the railing above the media panel; and in one fluid motion, I was over the edge and sailing down to the table behind which Jack was standing. I heard a scream from the audience, then the table crashed under the impact of my feet. I rolled onto the stage. The people on the panel, shoved away from the collapsing table, yelling. Jack's face showed astonished amusement. "Pierce?"

"Where is my son?!" I yelled with a fury I had never before felt.

"What are you doing, Pierce?" asked Jack. I lunged toward him, my fist connecting with Jack's jaw with all my strength. He toppled backward off the stage and sprawled on the ground.

"Pierce, what is going on?" questioned Mr. Turnbow.

Cameras were flashing, and I turned to the crowd, yelling, "Jack Jones ordered the murder of my wife and her brother, Cole Trace, and Don Parker killed them. Now they've taken my son." The officers near the entry were running toward me. I jumped from the stage and pushed the button on the wall that opened the far hangar door that led to the surface behind Paralight. I pushed through the media and the audience. The employees of Paralight were, for the most part, on their feet, stunned by the events on the stage. They didn't try to stop me as I pushed past them with the police in pursuit. I sprinted to the X1 on display next to Stormlight, leaped aboard, fired up the engines, and, just as the police reached the hovercraft, circled it around, smashing the rear side into their chests, sending them sliding backward across the floor. I thrust the X1 through the door and up the ramp, and I was quickly in the upper hangar. The large doors to the surface hanger were open, and I swerved out of the hangar. The office buildings were a blur as I sped past them; and Alex, in the guardhouse at the gate, gawked at me in dismay as I blazed out of Paralight and onto the streets. I pulled out the cell phone and dialed 911. A police operator answered and I demanded, "Get me Lieutenant Drake!"

"This is not the line to the police headquarters..."

"I don't care! Get him now! My name is Pierce Black. He'll take my call."

"Hold, please."

I swerved in and out of traffic; and a few moments later, I heard "This is Drake."

"Drake! They've taken my son! Get to my house!"

"Pierce?"

"Jack is responsible. He's taken my son!"

"Pierce, you need to turn yourself in," he said sternly.

"I'll turn myself in! I'll tell you everything! Just get to my house now!" I hung up and concentrated on flying. I zigzagged through the traffic and roared up the on-ramp to the freeway. I decided to give the X1 the ultimate test and pushed the thrust to full speed. I sped down the freeway and skimmed past several cars. I took the side mirror off a pick-up truck, and my front right propulsion jet jammed into the front bumper causing me to spin in front of a diesel truck. I put all power in the left jets, and it stopped the spin. Another full thrust pulled me away from the diesel. I regained control, but the propulsion jet was bent slightly, which caused the steering to slide. I had lost the tight cornering ability the techs had worked so feverishly to create, but I was still in control.

I exited near my neighborhood but could not corner correctly and slid across traffic lanes, smashing sideways into an SUV. I thrust the engines and took off down the street sideways, dragging two of the propulsion jets along the asphalt leaving a stream of sparks behind me. Cars swerved to avoid me; and at the next intersection, a sedan sideswiped me. I lost control, and the hovercraft slid into a light post, sending it toppling to the ground. I jumped away from the twisted metal and sprinted down the street. I sped faster than I had thought possible and felt as though I was hovering above the ground. The glow again emanated from my body, and time slowed down as I raced past homes and trees to my house. As I rushed through the broken front door, the world around me sped up to normal.

Inside Janet was sitting on the sofa, holding a blood-stained cloth to her forehead and crying. "I tried to stop him," she said.

"Are you okay? Let me see your forehead." I gently pulled her hands back to see a deep gash above her right brow.

"I couldn't stop him," she continued. "I tried, Mr. Black. I really tried."

Her cell phone rang, and we both looked at it on the table. No name showed on the screen, just a number.

"You recognize that number?" I asked.

"No," she said.

"Answer it," I instructed.

She picked up the phone, "Hello?" After a pause she held it out to me, "It's for you."

I put it to my ear, "This is Pierce."

"Not a good move, Pierce," said Jack, his voice stone cold. "You bring me the tape and all copies, or Danny will not live to see the sun set. I will call you in one hour and tell you where to bring them. Do not let me down."

"Cole gave you everything, and you still killed him," I countered.

"That's the past. Concern yourself with your son."

"Even if I bring you all the copies, how can I know you'll let us live?"

"You can't, but you have no choice," he said. He was quoting my own words when I had made the deal with him. I could hear his smile through the words. The phone went dead, and I stood in silence in my shattered house without my son.

Chapter 17

I handed the phone back to Janet. I had one hour to get the tape of the conversation between Jack and Cole and take it to Jack so he could destroy the evidence connecting him to the murders. The problem was that there was no evidence.

"What did he say?" Janet asked.

Without answering, I looked at the lock on the door. The masked man in black had smashed through the front door, breaking the lock. I turned the doorknob. The latch was bent and twisted, the door frame was splintered. There had been no sign of the break-in when I had inspected the front door with Johnny and Vanessa, but now the evidence was right in front of me.

"Janet, the man who took Danny was wearing all black?" I asked.

"Yes," she answered.

"He had a black mask?"

"Yes, a ski mask, I couldn't see his face…"

"And he smashed through the front door?"

"Yes," she answered. "I tried to stop him, and he hit me. He knocked me down and took Danny."

Danny had explained, *"The past is clear, the future blurry."*
During the stake-out, the man in black had been blurry although
the house and the trees were clear. It made sense. The man in
black had been blurry because he did not exist at the time of the
stake-out. I had seen the future, and it had happened just as I had
seen it. If I had seen the future once, I could do it again.

I sat down, closed my eyes, and focused on Danny, con-
centrating all my energy on the idea of where Danny was and
what was going to happen to him. The walls around me turned
to wisps of light and reformed into a dingy bedroom. The walls
and room were clear and vivid like all of my visions, but on the
floor was Danny's blurred figure, tied and motionless on a mat.
His body was transparent, and I could see the dirty mat under
him. I understood that this was the future. Danny was staring
at the wall and looked very uncomfortable. My heart ached for
him. I knelt down beside him and tried to touch his cheek. My
hand went through his cheek. Danny was helpless, and I was unable to help him.

I left the room and walked down a hallway to the battered
living room. On a chair facing the front window was the blurred
figure of Don in black, watching the front yard intently. Beside
him on the armrest of the chair was a gun with a silencer. To find
out where I was, I ran through the front door and onto the dried
grass of the front lawn. The sun was setting. I immediately knew
the place. It was in Scottsdale, not far from the freeway. The red-
brick house was small, rickety, and abandoned. A blurred and
slightly transparent police car stopped at the curb a short distance from the house. Johnny Drake and another officer, both of
them blurred got out and looked around. I saw a blurred image
of myself climbing out of the rear seat. The three blurred figures

slowly moved down the sidewalk, avoiding a direct line of sight to the house. I saw another blurred police car drive down the street from the other direction and stop at the curb. Two blurred officers stepped out of the other car and looked to Johnny for directions. Johnny gestured for them to proceed slowly.

I turned to see Don staring through the living room window at the left side of the yard where Johnny was approaching. He picked up his gun. I looked back at Johnny. He signaled for the other police officers to circle through the neighbor's yard to the back of the house. The officers moved in that direction and Don retreated into the hallway leading to the bedroom. Johnny peered around the bushes and looked through the window; seeing no movement, he rushed for the front door in a crouch, with the second officer and me following. I stepped into the house through the door and went down the hallway. Don was in a back room, opposite the room where Danny was. He had seen the officers approaching and had opened a window slightly. The officers had not seen him and leaped over the low fence dividing the yards. Just as the second officer cleared the fence, Don fired twice. Both officers dropped to the ground. Don returned to the hallway and waited.

There was a knock at the front door. Don waited a moment longer, leveled his gun at the door and fired six shots, then rushed to the door and kicked it open. It splintered off the hinges, smashing into Johnny who was mortally wounded, with blood gushing from bullet holes in his chest and neck. The other officer had also fallen back with a chest round. The blurred figure of me was clutching a bleeding shoulder. Don fired again into the officer, grabbed me, slammed me into the brick exterior wall, and dragged me inside. I was moaning as he dragged me down the hallway and into the room with Danny, unable to struggle.

Don threw me down next to Danny. The blurred image of me put my arms around my son. "Let him go," I told Don. "Do what you want with me."

"This is over," said Don and shot Danny in the head.

"No!" screamed my blurry image. I clutched Danny, screaming, "Not you, Danny. Not you."

Coldly, Don fired three bullets into my blurry image. My blurred body struggled for breath and clutched harder to Danny, then went limp. As I watched, tears streamed down my face. Don, without emotion, unscrewed the silencer from his gun and left. I watched, paralyzed, as the blood drained from our bodies, pooling on the floor. A soul-wrenching scream burst from my throat, and the dingy walls of the house burst into a flash of white light, ending the vision. I was back at my house screaming.

"Mr. Black? What's wrong with you! Mr. Black!?" screamed Janet. I heard her frightened voice and struggled to regain control. "Mr. Black, are you okay?"

I was shaking with rage and torment, unable to speak.

"Please, Mr. Black, are you okay?"

I stood up but fell back to the floor. My balance was gone. Leaning against a chair, I pulled myself to my feet; and as I did so, I saw a police car parked in front of my house. Johnny Drake and the other officer I had seen with him in the vision were walking to the door. I knew what was going to happen. They were going to die. I was going to die, and so was Danny. I could not let it happen.

"It's got to change," I said to Janet. "It's got to change!"

"What?" she demanded, confused.

"I'm not letting Danny die," I said as the doorbell rang. The future had not yet happened, and I would make it change. The fury in my soul mounted, and I unleashed it. I yanked open the damaged door, put all my weight behind my fist, and punched the officer standing next to Johnny. He staggered backward and collapsed to the ground. Johnny stood paralyzed, gaping at me. I leaped to the officer's side, pulled out his gun, and leveled it at Johnny. He blinked and put his hand on his gun.

"Don't do it!" I screamed.

Johnny dropped his hand.

"Give me your gun," I demanded.

"You're making a big mistake, Pierce."

"Give it to me now!" I insisted. I fired a shot past him and into my lawn.

He carefully pulled the gun from his holster and handed it to me, butt first. I put the gun in my belt and stepped past Johnny. I glanced back and saw Janet in the doorway, a look of stunned horror on her face, still holding the blood-stained cloth to her forehead.

"Keys to the car," I demanded.

"You don't want to do this, Pierce," said Johnny.

"The keys," I said firmly.

Johnny reached into his pocket, pulled out his keys, and handed them over. I ran to the cruiser and started it. I fumbled through the buttons, turned on the siren, put it in gear, and slammed my foot on the gas. The sirens and lights blared, and the wheels screeched as they spun. The patrol car careened down the street. I looked in my rearview mirror. Johnny was standing in the street yelling at me.

As I rounded a corner out of my subdivision, I turned on the police radio and announced, "I have just stolen Lieutenant Drake's police car, and I want to speak with Vanessa Trace of the district attorney's office."

"You have stolen Lieutenant Drake's squad car?"

"Yes. Call me when you have Vanessa Trace."

"I can't do that."

"Tell Drake I will speak only with Vanessa Trace," I said and hung up. I saw another police car driving toward me, lights flashing and siren blaring and swerved the police car I was driving over the curb and into a park. I accelerated across the grass and hills and screeched onto the street on the opposite side. The police officer in the other car followed with one hand on the steering wheel and the other on his radio. I saw another police car coming down the street from the other direction. As I accelerated, the second police car swung around and pursued me along with the first. I continued swerving through traffic. Other police cars joined in. I counted seven cars by the time I heard Vanessa's voice on the radio.

"Pierce, this is Vanessa."

I picked up the radio, "They took Danny!"

"What are you doing, Pierce?"

"Don broke into my house, hit Janet, and took Danny!"

"Pierce, you stole a police car?"

"Vanessa, it was a blur. I saw the future," I said.

"What are you talking about?"

"At my house, the man in black was a blur. It was the future."

"You're not making sense, Pierce," she said.

"Danny explained it."

"Danny can't speak."

"He spoke to me," I insisted.

"You have to listen to me, Pierce. What you're doing now will not help anything. You have done the worst possible thing. You need to stop," she pleaded.

"I'm changing things."

"Not one thing you have said has made any sense," I could hear desperation in her voice.

It was too hard to explain. I would have thought I was crazy, too, hearing what I was trying to explain to her. "I'm rescuing Danny. That's the only thing that makes sense." I hung up the radio and flipped the off switch. I turned a corner onto a large main road and saw a police helicopter hammering overhead. I stepped on the gas and sped ahead, siren wailing. More police cars swarmed onto the main road from all directions. I turned onto another big street and sped through a red light. A car hit the back end of my police car, sending me screeching around the corner. I continued down the street and pulled onto the freeway. Behind me was a sea of red and blue lights.

Two other helicopters appeared above—one police and the other a news station. I turned the police radio back on and kept driving, swerving through traffic. Johnny's voice came through the radio.

"Pierce, can you hear me?" said Johnny. I picked up the handset; and as I did, I saw a police barricade set up across the freeway in front of me. "Pierce, tell me what you want. Why are you doing this?"

"I'm getting my son," I said flatly. "Order the cars in the blockade to move out."

"This isn't the way to do it. Stop the car, and I'll help."

In the vision, Johnny and I had approached the house together. If I stopped, Johnny would help, but we would not survive. "If I do, we're all dead," I told him.

"Stop the car!" he repeated.

"I'm not stopping the car, and I don't want to hurt your officers. Tell them to move!" I pressed the accelerator to the floor
and the car leaped ahead. At the blockade, officers holding riot
guns and shotguns ran for cover. I aimed for what I thought was
the weakest point and battered my way through the two angled
two police cars. They spun aside. The hood on my car was man-
gled and blocked the center of my vision, but the car kept going.
I saw the exchange for the 101 freeway and took it. I was very
close to the house where Don was holding Danny.

I pulled off the freeway and careened through the residential
area. Police cars flooded the streets, and the helicopters were
now flying lower. I saw the street where the abandoned house
stood, turned onto it, and accelerated. The house came up quickly, and I veered over the curb of the neighboring house, tore
through the bushes separating the yards, and smashed directly
into the living room where Don had been sitting. The impact
made a deafening sound as the vehicle ripped apart metal and
brick. My head smashed forward into the deploying air bag, daz-
ing me. Bricks, shards of wood, and sheetrock smashed through
the windshield and cut into the passenger seat. Dust was everywhere as the car came to an abrupt stop. I struggled to stay conscious and, through adrenaline-enhanced will, kept my bearings.
I unsnapped my seatbelt and shoved open the driver's door with
my foot. Metal scraped on metal, the shriek filling the room. The
dust was suffocating, and I could not see as far as the walls in
front of me. I knew where Don had been; he had been sitting in

the chair across from the window. I climbed to the top of the police car and jumped blindly into the dust. I landed near the wall of the living room and groped around, coughing. I felt an arm. It was Don, unconscious. I gripped his throat, my hands moving on their own.

Then consciousness came into him. I felt his neck muscles flex, and his arms slammed between mine, hitting me in the jaw and forcing my hands loose. He shoved me away, and I flew backward toward the hallway. He was on me in an instant, and we rolled down the hallway in a vicious battle. My arms flailed at his face, and I tore a deep scratch that reopened the cut on his cheek that I had made hitting him in the simulator room. The air was clearer in the hallway, and he saw who I was.

"You're a dead man," he said. He grabbed my neck. I could feel my windpipe collapse under his grasp. I hit at him but to no avail. He was too strong. My punches were getting weaker, and I could feel my energy fading. I would be unconscious in a few moments. I forced myself to think. I could not beat him physically. He was much stronger, and I was dying. I had to do something else. I closed my eyes and thought of Sarah and her night terrors.

I grabbed Don's arms, opened my eyes, looked directly into Don's soulless eyes, and focused on Sarah as she lay in the small white room in the Kensington Mental Hospital. The ripples spread across the walls behind us, and I saw the materials of the walls transform into wisps of light that reformed into the walls of Sarah's room. There was no dust at all. We were both lying on Sarah's bed. Don looked around confused, relaxing his grip, and saw the creatures around him. The main creature pulled back its cloak, revealing the dark, devilish face. Its spine-chilling roar revealed razor-sharp teeth. It crouched to lunge at Sarah. It then did an interesting thing. It looked at me, then at Don. I looked at another of the creatures on the wall above us, and it was also staring directly at me, not Sarah.

"What the...?" said Don in confusion. The main creature lunged and sank its teeth into Don. He screamed and fell sideways. I pulled myself out of the vision, and the blinding white light flashed. We were again in the hallway of the dingy house. Don was screaming—his hands protectively covering his neck as the vision disappeared from around us. I yanked the gun out of my belt and leveled it at Don's head. My finger tightened on the trigger, and I thought of him coldly shooting Danny and me in my vision of the future, throwing Marty into the ocean, heaving Cole over the side of the road above Lake Pleasant, and Catherine in the ambulance. I had the power to take the life of the person who had ended so many lives. He had been trying to kill me, only moments earlier. It would be self-defense to kill him. My finger would not tighten on the trigger. Whether it was a moral compass telling me not to become a killer or whether I thought that ending his life quickly was not punishment enough, I could not tell, but I did not shoot him in the head. Instead I shot him in both shoulders and both legs, the four shots blasting through the small house. Blood gushed. He screamed in pain. I threw the gun down, grabbed his limp body, and smashed him against the wall, splattering his blood everywhere, then slammed him against the ground.

Police officers swarmed in the hallway, pulled me away from Don, and shoved me to the floor. Someone wrenched my hands behind my back, and I felt the handcuffs. I looked down the hallway and saw Danny on the mat. Officers knelt beside him, untying the cords on his hands and feet. He was safe. Danny was alive. I had changed the future. I relaxed. I felt happy as the officers dragged me to my feet and hauled me out of the small house. I had changed the future. I had saved my son.

Officers were screaming for an ambulance; and as I came out of the house, I realized the scale of what I had created. Helicopters were flying overhead. I counted seven. Two were police helicopters, and the others were news stations. A sea of police and emergency vehicles filled the street as far as I could see. I willingly sat on the porch of the house under the strict watch of several officers as others secured the area. An officer carried Danny out of the house and placed him in the back seat of a police car and Johnny Drake walked up to me.

"Lieutenant Drake, that's my son, and he's alive," I said, pointing with my chin toward the police car with Danny in it. I continued, "I'm sorry for what I did, but I needed to get him. This was the only way."

"Don't move an inch," he said. He turned away and began asking the officers standing by about the crime scene.

The police car with Danny in it pulled away from the curb and slowly made its way out of the neighborhood. I knew Danny was safe, and I was content with the decisions I had made. I would face the consequences of my actions, and I would do all in my power to assure that Jack and Don would sit in prison cells for the rest of their lives.

Somehow, Vanessa was there, walking toward the house carrying her briefcase. I could see relief in her eyes as she approached. A stern officer stepped in front of her, ordering, "Stay back."

"I'm his attorney," she said. "He has rights, and I am one of them."

How appropriate, I thought. *I have the right to Vanessa.*

The officer stepped aside, and she sat down next to me, "You know how to attract a crowd," she said.

"Yeah, it worked. I still have a son."

"You do," she smiled.

"Don was going to kill him," I said. "I saw it."

"I believe you," she said, then added regretfully, "I don't think there's any way I can help you out of this, Pierce."

"I'm not too worried," I said; and as I said it, I believed it. I felt nothing but relief—my son was alive. I felt confidence that everything would be okay. I searched for the reason for my confidence and found it: "You believe me?"

"Yes, I do."

The EMTs wheeled Don out of the house and loaded him into an ambulance that left with a police escort. Johnny led me to a police car. Vanessa followed closely; and as Johnny tried to close the door, Vanessa laid her hand on it.

"Vanessa, don't interfere," he ordered.

"I'm not interfering. I'm his attorney," she retorted.

Johnny rubbed his creased brow. "You're his attorney?"

"I am, and I'm going to make sure he's treated fairly."

"I have the right to her," I said with a smile.

"He does," she confirmed.

Johnny paused, looked at the helicopters circling overhead, and stepped aside, allowing Vanessa into the car. "She's with him," he instructed the driver.

Vanessa took my arm. It was comforting to have her next to me. The sun was setting as we drove toward downtown Phoenix.

Vanessa rested her head on my shoulder. The warmth of having her near me spread through the car. I felt whole, knowing that Danny was safe and Vanessa was next to me.

My world was complete.

Chapter 18

The police car pulled to the curb in front of the police station and the crowd converged. Camera lenses bumped and scratched against the windows, and reporters pushed forward to see into the back seat. I held Vanessa's hand and was enveloped with a surprising calm considering my situation. Officers from the police station forced the crowds of reporters, cameramen, and media personnel to the side and cleared a pathway into the building. Vanessa gave me a reassuring look and stepped out of the police car. I followed, and questions flared from all directions.

"Did you fire the gun?" asked a blurred face to my right.

"Is your son okay?" questioned a woman stretching to see over an officer's shoulder.

"Did you murder your wife?"

"No comment," Vanessa responded.

"Did you murder Cole Trace?"

"Are the allegations true?"

"What were you thinking?"

"No comment. He has no comment," Vanessa responded repeatedly as we pushed past the mass of media and into the station.

Johnny was already there. He directed us to a conference room and said, "Please take a seat, and don't worry. The cameras are off." Vanessa and I took a seat as he turned to the other officers and said, "I need to talk to them alone." He closed the door behind them, sat down across from us, took a deep breath and said, "You had better tell me everything because there's a hornet's nest outside this room bigger than anything I have ever seen. If I'm not on your side, your life is over."

He was right. I had just committed crimes that could keep me locked up for the rest of my life. He needed to understand that I did it to save lives—his included. I was not the murderer he thought I was. I had changed during the speed of light test flight, and my mind was no longer confined in the same way his was.

I looked at Johnny and said, "When you close your eyes, the world around you disappears and is replaced with a calm blur of avoidance. I did that with my life. I closed my eyes and refused to see what was happening around me, and, as a result, I lost and gained everything. I know that's an odd statement, but it's true."

"You closed your eyes?" stated Johnny. "That's all you can say? You resisted arrest. You attacked police officers, Pierce."

"There is more to this than you can imagine," I answered.

"Try me," he said.

I cupped my hands over my eyes and the world around me went black. Slowly light appeared, and I could see blurred images. Danny's face came into focus. He was smiling. I understood his thoughts, and he was right. I had a way to prove the truth that

Johnny would believe. I took my hands from my eyes, reached across the table, and grabbed Johnny's forearm.

"Don't close your eyes," I said, "I'll show you."

"You'll show me?" he asked.

"Just do as I ask. Keep your eyes open," I said confidently as I looked into his eyes. I concentrated on the day of my anniversary, and clear images formed in my mind. He stiffened and I could feel the connection I was making flow from my hand to his arm and into his mind.

"What are you doing?" he demanded, alarmed, as I saw the now-familiar shimmer of energy lift off my skin and ripple through the air around me. Johnny's eyes widened. The solid table top below our arms rippled, and sinews of light rose from the surface. It dematerialized into threads of soft light that streamed down to the floor, and green, manicured blades of grass grew from the white tiles. The color spectrum in a single blade of grass was hypnotizing. Johnny's head cocked back in disbelief.

"Look around you," I answered. The walls of the small room disintegrated into wisps of light that reconstructed themselves into a sidewalk stretching along the roadside, and blue skies stretched over our heads. The sharpness and brightness of the colors around us should have been blinding but instead were comfortable and natural. When the transformation was complete, we were standing outside the quaint whitewashed café with the outdoor seating area.

"What is this?" he asked, astonished.

"This way," I said. We walked toward the café and I saw myself sitting at the table across from my wife, who was speaking while my eyes were closed, covered by my palms. The morning sun glowed on her smooth skin, and the blue desert sky enhanced the azure of her eyes. A breeze stirred the long, dark hair on her tanned shoulders and framed her prominent cheekbones and arched brows. The ambiance of the small café with hand-painted artwork and whitewashed walls accentuated her beauty.

"That's you?"

"Yes, and Catherine, my wife," I said as my heart wrenched inside me, "This was our anniversary."

Catherine was talking, "Everything Cole said is true, Pierce—all of it. It's coming together. The case is solid. The banks have confirmed the transactions, and Cole has made head-way with the witnesses. We're getting together this afternoon to connect the dots."

Johnny stammered, "This is what you meant when you told me you dreamed it?"

"It's more than a dream, Johnny. This is the past. This is the day she died. She was working with Cole on a case against Paralight that would expose it for misusing funds earmarked for a military project to create the speed of light plane. It also falsi-fied the results of the first speed of light test with the monkey to convince the investment group to provide the funds needed to cover the trail."

I again put my hand on Johnny's arm, and the images of Catherine and me sitting at the table rippled and turned into wisps of light which reconstructed into a dark street corner on a rainy night. Johnny put his hand out to catch the rain, but it went right through his palm. "This is the past again?"

"The night of our anniversary. I was driving with Catherine." Headlights approached from down the street. "That's my car."

Catherine's Lexus entered the intersection and was broad-sided with a deafening crash by the car Don was driving. The

Lexus spun and smashed into the building near where Johnny and I were standing. Catherine's body hung out of the shattered window, and my body slumped unconscious in the driver's seat. Johnny rushed to Catherine and reached for her, his hands going through her body.

"You can't help her," I said.

Don unstrapped his helmet and pushed his door open. It grated—metal against metal.

"That's Don Parker?" said Johnny with disgust.

"On orders from Jack," I said.

I saw fury in Johnny's eyes as Don walked to the Lexus, leaned in close to examine our unconscious bodies, then turned and jogged away. I walked to Johnny and put my hand on his arm again. The world around us changed to the back of the ambulance where we watched Catherine die in my arms.

"I did not murder her," I said to Johnny.

He swallowed hard. "I'm sorry."

I touched his arm again and took him to Lake Pleasant on the horrible night of Cole's murder. Johnny's face contorted as he watched Don coldly throw Cole over the edge of the road and into the water below. Then he watched Don throw the helpless Marty Sobisky into the ocean. The next scene was the cement room in the underground parking lot where Jack and Don forced me to my knees, and Don prepared to execute me. Johnny watched, riveted, as I threatened Jack and negotiated for my life.

"Jack orchestrated the murders," Johnny said, staring at Jack. "He lied to me and I believed him."

I put my hand on his shoulder, and the light around us flashed into bright white, bringing us back to the present, in the small police conference room.

I lifted my hand from his arm but said nothing, letting Johnny absorb this new information. He sat back, looked intently at me and then at Vanessa, then took several deep breaths. His large hand rose to his brow, and he rubbed it hard, pushing the skin between his eyes into deep folds. He looked at Vanessa, "You've seen this?"

"I saw Cole's death," she answered.

Again came a long pause. Johnny took another deep breath. "I have two criminals I need to arrest." He looked at me. "Pierce, all charges against you are dropped. Please accept my apology."

"Thank you," I said. I felt the exhilaration of freedom and Vanessa was beaming.

"Will you assist me in the investigation leading to the arrest of Jack and Don and anyone else involved in these crimes?"

"I will," I said.

"I can help, too," interjected Vanessa. She lifted her briefcase to the table and withdrew a folder. "I have the case and investigation outlined in this brief."

"One moment," interjected Johnny as he stood up. "I'll get my detectives in here so we can all go over the case and I can make assignments."

"Not Calloway," asserted Vanessa. "He's involved with Jack."

Astonishment crossed Johnny's face then he looked to me, "You've dreamed that?"

"I have," I answered.

Johnny slowly nodded and left the room. Soon Vanessa was explaining to five additional detectives the misuse of funds, the cover-up of the monkey's death, the witnesses of the monkey's death, the murders of Cole and Catherine, the firing of employees connected with the crimes, Marty Sobisky's disappearance and death, and finally Jack's steps to frame me for the murders. Johnny gave assignments to each detective, and they left.

"You've had a rough few days," Johnny said to me.

I smiled, "Yes, I have."

"I hope you don't mind resting, because I'll need you out of the reach of the press. You and Danny will need to be under our protection for a while."

"Sounds very good to me."

"A while" turned into three days. Danny and I were taken to a rather nice hotel with all we could order delivered and twenty-four-hour police protection. The media went into a frenzy about the chase and kidnapping. The whole world was watching and wanting answers that Johnny Drake supplied strategically. Johnny, Danny, Don, and I were on every station, and the world waited day by day for breaking news. Jack Jones was arrested on charges of conspiracy to murder, kidnapping, and securities charges. Don was charged with murder, conspiracy to murder, and kidnapping. Calloway was also arrested for corruption and bribery. Many people inside Paralight were connected to the crimes, and I worked with Johnny and Vanessa in putting the pieces together. They verified the information gathered through my vision of Cole and Catherine as they assembled evidence against Paralight. Witnesses, including Keri, Howard, and Raymond were willing to testify. Mr. Turnbow fully cooperated with the investigation and released pertinent information to the media and investigators. He said he was determined to root out all corruption in the company and move forward as a leader in the technological industry.

At Cole's funeral service, Vanessa and I were able to say that Cole and Catherine had put together the case against Paralight and that, because of Cole's efforts, the fraudulent activities of company executives had been exposed and the murders to cover them were being solved. The alleged murderers were in custody and Cole had been redeemed.

Kendall went into a coma similar to mine following his test flight; and in the mix of negative media, Mr. Turnbow turned most of the attention to me as the first successful test pilot for the speed of light plane. I was "the first man to become light."

On top of the glamorization surrounding Paralight's crimes and my role in saving Danny, my celebrity status was astronomical. I was compared with icons such as John Glenn and Neil Armstrong. At a second press conference, I sat next to Mr. Turnbow as the media questioned me about the speed of light plane. They had been instructed not to ask any questions about the investigation. One of the questions was my thoughts of the significance of the speed of light technology. I answered, "Flying the speed of light is physical proof of our unlimited minds." The media seized this quotation, and it appeared everywhere. Not long after the interview, in a restaurant I saw a teenager wearing a black shirt with an image of a man running in a flash of light: "Physical Proof of Our Unlimited Minds—Pierce Black."

The focus on the speed of light technology brought welcome relief to Mr. Turnbow and the board of Paralight as the scandals and criminal activities were taken out of the direct spotlight. I was asked to appear on many talk shows, but after the first half dozen, I set limits to my appearances and returned to work at Paralight. It felt good to be at home with Danny, and I wanted to return to a normal life. Entering and leaving Paralight I would encounter small groups of reporters but the crews appearing at my house waned considerably as time went by. Kendall remained in a coma at Kensington, and Paralight purchased a new Saab that would be waiting for him when he regained consciousness.

One Friday night I came home early because Janet had a date. As I drove down my street, I saw a news crew talking to Carl, the police officer with the day shift watching my house. Johnny Drake had ordered a constant police presence to keep the peace and protect my family. Carl knew which people to allow into my house. I stopped the car and spoke with a reporter for a moment. She was pleasant and appreciated my willingness to answer a few questions. I felt it was fine to spend some time and be personable in all situations, but I loved the fact that I did not have to wade through frenzied media as I had immediately following the kidnapping and the public release of the speed of light plane. My life was slowing down, and it felt good. As I walked to the door, Janet opened it.

"Thanks, Mr. Black," she said excitedly. Her make-up was perfect, and she was dressed to enchant. "He looks like Edward!" she exclaimed as she ran off with her make-up bag under her arm.

"You have fun tonight," I said, as she darted past me and ran down the street to her house.

Danny was sitting on the sofa watching the wall as the television blared. I picked up the remote, hit mute, and squatted in front of Danny. "Great to see you, Danny. It looks like it's you and me tonight." On the chair was *Richard III*, and I picked it up and sat down. "Do you want to read this? Maybe we can finish it tonight." I looked at him, and he continued to stare blankly at the wall. "Agreed!" I said, "Let's do it."

I started to read; and as I did so, several of the letters again came off the page and rose in the air before me. They spelled out, "Richard is a lot like Jack, isn't he?"

I smiled and said, "He is, and I hope they meet each other soon." The doorbell rang, and I looked out the window to see Vanessa carrying two plastic bags. "It's open," I called, smiling.

Vanessa came in. "I thought the two of you might like some dinner."

"I think we'd be open to that."

"I looked for the greasiest and most harmful things on the Chinese menu."

"I like someone who knows how to order," I said.

Vanessa's eyes went to the muted television that was showing a news report. A photo of me appeared in the corner above and to the right of the anchorwoman. "How long do you think it will be until you're not the main topic of every conversation?"

"We are quite interesting, aren't we, Danny?"

As she was opening the different boxes of Chinese take-out on the coffee table, she commented, "Danny's interesting, but what's so interesting about you?"

"I have an itch on my back. That's interesting," I said as I leaned forward to put my back in her view, "It's just below the shoulder blade and too high to reach."

Vanessa paid no attention to me but looked at the air in front of me. "Danny, I have always liked you, too," she said to Danny.

I followed her gaze and saw the floating letters: "Dad, I have always liked her."

"You see it?" I asked in confusion.

Vanessa smiled and said, "It's incredible, isn't it?" She held her hand out in the air and waved it through the letters. They moved smoothly around her fingers and then returned to their original position. She laughed, "I think I'm going crazy."

"I think you are," I said in astonishment. "And you're in good company."

THE END

Lee Baker is a novelist and a screenwriter. Many of his works have started in screenplay form and are in development as feature films. Two illustrated books, *Beau and the Beanstalk* and *Humbug, A Christmas Carol*, have been created from his stories with plans of becoming 3D animated films. Book two for the Speed of Light series is underway and keep your eyes open for the other stories by Lee Baker in print and on the screen.